A Churn for the Worse

LAURA BRADFORD

BERKLEY PRIME CRIME, NEW YORK

BERKLEY
PRIME
CRIME

An imprint of Penguin Random House LLC
375 Hudson Street, New York, New York 10014

A CHURN FOR THE WORSE

A Berkley Prime Crime Book / published by arrangement with the author

ISBN: 978-0-425-27303-6

PUBLISHING HISTORY
Berkley Prime Crime mass-market edition / March 2016

PRINTED IN THE UNITED STATES OF AMERICA

10 9 8 7 6 5 4 3 2 1

Cover illustration by Mary Ann Lasher.
Cover design by Sarah Oberrender.
Interior text design by Laura K. Corless.

Penguin
Random
House

WITHDRAWN

More Praise for the National Bestselling Amish Mysteries

"The best cozy mystery debut I've read this year."
—Harlan Coben on *Hearse and Buggy*

"The characters are interesting and delightful. The setting in the wonderful town of Heavenly, Pennsylvania, is just that, heavenly. Mixing Amish and 'English' town folk is intriguing . . . I recommend this book to any reader interested in Amish novels, cozy mysteries, or who just wants to read a fabulous book."
—Open Book Society

"Delightful . . . Well-portrayed characters and authentic Amish lore make this a memorable read."
—*Publishers Weekly*

"Bradford concocts a clever whodunit . . . Her characters possess depth."
—*Richmond Times-Dispatch*

"An engaging amateur sleuth that interweaves Amish society with an enjoyable whodunit. Claire is a terrific protagonist whose wonderful investigation enables readers to obtain insight into the Amish culture."
—Genre Go Round Reviews

"The Amish customs and traditions are fascinating and blend nicely into the mystery, while the author's ability to provide an authentic sense of community makes this story engaging."
—*RT Book Reviews*

"Engaging characters fill this well-plotted mystery. The Amish community of Heavenly is realistically depicted and English (as the Amish call non-Amish) characters are woven into the community in believable ways."
—The Mystery Reader

For Joe.
I'm honored to call you friend.

Acknowledgments

While the stories that comprise the Amish Mysteries come to life in my imagination, there are times I turn to other people to enhance certain aspects. That was certainly the case in this book as I worked to create the featured horse. A huge thank-you goes out to reader Valeria Cannata for answering my endless (and I do mean, *endless*) questions about horses. Her help was invaluable to me and her love for her own horses was palpable in every correspondence we shared.

I'd also like to thank all of my readers for supporting this series by buying each book, spreading the word, and sending me such nice notes via my website and/or my Facebook author page. Knowing that folks love Claire and Jakob as much as I do is heartwarming.

Finally, if you enjoy my writing, I hope you'll check out my new series: Emergency Dessert Squad Mysteries. Information about it can be found on my website: laurabradford.com.

Chapter 1

"Penny for your thoughts?"

Claire Weatherly lifted her cheek from its resting spot against Jakob Fisher's chest and smiled up at the handsome detective. "If I was thinking something, I'd tell you for free. Really, I'm just enjoying sitting here with you and looking out at *that*—" Sweeping her hand toward the lush green fields in the distance, Claire dropped her sandal-clad feet back onto the floor and brought their rhythmic motion to an end. "Every time I think I've picked my favorite season here, the next one rolls in and I change my mind all over again."

Jakob's attention traveled across the very fields he'd once walked as a child, an odd expression momentarily claiming the peace he'd worn so easily only moments earlier. "Summer was always hard work. The second we'd harvest one crop, we'd prepare the field and plant the next. But when we got to play it was"—he cupped his hand over his mouth, only to let it slide slowly down his clean-shaven chin and back to its original spot atop the swing's armrest—"the *best*."

"Tell me," she said, scooting to the opposite end of the wooden swing so she could have an uninhibited view of his face as he spoke. "Leave nothing out."

His smile was back, along with his focus. "When I was really little—like two or three—I loved jumping in the hay. Skinned my knees a few times before I got good at gauging how much hay was needed for a soft landing." He laughed at the memory, the warm, rich sound rivaling the effects of the setting July sun on the left side of her face. "Then, as I got a little older, summer meant walking down to Miller's Pond and spending a few hours catching frogs with Benjamin. We'd search high and low for the two biggest frogs we could find, place them on the ground, and then try to make them race one another back to the pond."

She tried to imagine the two grown men as eight-year-olds, their pant legs rolled up to their knees, their heads covered by the same straw hats worn throughout the Amish community of Heavenly, Pennsylvania, and beyond. Any momentary success she had, though, was quickly marred by the reality of what had happened to that childhood friendship not more than three or four years later—a downward spiral that had only recently begun to show the faintest signs of a reversal. Or as much of a reversal as there could be when one's core beliefs demanded he not speak to the other.

"But the best part of summer was getting to go to the lake with Martha and, later, Isaac. Skipping stones, making paper boats, wading in to our knees . . ." He linked his hands behind his head and stretched his feet out along the wooden boards of the front porch. "I was incredibly blessed in the sister and brother department, that's for sure."

"Do you ever regret your decision to leave?" It was a question she'd wanted to ask many times over the eleven months she'd known the police detective, yet, until that very moment, she'd never had the courage. Still, she couldn't help but brace herself for the possibility that his answer might reveal a regret she'd have to learn to live with if their relationship continued to progress at its current rate.

His elbows moved side to side along with his head and she felt her body sag with relief in response. "No. I was meant to be a cop. I just wish I'd come to that realization before baptism. If I had, everything would be different." His eyes returned to the fields in the distance, but Claire knew his thoughts went beyond the greenery of the crops to a mental space that held not only his sister, Martha; his niece, Esther; and Esther's husband, Eli; but also his brother, Isaac; his mother; the rest of his nieces and nephews; and, perhaps, even his father.

Closing the gap between them with one small scoot, Claire guided Jakob's hands down to his lap and gave them a gentle squeeze. "At least with Heavenly Treasures, you can see them from time to time."

"True. Your gift shop and its connection to Martha and Esther has been a godsend in that regard. But there's something else I'm grateful about when it comes to your shop."

She felt the twinge of excitement caused by his thumbs as they gently massaged the backs of her hands, and willed herself to remain in the conversation. "Oh?"

"It's because of your dream to own that shop that I have you in my life."

"Knock, knock . . . Is there room for one more out here?"

Claire held Jakob's gaze long enough to acknowledge the magnitude of his words and then peeked around the back of the swing to nod at the woman standing in the front doorway of Sleep Heavenly Bed and Breakfast with a magazine in one hand and a plate of cookies in the other. "There's always room for you, Aunt Diane. Especially when you have cookies," she teased, releasing Jakob's hands from her grasp as she did. "Come. Sit. Please."

Jakob turned his head to follow the sixty-two-year-old's trek across the porch and over to the wicker settee on their left. "We were hoping you'd have some time to come out here and sit with us before nightfall, Diane."

With any other man, Claire would have to doubt his words, especially when her aunt's entrance had come at such an emotionally charged moment, but Jakob was different. He meant what he said, and he, more than anyone else, knew the importance of Diane's place in Claire's life. The fact that Diane treated Jakob, as well as everyone she came in contact with inside or outside the walls of her inn, like family made his response second nature.

"I have to admit, I could have been out here thirty minutes ago, but I got lost in *this*." Diane sank onto the floral cushion and waved the magazine in the air.

Jakob leaned across the armrest of the swing to read the title stretched across the cover photograph depicting a large brown horse and its sixty-something male owner. "*The Stable Life?*"

"It's been my favorite magazine since Claire was a little girl," Diane said.

"It's true. That's the one magazine I couldn't cut up for

a school or camp project." Claire directed her aunt's gaze toward the inn's nearly empty parking lot. "I was surprised to see everyone head out so soon after dinner tonight. Is there something going on somewhere?"

Slowly, Diane lowered the magazine to her lap and held out the plate of cookies for Jakob to take and share. "The writer, Jeremy, and his photographer, Hayley, headed into town for coffee and to get some material for that online thingy they do."

"It's called a blog," Claire interjected. "Theirs is apparently centered on travel or something like that. And Hank—the small-business guru? Where is he this evening?"

Jakob set the cookie plate on his lap and waited for Claire to pick one first. "Small-business guru?"

"That's just my terminology," Claire said, before taking a bite of the still-warm chocolate chip treat. "Mmmm . . ."

"Mr. Turner is actually a teacher at a small community college in Wisconsin, I believe." Diane waved away Jakob's offer of a cookie and continued on, her knowledge of her guests and their backgrounds, no matter their length of stay, impressive. "He's here doing research about the many cottage businesses that put food on the table in Amish homes. He's hoping to use what he learns as a motivator for his students when classes resume in the fall."

"If he's from Wisconsin, why did he travel all the way to Lancaster to do his research?" Jakob asked. "There are Amish communities in his own state."

Diane settled all the way back against her chair and lifted her chin to the evening breeze. "He wanted to come here—to the first substantial Amish settlement."

"Okay. That makes sense, I guess," Jakob said, nodding.

"He's an interesting man. Really seems to care about his students." Diane gestured up to the second floor. "In fact, I believe he's upstairs in his room right now, plugging his day's notes into his computer."

Jakob finished his first cookie and moved on to a second, his appreciation for Diane's baking skills earning him a smile from the woman in the process. "Sounds like an interesting crew. How long are they here?"

"The blog duo arrived today while I was at the gift shop, and Hank—Turner—checked in yesterday." At Diane's nod, Claire stood and wandered over to the railing, the sun's descent in the western sky beginning to pick up pace. "But there's more. A full house, in fact, isn't there, Aunt Diane?"

"That's right. Bill Brockman is a travel agent from Kentucky who is thinking about sponsoring a trip to Heavenly next spring. He's here to decide if he should go ahead with it, which is why he's out and about right now. He wants to see what the town is like at various times throughout the day." Diane looked down at her magazine and then back up, first at Claire, and then at Jakob. "And then there's Jim Naber, the consultant hired by the town to determine if there are any other ways to attract tourism dollars to Heavenly. He missed out on dinner on account of an invitation to the mayor's home."

Jakob joined Claire by the railing and draped his arm around her shoulders. "I wish they'd quit with all of that. We have just the right amount of tourists. Any more, and Heavenly is going to lose that special something that makes people want to come here in the first place."

It was a fear Claire knew they all shared. Heavenly was

the perfect blend of the past and the present, thanks to its Amish residents on the western side and their English counterparts on the eastern side. In between, along Lighted Way, the two lifestyles mingled, complementing and benefitting each another in ways that went well beyond the financial aspects of the Amish- and English-owned shops and cafés that lined the thoroughfare.

"All we can do is say a prayer that Heavenly remains as it should," Diane said. "So people like Judy Little, the last of our current guests, who is now off on a long walk, will see fit to come back a *third* and a *fourth* and a *fifth* time."

The approaching *clip-clop* of a horse's hooves made them turn, as one, toward the driveway. Sure enough, a gray-topped buggy, common to Lancaster County Amish, turned into the parking lot and stopped in front of the hitching pole Diane had insisted her inn have, despite the rarity of an Amish guest.

"Are you expecting someone?" Claire asked of her aunt while simultaneously leaning over the railing in the hope of gaining a glimpse of the driver.

"No. But—"

"Wait!" Claire straightened up and made a beeline for the steps. "That's *Annie*! Driving a buggy by *herself*!"

At the base of the steps, Claire turned right and headed across the top of the driveway and into the parking lot. When she reached the side of the buggy, she smiled up at the kapp-wearing sixteen-year-old inside. "Annie Hershberger, what is this?"

"Dat said I could hitch my new horse to his buggy and come say hello."

"Hello." Claire took a step back to allow the girl enough

7

room to exit the buggy and then followed her to the hitching post. "I didn't know you were driving a buggy already."

"That's because I wanted to surprise you." Annie secured the horse and buggy to the pole and then turned to the sturdy brown horse, her voice adopting a slight singsong quality as she opened her palm to reveal a round, red-and-white-striped candy. "Yah. This is for you, Katie. For doing such a good job."

Claire looked from Annie to the horse and back again, the joy in her employee's face impossible to miss. "This is your horse?"

"Yah. Her name is Katie. Dat took me to pick her out on Saturday. She is gentle and sweet, and she likes peppermint candy just like me."

In a rush of motion just over Claire's left shoulder, Diane stepped forward and ran her hand along the side of Annie's horse. "Oh, Annie, she is beautiful."

Annie rocked back on the soles of the black lace-up boots barely visible beneath her simple aproned dress and beamed. "Yah. There were many horses to choose from that day, but I knew at once that Katie was for me. It was that way for Henry, too."

"Henry?" Claire felt Jakob's presence behind her and reached for his hand, pulling him into the circle made by Annie, Diane, Katie, and Claire.

"Yah. Henry Stutzman. He took Mary home after the sale. Mary is a bit bigger and is more black than brown, but she is a good horse, too."

"Does it make you nervous to go off with Katie and the buggy by yourself?" Claire asked.

"Nah. I have been practicing for some time."

Jakob relinquished Claire's hand in favor of the horse. After saying something into the animal's ear in Pennsylvania Dutch, he turned back to Claire with an explanation for Annie's apparent confidence. "Very often, Amish children are given a miniature horse when they are eleven or twelve. The horse is hooked up to a pony cart for the child to practice with. Younger siblings get a kick out of it because it means lots of rides around the farm."

Annie's eyes skirted Jakob's en route to Claire's, the girl's unease with the detective's former Amish status juxtaposed against her own as the bishop's daughter lessening a little each day. "I gave rides to Smokey, the barn cat. I only tipped him twice."

"That's pretty impressive. I tipped my sister, Martha, at least a dozen times." Jakob flashed a brief smile at the girl and then turned his attention back to the horse. "How many horses were there on Saturday?"

Annie's index finger shot out as she mentally calculated her answer. When she was done, she said, "Nine."

"You get her out at Weaver's place?" Jakob asked.

"Yah."

Claire stepped closer to the buggy, trying to remember everything Leroy Beiler had taught her about approaching a horse. But before she could employ any of her knowledge, Annie dropped a peppermint candy into her hand. "Here. It is the best way to become friends with Katie."

"Shouldn't she be eating a carrot or something?"

Diane, who was still fawning over the horse, laughed. "Carrots are a hit, sure. But hard candy—in particular, peppermint? That's a horse's equivalent to you and chocolate chip cookies."

"Hmmm . . . Interesting." She held the candy in the palm of her hand and offered it to Katie. Sure enough, the horse helped herself with no prodding necessary. "Wow."

"Diane's right. It is like you with chocolate chip cookies," Jakob said.

She pulled her hand back, wiped it along the side of her slacks, and then used it to swat Jakob's arm. "Hey!"

"There's a horse in one of the more recent issues of *The Stable Life* who actually has a penchant for a candy called Root Beer Barrels." Diane gave the horse one final pat on the side of its long neck and then came to stand between Annie and Claire. "The other horses in the owner's stable had no interest in that flavor. If they were given one, they'd spit it out. But this particular horse—a Standardbred racer like Katie here—loves them so much she'll stick her nose in her owner's pocket looking for them."

"I never realized you were such a horse enthusiast, Diane," Jakob said as he pulled Claire in for a side hug.

Claire leaned into the hug, smiling up at him as she did. "Remind me to show you her bedroom one day. It's covered in pictures of horses."

"Have you always loved horses?" Annie asked, pulling her gaze from Katie and fixing it, instead, on Claire's aunt. "Since you were young?"

"I've loved them since I was ten years old and accompanied my grandfather to my very first harness race." Diane's voice took on a faraway note that had Claire trying to imagine the scene no doubt playing in her aunt's thoughts at that exact moment. "Oh, Annie, there was nothing I wouldn't have done to have a horse of my own back then. *Nothing.*"

Chapter 2

Claire lifted the platter-sized plate of homemade cin-namon rolls from the counter, waited for Diane to claim the pitcher of freshly squeezed orange juice, and then followed the woman through the kitchen doorway, down a short hallway, and into the dining room. When they reached their final destination, they parted company like the well-oiled machine that they'd become, each taking an opposite end of the large colonial-style table and making their way around it in a counterclockwise direction.

"Now, don't those look delicious." Hank Turner, the community college teacher from Wisconsin, leaned to the side to afford Claire better access to his plate. "I haven't had a cinnamon roll in entirely too long."

Judy Little, the one returning guest among the six bod-ies assembled around the table, flashed a smile at her now-filled orange juice glass and then up at Claire's aunt. "Even if you *had*, it would pale in comparison to Diane's."

Claire peeked across the table in time to see the innkeeper blush, a reaction that was as much a given as any her culinary efforts got no matter the meal or the guest.

"Then I'm even more excited to try it." Hank abandoned his egg-and-cheese casserole long enough to sample the icing-topped treat. One bite in and he proved himself a believer. "Wow. I mean—*wow*!"

Continuing around the table, Claire deposited a cinnamon roll on each of the next five plates and then set the remaining rolls in the center of the table. A quick check of everyone's coffee cups showed no refills were necessary, and she turned her attention to the rest of the guests.

"Did you sleep well, Mr. Brockman?"

The travel agent paused, his second piece of bacon a mere inch or two from his lips, and nodded. "Please, call me Bill. And yes, very well, thank you. This town is very peaceful."

"Perhaps that's something that will appeal to your clients," Diane mused as she finished pouring juice and set the empty pitcher down on the narrow buffet table in the corner.

"It certainly helps me narrow in on the demographic most likely to enjoy Heavenly." Bill nibbled on his bacon and then dropped the remaining piece back on to his plate. "Question. A lot of the Amish farms have shingles out front announcing a business. I saw one that mentioned candles, one that actually sold homemade salsa, and another that caned chairs. I always thought farming was their business, no?"

Armed with the knowledge that had brought him to Heavenly in the first place, Hank Turner, the well-dressed forty-something at the far end of the table, pulled his spoon from his tea cup and set it beside his plate. "The Amish boast over two thousand cottage businesses in Lancaster County alone. The businesses run the gamut from the types you just mentioned, to equipment repair, horse sales, deer farms, the manufacturing of various buggy components, furniture, and on and on. They are extremely resourceful people."

"Why did they move away from farming?" Bill asked, leaning back in his chair and turning his attention to Diane.

"The Amish population is doubling every twenty years. Which means they are, essentially, running out of farmland. So if a young married man doesn't have enough land to farm, he either moves to another Amish settlement in another county or another state, or he finds another way to make a living." Diane grabbed the coffeepot and topped off a few mugs. "The shingles you saw, Bill, denote those businesses that sell directly to the public."

Hank reached into his jacket pocket, plucked out a small notebook and pen, and began to write, his hand pausing midway across the page. "Businesses that sell directly to the public?"

"Like the salsa shop, and the chair caning shop Mr. Brockman—I mean, *Bill* mentioned a moment ago." Claire came around the table to stand beside her aunt, her internal clock acutely aware of the limited window she had to get to Heavenly Treasures in time to ready the store for its ten o'clock opening. "Others, like a business that makes buggy tops, would only sell to a shop that puts the buggies together."

"Ahhhh. I get it." Hank flipped a page in his notebook, jotted a few more notes, and then placed it and the pen back into his pocket.

"So if you see a shingle out front, you can just go right up to the barn or the outbuilding or whatever?" Bill asked.

Diane and Claire nodded in unison, with Diane providing the verbal accompaniment. "That's right. A shingle out front is an invitation to come onto the property."

"Could I have another one of those rolls?" Jeremy Stockton, the blog writer and youngest person at the table, straightened in his seat and pointed over the floral centerpiece that blocked his view of the platter. "They were really good."

Claire retrieved the plate from its spot on the opposite end of the table and carried it around to the mid-twenty-something. She placed a second roll on his plate and smiled at his slightly older coworker, Hayley Wright.

"Have you been getting some good pictures for your blog?" Claire asked.

"A few, I think." Hayley traced her finger around the edge of her orange juice cup and then lifted her blue eyes to Claire's. "I understand the Amish don't like their pictures being taken?"

"That's true. They see photographs of themselves as being graven images, something that is in direct violation of the Ten Commandments."

Hayley leaned forward, cocking her head slightly as she did. "But surely they know tourists are taking pictures of them . . . their farms . . . their buggies . . . their horses. . . . their everything, right?"

"Of course," Diane interjected, as she moved in beside Claire. "But they don't take them, they don't keep them, and they don't pose for them. They can't control what the world around them does." Diane placed her hand on

Claire's shoulder and lowered her voice to a near whisper. "It's getting late, dear. You really should be heading out. I'll finish up here."

Claire followed Diane's pointed look to the small wall clock just outside the dining room and bit back the urge to groan.

Nine thirty-five.

So much for getting things done before unlocking the front door . . .

Reaching behind her back, she untied the strings of her apron, pulled the fabric from around her waist, and folded it neatly in her hands. "I have to excuse myself for now as my shop is set to open in twenty-five minutes. If you find yourself on Lighted Way at any point today, I highly recommend a stop at Shoo Fly Bake Shoppe. Ruth Miller, the young Amish woman who runs it, is an absolutely *amazing* baker."

"As good as Diane here?" Jeremy asked around the last remaining bite of his second cinnamon roll.

"Better." Diane took the folded apron from Claire and shooed her toward the hallway. "Now skedaddle, dear. We'll see you back here in time for dinner."

She spotted his car the second she stepped out the back door, the increasingly familiar sight no less exciting than it had been the first time Jakob had shown up and driven her to work. But this time, the excitement was mixed with relief.

"Aren't you a sight for sore eyes," she said as she approached the car.

"Sore . . . or *late*?"

She poked her head through the open driver's side window, whispered a kiss across his lips, and then ran around the back of the car and into the passenger seat. "Actually, thanks to you, kind sir, I think I'll be right on time."

"Good news for your customers, bad news for me." Jakob shifted his unmarked car into drive and pulled out of the inn's narrow parking lot and down the winding driveway.

"Bad news for you?"

"That's right." At the end of the driveway, he turned left and headed toward Lighted Way—the thoroughfare that not only linked the Amish and English sects of town but also served as a place where both groups interacted, each true to their own way of life. "I was kind of hoping we'd have a few minutes together."

She smiled across the center console at him. "I'm sorry. I didn't know you were outside."

"I wanted to surprise you." He took his right hand off the steering wheel and reached for Claire's, who gave it willingly.

"And you did. I just got busy with Diane and the guests. They were a chatty bunch this morning."

"Nice folks?"

"You know Aunt Diane, she's a magnet for nice people." She squeezed his hand, then pulled hers away so he could focus on the change from pavement to cobblestones that denoted the Lighted Way shopping district. Even now, after nearly eighteen months in Heavenly, Claire still felt a twinge of excitement and awe at her ability to call the quiet town home—a place where her tastes and interests didn't stick out as being hokey or silly. "But maybe, if you're not too busy at the station this afternoon, we could have lunch together. Annie is scheduled to come in around noon and stay with me until closing."

"You're on."

Jakob slowed the car to a crawl to allow a buggy to enter the flow of traffic from the alleyway between Heavenly Treasures and Shoo Fly Bake Shoppe and waved at the familiar hatted man who now sported a beard where a year earlier there had been none.

Claire held her breath a beat to see how Eli Miller would respond, but true to the Amish man's nature and his marital status with the detective's niece, he returned Jakob's gesture with a slight nod and a smile.

She retrieved her purse from the floor beside her feet and rested her hand on the door handle as Jakob pulled to a stop in front of Heavenly Treasures. "If you get to work and find that something has changed and lunch isn't an option, maybe we can go for a walk after dinner or something."

"We can do that, too. But nothing is going to change."

"You sound mighty confident of that, Detective," she teased.

Jakob shrugged and then leaned across the seat to kiss Claire. "I am. Things have been blissfully quiet around this town lately. The way it should be."

Chapter 3

Claire placed the Amish doll in the bag alongside the hand-drawn note cards and lavender-scented candle and handed it to the gray-haired woman on the other side of the counter. "I hope your granddaughter enjoys the doll."

"I'm sure she will. It's absolutely darling." Transferring the bag to her left hand, the woman widened her eyes as she took one last look around the shop. "There are so many things in here I'd love to take home, but my husband would have my neck if I did."

"There's always next time."

Bringing her gaze back onto Claire, she nodded. "And there *will* be a next time. This town is lovely. Only"—the woman lowered her voice and leaned across the counter—"next time, I want to stay in that beautiful Victorian bed and breakfast just up the road."

"Sleep Heavenly."

"Yes, that's the one."

Claire opened the drawer beneath the register and fished out the tri-fold brochure she'd helped Diane create over the winter. The picture of the inn on the cover, as well as the interior shots she'd snapped for the center section, beckoned as planned. She held the brochure out to the woman. "I have it on good authority that you won't be sorry if you do."

"Oh?" the woman asked, glancing down at the brochure.

"My aunt owns the inn, and I can attest to the fact that her guests are always sad to leave."

"I'll have to make sure to tell my husband that."

"Does your husband like to eat?"

"Does he ever . . ."

"Then make sure to add in the fact that Aunt Diane's dinners are out of this world. And I mean, *out of this world*. My favorite is the pot roast."

The woman's face glowed with pleasure. "You just spoke the magic words, young lady. Thank you."

"My pleasure." Claire closed the drawer, walked around the counter, and accompanied the woman toward the front of the shop. "Now go home and see your granddaughter."

At the door, the woman peeked inside her bag and then back up at Claire. "And this doll was made by a real Amish woman?"

"It was, indeed. By my friend Esther, in fact. She worked here at the shop with me until last December when she got married."

"An Amish woman can work in an English store?"

"Sure. But once she marries, her focus must turn to her

19

home, her husband, and the children they will soon have."
It was funny how, after all these months, her voice still
hitched over losing Esther from the shop. Granted, they still
saw each other once or twice a week, but she missed the
day-to-day interaction with her friend.

"Very interesting. Thank you." The woman headed out
into the summer heat and made a beeline for a similarly
aged man seated on a bench in front of the shop, the Sleep
Heavenly brochure in one hand and her purchases in the
other.

"Good afternoon, Claire."

Stepping back into the shop, Claire closed the front door
and turned toward the Amish teenager standing just inside
the back hallway. "Hi, Annie. Ready to . . ." The words
fell away as she took in the dark shadows surrounding
Annie's bloodshot eyes. "Annie? Are you okay?"

"My heart is heavy."

Claire met the girl in the center of the shop and then
motioned her over to the pair of stools just inside the partial
enclosure made by the counter. Gently, she liberated the
simple lunch pail from Annie's trembling hands, deposited
it on a shelf not visible to customers, and patted the top of
the stool. "C'mon, sweetie. Sit. Tell me what's wrong."

Pitching forward on the stool, Annie dropped her head
into her palms. "Henry will now know what I know."

"Henry?"

"Henry Stutzman. My friend. He is sixteen, like me."

"Oh, wait, Henry is the one you mentioned last night—
the one who just got a new horse, too, right?" Claire
perched on the edge of her stool and waited for Annie to
lift her head.

"Yah. Her name is Mary."

Hooking her finger beneath Annie's chin, Claire lifted the girl's gaze to hers. "So what has you so upset?"

"It is hard to not have Mamm. My sister, Eva, tries, but it is not the same. Eva has her own family and does not need to worry about me." Annie wiped her eyes with the back of her hand and then inhaled sharply, as if she was trying to muster the courage she needed to continue despite the sadness in her voice. "I know it will be hard for Henry to not have his dat."

"Your friend lost his father?" she asked, honing in on the part of the conversation that had Annie so upset.

"Yah. Last night."

"Oh, Annie, I'm so sorry. Was he sick?"

Annie sniffled and shook her head. "No. He was hit by a shovel."

Claire drew back. "A shovel?"

"Yah. Henry found it near his dat's body. In the barn. There was much blood. Much sadness."

"I don't understand—"

"Dat woke me in the middle of the night to tell me he was going to Henry's farm. When he told me why, I asked to go, too. I did not know what I could do, but I knew I wanted to help. When we got there, Dat spoke to Henry's mamm, Henry's brothers and sisters, and to Henry, too. Henry's mamm cried many tears." Annie took another breath and then stepped down off her stool, her legs displaying much of the same shake Claire heard in the girl's words. "It is when Henry left to get air, that I followed him onto the porch. I tried to find the words that comfort, the words my dat is so good at speaking, but I am not good at that."

21

"I'm sure you being there was a comfort."

Annie traced her finger along the countertop, shrugging as she did. "When I could not think of enough things to say, I listened. He talked of memories of his dat, and he talked of the work they had finished that day." When she reached the edge of the counter closest to Claire, Annie pulled her hand back. "It was after he talked of the crops that he said it."

"Said what?" Claire asked.

"Henry knows he is to believe his dat's passing is God's will. But that is hard for him to do when he believes it is his fault."

"His *fault*?" Claire echoed.

"Yah. His dat went out to check on Henry's horse. To make sure she was settled for the night. It was a job for Henry to do but Henry was playing a silly game with his brothers and did not go."

"Okay . . ."

"It is then, in the barn, that Henry's dat passed."

"Wow." It was almost more than she could process at that moment, but still she tried. "I'm surprised Jakob didn't mention this when he drove me to work this morning."

"Your detective does not know." Annie wiped her eyes one last time and then smoothed down the sides of her mint green aproned dress. "I have spent too much time talking. It is time to work. What would you like me to—"

Claire pushed through the fog left in her brain by the young girl's words and brought the focus back on Henry Stutzman and his deceased father. "Why not? A man is dead."

Pausing her hand above the clipboard of items to be

attended to that day, Annie turned a questioning eye in Claire's direction. "I do not understand your question."

"Why wasn't Jakob called? He's a *detective*, Annie. Henry's father is dead."

"There is nothing to tell the English police."

Claire followed the girl's attention back to the clipboard, the dozen or so tasks listed on the lined paper no longer important. "*Nothing to tell the police?* Are you serious? A man is *dead*, Annie."

"It was an accident," Annie said, shrugging. "It was God's will."

She walked over to the clipboard, removed it from Annie's hands, and tried to make her employee grasp reality. "Annie, shovels don't jump up and hit a person in the head all by themselves. Even if he stepped on one that was out of place, it shouldn't have reached up high enough to hit him in the head. Unless he was a small man."

"Henry's dat was tall. He had to duck to fit through many doors."

"I rest my case." Claire crossed to the wood-paneled upright in the center of the store only to retrace her steps back to the counter and her employee. "Annie, we have to tell Jakob. Now."

The sentence was barely past Claire's lips and Annie was already shaking her head. "Dat would not approve."

"Annie, this isn't about your father's feelings for Jakob or the general distrust the Amish have for the English police. This is about a man who didn't die a normal death. A man who should be alive right now, raising your friend." It was quick, fleeting even, but still, Claire saw it. Annie

23

had doubt. Armed with that realization, Claire plowed ahead. "You know I'm right, Annie. You have to."

Nibbling her lower lip inward, Annie shifted her minimal weight from one boot-clad foot to the other and then froze. "Dat would not want me to call the police."

Again she sought the teenager's hands and held them tightly. "You don't have to, Annie. *I* will."

Chapter 4

The second her feet transitioned from the cobblestones to the fine gravel roadway that wound its way through the Amish countryside, Claire felt the day's tension slipping away. The reaction was a given, of course, but still she couldn't help marvel at the shift and its reason.

Prior to moving to Heavenly, she'd never realized just how much the hustle and bustle of life in New York City had weighed on her heart and her psyche. Sure, a sizeable chunk of that was more about her failed attempt at marriage than it was about a city and its people. But there was no getting around the fact that her heart was lighter just being in a place where people knew her name and treasured her company.

These days, when she needed to clear her head of everyday clutter, instead of holing up inside a one-bedroom apartment that was never completely immune to other people's music or the wailing siren of emergency vehicles in the distance, she could lace up her sneakers and head straight for the most peaceful place she'd ever experienced.

Here, on the Amish side of Heavenly, she could lose herself in the sounds of nature instead of man—cows mooing, birds tweeting, and crickets coming to life as dusk slowly inched its way across the sky. Most of the farms she'd passed thus far were relatively quiet, the men and the boys who tended their fields likely now assembled around the kitchen table in their homes, enjoying dinner and sharing details of their day with the rest of their families. There were a few farms, of course, that still seemed active, with their owners trying to squeeze every last minute of work time from the long summer day, but even in those instances, she knew it wouldn't be long before they, too, turned their attention inside the home.

It was a part of the Amish life she admired, and a part she very much wanted to emulate when and if she ever remarried and started a family of her own.

Like clockwork, Jakob's amber-flecked hazel eyes appeared in her thoughts and elicited a smile from her lips. So many times over the last few months, she'd found herself daydreaming about the faces of Jakob's future children—their sandy blond hair, their dimple-accompanied smiles, their broad shoulders, their knee-weakening laughter, and their unwavering sense of right and wrong. Sometimes, their blond hair would take on an auburn tint more like their mother's . . .

Shaking the not-so-ludicrous thought from her head, Claire followed the bend in the road, taking in the name on the next mailbox she saw.

Stutzman.

Annie's friend . . .

Her pace slowed enough to afford a view of the family home in the background and the driveway in the fore-ground. Careful not to run into the mailbox, Claire took a mental count of the buggies tethered to trees on both sides of the narrow, winding driveway. Sure enough, nearly half a dozen people from the community had amassed on the Stutzman farm to lend a hand in the wake of tragedy. The women, Claire knew, were inside the two-story home, mak-ing dinner, helping with the youngest children, and lending support to the deceased's wife. The men were likely in the barn tending to animals or out in the fields with Henry and the other boys helping wherever they could.

She craned her head up and around the buggies in search of Jakob's car but came up empty. If he'd been there—as she suspected he had—he'd moved on, taking his notes and his finely tuned gut back to his office inside the Heavenly Police Department. Whatever he had or hadn't found in the Stutzmans' barn would remain a ques-tion mark for her until he reached out via a call or text.

Glancing at her watch, Claire continued toward the one farm that made her feel lighter and happier than all the rest. Step by step she made her way past farms she knew, and farms she didn't, the day's final rays still warm on her face. As she walked, she tried to imagine what Esther and Eli were doing at that moment . . .

Would they still be eating dinner?

Would they be sitting on their front porch, talking about the baby that was due to arrive in a little over two months?

It went through her head, for just a moment, to turn

around and head back to the inn. After all, Esther and Eli were still relative newlyweds. After a long day out in the fields and in his woodworking shop, maybe Eli just wanted to have Esther all to himself . . .

Yet she kept walking.

She didn't know why, exactly, but she knew she needed time with Esther—time to laugh, time to catch up on each other's lives, time to soak up the positive, upbeat aura that was her former-employee-turned-friend and Jakob's niece.

It wasn't that anything was wrong in her life; quite the contrary, in fact. Life was good, great even. And if that wasn't the case, she had Aunt Diane and Jakob ready to lend a listening ear and a supportive shoulder at the drop of a hat.

No, Esther was different. Esther was the girlfriend Claire had been too busy to find in her twenties. Now that she had an Esther in her life, she found she needed that kind of friendship in much the same way one of Aunt Diane's potted plants needed water and sunlight.

A half mile or so down the road, she turned down the driveway marked *Miller*, the sound of Eli's happy greeting from inside the barn only serving to solidify her decision to come.

"Hi, Eli," she called back, making her way down the driveway and over to the large white building on the left. "Working late, I see . . ."

Eli stepped out of a stall toward the back of the barn and closed the gap between them with several easy strides, his mop of blond hair escaping around the edges of his straw hat. "It is good to see you, Claire. Esther will be pleased."

"How is Esther feeling?" she asked.

"Esther is fine. You must go inside and say hello."

"I won't be interrupting anything?"

"You do not interrupt." Eli thumbed the back side of the nearly seven-month-old beard that served as his wedding ring and nodded toward the house. "Tell Esther I will be in soon."

"I'll do that." She watched him return to the stall from which he'd come and then made her way up to the house, the smell of warm chocolate chip cookies wafting through the first-floor windows of the couple's home.

When she reached the door, she knocked, the answering sound of Esther's footsteps igniting a smile that claimed far more than just Claire's mouth. She did a little dance atop the welcome mat as the door swung open.

"Claire!"

"Esther!" She accepted Esther's hug and held it for several long moments before stepping back to take in her friend's burgeoning belly. "Look at you! That baby is really growing!"

"That is what I keep telling Eli, but he thinks it might be the cookies I keep making." Esther's gaze dropped to the floor momentarily, only to return to Claire's with a side order of crimson cheeks. "I do not know why, but I can't stop thinking about cookies."

Claire laughed. "It's called pregnancy cravings. And it's normal, from what I've read."

Esther peeked around Claire and surveyed their immediate surroundings, her voice dipping to a whisper. "Yesterday, it was oatmeal cookies. Today, it is chocolate chip. It does not stop."

"I could smell them the moment I left the barn and started in this direction," Claire said.

"They are fresh out of the oven. Would you like one?" Then, shaking her head, Esther motioned Claire to follow her inside. "Of course you want a cookie. You always want cookies."

"And cake . . . and brownies . . ." She closed the door and trailed her friend through the large, sparsely decorated front room that served as a worship space when it was Eli and Esther's turn to host Sunday service. "I wish I could say I've changed in that regard since you left Heavenly Treasures, but I haven't."

"I am glad." Esther led Claire into the kitchen and over to the handmade wooden table in the center of the room. Once she was settled on one of the two long benches Eli had crafted to accompany the table, Esther retrieved the plate of cookies from the counter and set it in front of Claire. "It is good to see you."

She bit into the still-warm cookie and moaned. "Oh, Esther . . . These are delicious."

"They are the same cookies Mamm makes."

"How is Martha?" she asked, taking another bite.

"Mamm is good. We visited for a time this morning when she and Dat came to see Carly."

"Who is Carly?"

"Carly is the horse Eli has bought to pull the buggy."

She refrained from a third bite long enough to consider her friend's words. "What about Minnie? She does a fine job pulling your buggy."

"Minnie is slowing down. Eli worries the buggy will soon be too much for her to pull. Carly's leg should be better by the time the baby is born. When it is, she will pull the buggy."

Securing a second cookie, Claire scooted the plate across the table to Esther. "There's something wrong with the new horse's leg?"

"Eli says it is just a strained tendon. It will heal."

She couldn't help but wonder if Esther was able to read between the lines of Eli's new horse purchase. Sure, maybe Minnie was slowing down. Maybe it really was time to relegate her to second-string buggy-pulling duties. But Claire suspected the real reason lapped at the edges.

Eli was a protector, plain and simple. He felt it his duty to look after the womenfolk in his life—his wife; his twin sister, Ruth; his mother; and even, to some degree, Claire herself. The purchase of a younger, stronger horse to transport his wife and new baby around made perfect sense.

"Eli is a good man." Claire looked around the impeccably maintained kitchen and tried to imagine a half dozen or so children sitting on the same benches where Esther and she now sat. Some of the faces she envisioned favored Eli, with his blond hair and ocean blue eyes. Some were the spitting image of Esther, with her soft brown hair, inquisitive eyes, and propensity for leaving her kapp strings untied. All came together to underscore the part of the Amish culture Claire envied most—the large families and the closeness they shared.

Aware of Esther's gaze, Claire brought her thoughts back to the present. "I am sorry to hear about your neighbor. Did you know him well?"

Esther set her half-eaten cookie on a napkin and rested her hand atop her stomach. "I did. He is with God now."

"How is his wife? His children?"

"Mamm and Dat stopped on their way to see me. They say Emma is looking after the children. She is a strong woman." Esther glanced toward the hallway and then back at Claire, her eyes wide, her voice hushed. "I could not be strong if I lost Eli."

Pushing her own napkin to the side, Claire reached across the table and covered Esther's free hand with her own. "There is no reason to even think of such a thing. You and Eli are going to live a long and happy life together. I just know it."

"I pray that is God's will."

She contemplated a third cookie but opted to refrain, her thoughts traveling back through the day. "I called Jakob about what happened."

The faintest hint of a smile twitched at the corners of Esther's mouth at the mention of her uncle. In public, with her Amish brethren around, Esther abided by the Ordnung and its unwritten rules that mandated she shun her uncle for having left their community after baptism. But in private, or around those who knew better, Esther was beyond thrilled to have Jakob in her life again.

Fortunately, Eli not only understood that, but also shared his wife's feelings.

"I felt he should know," Claire added. "As a detective."

Esther's eyebrows furrowed in confusion. "I do not understand."

"The way the man died . . . it didn't sound right to me."

"The shovel hit his head," Esther said. "It hit him hard."

"Wayne was a big man—a tall man. If he were to step on the handle, it would hit his stomach, not his head," Eli said as he strode into the kitchen and over to the sink to wash his hands. When they were dry, he joined them at the table. "I am glad you told Jakob."

Esther looked from Eli to Claire and back again. "You do not think Wayne's death was an accident, Eli?"

"I did at first. But this afternoon, when I was making that stool for Claire's shop, I see it does not make sense."

"But you did not tell me," Esther whispered.

"I did not want to worry you." He reached across the table for two cookies and handed one of them to his wife. "If something is not right, Jakob will know."

Oh, what Claire wouldn't give to have Jakob there with her, to hear with his own two ears the trust some of his former Amish brethren had in him. Granted, it could never make up for the pain of being shunned by the very people he left to serve and protect, but it was something . . .

Esther looked down at the cookie Eli had given her and quietly placed it back on the plate. "Do you really think it is true? That someone"—Esther dropped her hands to her lap and fiddled with the edge of her dress—"could hit Wayne like that?"

"I do not know, but I wonder." Eli swallowed his cookie and then turned his attention solely on his pregnant wife. As her gaze lifted to meet his, he nodded. "Carly took the carrot right out of my pocket."

The fiddling stopped as Eli's gentle words and reassuring smile worked their magic on Esther. "That is a good sign, Eli. She is eating."

"Yah."

Curious, Claire leaned forward. "Can I ask why you bought a horse that is injured?"

"It is only a strained tendon. She will heal in time."

"She is a wonderful horse," Esther rushed to add. "She has bright eyes."

"Bright eyes?" she echoed. "What does that mean?"

"To many, it means nothing." Eli rose from the wooden bench and crossed to the window above the sink. He surveyed his land for a few moments and then turned to face them once again. "To me, it means she is strong and with purpose. A good thing for one who will pull Esther and the baby."

"That makes sense—"

A vibration inside her front pocket cut her off midsentence and sent her scrambling for her cell phone. "I . . . I'm sorry. I forgot it was on." Claire glanced at the caller ID screen and instantly smiled.

"It is my uncle, yah?" Esther asked

"It is . . ."

"Please. Take his call."

"Are you sure?" she asked. "I know phones aren't something you—"

"You are English." Eli made his way back to the table, gesturing to the phone in Claire's hand as he did. "Please. He might worry if you do not answer."

Chapter 5

To the casual observer, nothing was amiss. They were at their usual corner table in Heavenly Brews, sharing a coffee (his) and a hot chocolate (hers), and engaging in the kind of chitchat that made it appear as if everything was fine.

But no amount of pontificating about the rising humidity or the rapid speed with which Esther's stomach was growing could erase the simple fact that Jakob was preoccupied. Claire sensed it the second he got out of his car to exchange a pleasant nod with his niece and her husband. Sure, the brief interaction had been positive, but still, beneath the smile and the elation that always came with a chance to see Esther and Eli, there had been an aura of heaviness.

Several times during the relatively brief drive back to Lighted Way, she'd thrown out a few seemingly innocuous questions in the hope of getting a feel for his state of mind, but he'd sidestepped every single one with a comment about a particular farm they passed or one of his own questions about her time with Esther and Eli.

When she couldn't take it anymore, Claire leaned around her mug of hot chocolate and plopped her hand in the center of the table, palm up. Like clockwork, he set his hand in hers.

"What's wrong, Jakob?"

Everything from surprise to knee-jerk resistance paraded across his face before his shoulders pitched upward in a halfhearted shrug. "Is it that obvious?"

"To everyone else in here," she said, lowering her voice, "probably not. But to someone who knows and cares about you, yes."

He pulled his hand back and draped it across his chin. "Do you think Esther picked it up?"

"What? That something is wrong? I don't know. I *do* know she was happy to see you, even if she, too, was a little preoccupied."

For a moment, whatever was bothering the man took a backseat to concern for his niece and propelled his upper body halfway across the table. "Is everything okay with the baby?"

She met his anguished eyes with the most reassuring smile she could muster. "Esther is fine. The baby is fine. Eli is fine. She was just a little taken aback to hear both me and Eli questioning the notion that Wayne Stutzman's death was simply an accident."

Jakob casually surveyed their immediate surroundings and then lowered his voice. "Are you saying that Eli thinks Stutzman was murdered?" he asked, looking back at Claire.

"Technically, he never said murder. But he certainly doubts the theory that the man somehow stepped on the handle of the shovel and wacked himself in the head." Tracing her finger around the edge of her mug, she mentally revisited the moment in question. "He, too, finds the man's height a reason for doubt."

Jakob sat up tall, took a gulp of his coffee, and then kneaded the skin just above his eyebrows. "Oh, there's doubt, alright. A *lot* of doubt."

"So I did the right thing in calling you about this?" she asked.

"Absolutely."

"Is that why you seem upset tonight?"

He took another gulp of coffee and then pushed the half-empty cup to his left. "I saw the body. There's no way he stepped on anything."

"Meaning?"

"Meaning someone hit him with that shovel hard enough to kill him."

Her answering gasp turned more than a few heads in their direction. "But . . . why? He's an Amish farmer. With what—five kids?"

"Seven." Jakob palmed his mouth, only to let his hand drop back down to the table with a thump. "We don't know the why, we don't know the who. We found nothing in the barn, and Wayne's wife and kids were all inside the house, playing a card game when it happened. They saw nothing and they heard nothing."

"Was he in a dispute with a neighbor, perhaps?" she asked.

"Stutzman has Amish neighbors on both sides. So, no."

She willed her thoughts to stay in the moment rather than follow an oft-visited path that had caused more than its fair share of heart-pounding nightmares over the past few months—nightmares she opted not to share with her aunt despite having woken the woman with their effects a time or two. Instead, she simply walked on the edge of the memory that spawned them. "The Amish snap, too, Jakob."

"I interviewed his neighbors this afternoon. They didn't do this. I'm certain of that."

"Then who? And why?"

He leaned against the back of his chair and, again, took in the room as a whole before responding. "Do you want my official response or my gut?"

"There's a difference?"

"Right now, in light of the mayor's push to increase our tourism appeal, there is."

"Meaning?" she prodded.

"Meaning my official response at the moment is this: What happened to Wayne Stutzman is an isolated occurrence. We'll, of course, seek to find justice, but we don't think the public has anything to worry about."

An odd shiver made its way down her spine and to her extremities despite the outdoor temperature that made her request for hot chocolate almost silly. "And *unofficially*?"

"I'm not entirely sure that last part is accurate."

"Y-you think the public is—is in danger?" she stammered.

"The general, visiting public? No."

She tried to get a read on what Jakob was thinking, but she got nothing. Nothing except tension, exhaustion, and—

Fear?

"Jakob, please," she pleaded. "Talk to me."

"I'm not sure what to say. I've got nothing to back it up. No evidence, no report, no letter or phone call confirming my suspicions."

"You've got experience and amazing instincts." She grabbed hold of her mug but stopped short of lifting it to her lips. Any warmth she'd hoped to gain from the move, however, was inconsequential in warding off the chill that now enveloped her entire being. "And you've got my undivided attention."

Jakob raked a hand through his hair and down the back of his head. "I'm worried this is a hate crime."

"A hate crime?" she echoed. "Against a farmer?"

"It could be. But it's more likely a hate crime against an Amish farmer . . . with *Amish* being the operative word in that sentence."

Oh, how she wanted to laugh his theory away, to believe that people who lived their lives as pacifists would be treated the same way in return, but she couldn't. Not any longer, anyway. Not since moving to Heavenly and coming face-to-face with reality.

Granted, the incidents of aggression toward the Amish were few and far between, but they weren't unheard-of the way Claire had once ignorantly believed. Now, thanks to nearly eighteen months as a resident of the quaint little Lancaster County town, she knew that impatient English drivers drove Amish buggies and the families they transported off roads and into ditches. She knew that Amish roadside stands—where the honor code was used—were robbed on occasion, the owner's money box and homemade wares stolen. And she knew that Amish children were sometimes taunted, their simple dress and even simpler lifestyle making them an appealing target for English counterparts with too much time on their hands.

"Has there been word of something similar happening in a neighboring town?" she finally asked.

Jakob shook his head.

"Did someone say something to make you think they're being targeted?"

Again he shook his head.

"Then why do you think a hate crime is even a possibility here?"

Slowly, he lifted his gaze to meet hers, the fear she'd seen reflected there only moments earlier now taking on a hint of sadness. "It's just my gut, Claire. The problem is trying to figure out what's driving that feeling. Is it something I registered on a subconscious level while I was at Stutzman's today? Or am I reaching for my old standby simply because I've got nothing else?"

She released her hold on the mug and reached for Jakob's hand again, the coolness of his skin a perfect match for the internal chill she couldn't seem to shake. "I've never known you to reach on anything, Jakob. You're careful, you're inquisitive, you're steady. Trust that. Trust *yourself*."

"I want to, Claire. I really do. But I can't discount the fact that I'm former Amish. Heck, the whole reason I became a cop was because I wanted to avenge a crime against one of my own. I believed, with everything I was, that John Zook was dead because he was Amish."

"And you were right."

"I was." He interlaced their fingers and sighed. "But

that doesn't mean that's the case all the time. Sometimes Amish are victims of crime for the same reason as anyone else—wrong place, wrong time . . . money . . . random violence, etcetera. It doesn't have to always be because they're *different*, you know?"

"You're right, it doesn't. But your gut is telling you something, Jakob. There's a reason for that."

"I get that," he said, his voice taking on a husky, almost strained quality. "I'm just afraid that reason is more about bias than fact."

She considered his words. "Okay, so why do people murder? Maybe that's where we need to start."

He shrugged even as he started rattling off the various reasons. "Revenge, greed, jealousy, drugs, property disputes, a need to protect, love, other felonies, and, as we both know from what happened this past spring, to keep a secret."

She shook off the last reason out of self-preservation and a desire to avoid a repeat of the previous night's nightmare and, instead, started at the top of Jakob's list. "Okay, let's consider revenge. Is there any reason to think someone wanted revenge on the victim?"

"No. I talked to Bishop Hershberger this afternoon and he said there were no problems with Wayne. He was not being shunned for anything and he wasn't in business with anyone." He extricated his hand from Claire's long enough to take a final gulp of what was now surely lukewarm coffee. "Then I stopped at Benjamin's."

"Oh?"

"I figured Ben might give me more thorough answers than the bishop had. And, although he elaborated more when prompted, he said all the same things—the victim was a good farmer, a good husband, a good father, and well respected inside the community."

"Greed? Jealousy? Any chance those are possibilities?" she asked.

He shook his head.

"I imagine it's safe to assume no property disputes or drug issues, yes? So what does that leave us?"

"A need to *protect*—which wouldn't be the case because Wayne was in his own barn—and . . . *love*. I asked his wife if he ever disappeared for unexplained bouts of time, but of course, he didn't."

"Could he have been killed by someone who was there to do something else?" she posed. "Like to steal something?"

"He was in the barn, remember?" Jakob said, not unkindly. "And his oldest son, Henry, did a thorough inspection of everything for me and said nothing was missing."

"Well, then I think it only makes sense that your gut is leading you toward a hate crime. After all, what else is there? Nothing else fits."

"Nothing else fits," he repeated. "Nothing. Else. Fits."

She squeezed his hand inside hers and hoped her smile offered whatever boost he needed to believe in himself and his instincts. "Follow your gut, Jakob."

"The mayor isn't going to like what my gut is saying."

"So don't tell him," she said. "Not yet, anyway. Tell him only if and when you have to."

Silence followed in the wake of her advice and she let it hover, unchecked. Jakob had a lot on his mind. If there was any chance her words were going to hit their target and take root, she needed to let him think, process.

When he finally did speak, it followed the very real thrill of feeling his lips on her hand. "Thank you, Claire. I needed this more than I can ever say."

"I'm glad." She pushed back her chair and stood. "Now, Detective, you need to get some sleep. You've got a gut to follow come morning."

Chapter 6

For the umpteenth time, the term *revolving door* went through Claire's head as she and Annie moved from one customer to the next, answering questions and ringing up purchases.

Two footstools . . .

A quilt . . .

Two hand-painted milk cans . . .

A half dozen or so Amish dolls . . .

Three scented candles . . .

An Amish-themed picture frame . . .

Four baby bibs . . .

On and on it went as tourists visited Heavenly Treasures to browse and left with a memento (or several) of their trip to Amish country. A few times, they even came back, their knee-jerk decision to walk away from a particular item proving ineffectual against the ticking clock that was their vacation.

"I do not think I have seen such a busy Thursday." Annie sank against the shop's front door, exhaling a burst of air through puckered lips as she did. "Michigan, Wisconsin, Florida, Tennessee. So many people come from such great distances."

Claire broke a roll of quarters into the appropriate compartment inside the register and then closed the drawer. "People are fascinated by the way you live, Annie. They're drawn to the simplicity."

"That is what Henry says, too." Annie parted company with the door and made her way over to the display of handmade baby bibs that had grown increasingly disheveled throughout the morning.

Claire took a moment to revel in the momentary lull in customers and the window of time it provided to catch up with the young girl. "How is he? I imagine this must all be so hard on him."

"He is the oldest. He must be strong for his mamm." A hint of crimson inched its way into Annie's cheeks as she fanned a handful of bibs across the top of the shelf and stacked a few others. "But I am worried for him. It is hard to accept God's will when it is your mamm or your dat who is gone."

Stepping around the counter, Claire crossed to the now-neatened baby bib display. "You care about Henry, don't you?"

Annie's response came via a nod that was so slight, so quick, Claire wasn't entirely sure she'd seen it at all. But, based on the girl's sudden fidgeting, she knew it was a safe assumption.

"I've never met your friend Henry, but I'm sure he's nice if you like him." Claire reached around Annie to straighten a stack of infant onesies, her thoughts jumping ahead to the list of items she'd ask Martha, Eli, and Esther to replenish.

"We are friends. That is all."

It was hard not to smile at Annie's need to backpedal, the memory of having done the same thing a time or two in her own youth pushing all inventory needs to the background. "Friends are good, Annie. We all need them—in good times and bad times. Henry is lucky to have you as a friend."

Annie crossed to the doll display and began arranging them in size order. "I am the one who is blessed. When Mamm died, everyone said it was God's will. I know that it was, but that did not mean I did not mourn. That was *Mamm*. I *loved* her." When she had the dolls back to the way they liked, Annie turned to Claire, her eyes bright with unshed tears. "Henry would ask how I was at recess each day. And if I cried because I missed Mamm, he would pat my back. Sometimes, he would even bring me cookies *his* mamm made for me."

"Henry sounds like a very special friend."

"Yah." Annie glanced at the shelves around her, instinctively righting candles, sorting place mats, and stacking calendars as she did. "That is why it is me who is blessed."

"I suspect you will be the same source of comfort for Henry at the loss of his dat, as he has been for you all these years." Claire hooked her thumb toward the counter and the stools they occasionally utilized for working lunches on busy days and chat-sessions on quiet days. "Let's take advantage of the lunch hour and actually eat, okay?"

Annie trailed Claire across the shop and around the counter. Reaching onto a shelf sheltered from the customers' view, the girl retrieved a small metal bucket with a piece of simple fabric that served as a cover. "I brought you a piece of cold chicken. My sister, Eva, made it for Dat and me last night."

Her stomach growled in response, earning her a welcomed laugh from Annie. "I take it you heard that?" Claire joked.

"Yah. It was very loud."

"Well, that's what happens when you mention chicken to a woman who slept through breakfast." She pulled her own brown paper sack from the same shelf and peeked inside. "I can offer you a handful of grapes in return."

"That is what makes *my* stomach talk." Annie took the grapes from Claire's outstretched hand and popped one into her mouth. "Do you have a good friend that *you* talk to?"

Claire took a bite of chicken and chased it down with a sip of water. "You mean besides you? Sure. I have many now that I'm living here in Heavenly."

"Who do you talk to when you are sad?" Annie nibbled at a cookie and then went back to the grapes, her gaze never leaving Claire's face.

"That depends on what I'm sad about, I guess. But mostly I'd have to say my aunt Diane or Jakob."

Annie stopped chewing. "But Jakob is not your friend. He is your boyfriend."

"He's both. And that's why I love him so much. He cares about me as a person every bit as much as he cares about me as a girlfriend."

"Do you think you are the same to him?"

"I certainly hope so." She lowered the chicken leg to her napkin and studied Annie, the girl's wide eyes and rapt attention connecting the girl's questions in Claire's head. "The person you choose to spend your life with, Annie, needs to care about you—your opinions, your dreams, your health, your being. And, likewise, you need to care for him in the same way."

"I care for Henry that way," Annie whispered. "I smile when he smiles, I am sad when he is sad, and I worry when he worries. It has been that way since we were in school."

"That's a good start."

"This morning, when I was bringing a plate of Eva's cinnamon rolls to Henry's mamm, I saw him. He was quiet."

Claire nudged her lunch to the side and propped her elbows atop the counter. "That makes sense. It has been little more than thirty-six hours since he found his father dead in the barn, right?"

"This was a different quiet. It was troubled, not sad." Annie reached across the gap between their lunches and sheepishly helped herself to a few more grapes. "After I gave the plate to his mamm, I stopped in the barn to check on Henry. I asked him what was wrong."

"And?"

"At first, he would not say. He just asked about me and how *I* am doing. But I did not answer. I said that it was *his* turn to talk and *my* turn to listen." Annie ate the rest of the grapes and then settled her back against the edge of the counter. "He knows he is to look after his mamm, but he must work many hours now to replace what is gone. I told him everyone would help."

"It doesn't make it easier, but he and his mother and siblings will find a routine as the days and weeks go on."

Annie waved Claire's words away. "It is not the routine,

it is the money that is gone. He will need to work many hours and many jobs to put that back."

"Wait. I'm confused. Put what back?" she asked.

"The money that is now missing."

She felt her breath hitch. "What money?"

"His dat's money. It is all gone."

Dropping her arms back down to the counter, Claire stared at her employee, the girl's words catching her by surprise. "I thought Henry told Jakob nothing was missing."

"The money can was in the kitchen, not the barn. Henry did not see that it was empty until this morning. He did not want to worry his mamm, but he knows he must tell her today."

"Does Jakob know this?"

Annie stuffed the rest of her lunch back into her pail and then shrugged. "I do not think so. I do not know how he could."

"We have to tell him, Annie, and we have to tell him right now." Claire slipped off her stool and retrieved her cell phone from the cupboard beneath the register. The previous night, they'd been lacking for motives. But now, in light of what Annie had just shared, things had changed.

"But why?"

"That empty jar might be as simple as Henry's mamm moving the money to a different location. Or, it could be connected to the death of his dat."

Annie sucked in her breath so hard and so loud, Claire had to strain to make out the detective's greeting in her ear. Fortunately for her, he repeated it.

"Claire? Are you there?"

"Yes, yes, I'm here."

"Is everything okay?"

"I'm not sure." She took a moment to reign in her own breath and to compose her sentence as succinctly as possible. "Annie spoke with Henry Stutzman this morning. It seems money is missing from their home."

"Missing?"

"That's what Henry told her," she relayed.

Jakob sighed in her ear. "Why didn't he tell me this yesterday?"

"Because he didn't realize it was gone until this morning."

"Okay, I'm on it." The creak of his chair in the background let her know the detective was on the move, whatever immediate plans he'd had prior to her call now shelved. "Thanks, Claire. This could be the break I've been looking for."

Chapter 7

With the toes of her right foot acting as a door prop, Claire hoisted the last of the boxes up off the back stoop and carried them into the long but narrow back room that served as her staging area for all of her shop's treasures, Amish or otherwise. There, she could cull through the occasional supply delivery, sorting the picture frames she would soon embellish into one area and the jars and pedestals she often used for her homemade candles into another.

"Claire? May I come in?"

Peeking over her shoulder, she smiled at the tall, blue-eyed man visible through the screen door. The afternoon sun beat down on his broad-brimmed straw hat and created an almost halo-like effect that fit the man well. His dark brown hair, visible beneath the inside edges of the hat, curled ever so slightly in the humid air.

"Benjamin, hi. Yes . . . please. Come in." Claire set the box down, wiped her hands along the sides of the jeans she'd donned to deal with the delivery, and crossed back to the door just as the Amish man stepped through it. "I didn't hear your buggy in the alley just now . . ."

"That is because Eli dropped me off on his way to Gussman's."

"I'm glad." And she was. Benjamin Miller was special. He was kind, he was gentle, he was considerate, and he was the kind of steadfast friend everyone wished they had. The fact that, at one time, he'd been willing to leave the only life he'd ever known in order to have one with her was simply the icing on one of his sister's second-to-none cakes. "Did you check on Ruth?"

"Yah." He gestured to a stack of napkins with his callused hand and, at her nod, plucked one off a shelf. Unfolding it to its true size, Ben used it to wipe the sweat from his high cheekbones. "She says it has been busy today. She has sold many pies and cakes."

"She always sells a lot of pies and cakes." Claire crossed to the boxes she'd stacked in the corner and retrieved her water bottle from its resting spot on the floor. She held it out to Ben. "Here. Finish this."

He started to protest, but when she placed it in his hand, he accepted, the water disappearing in a matter of two large gulps. "Thank you, Claire."

She took a moment to really take in his attire—black shoes, black pants, pale blue shirt, and suspenders. It was the traditional dress for Amish men like Benjamin, but still, it was July . . .

"I could turn on the fan in my office and we could sit in there for a little while if you'd like," she offered, gesturing toward the open doorway at the opposite end of the room. "It really helps on a hot day like this."

He smiled but remained standing in exactly the same place. "Do you need any help?"

"No. I'm fine." She guided his gaze toward the trio of boxes with her own. "I was just carrying in the last one when you appeared at the door."

"You should not carry such boxes. You should leave them for me or for Eli. We will carry them."

"Carrying my boxes into my store isn't your job, Benjamin." She turned back in time to catch the longing look he cast at the now-empty water bottle in his hand. Without giving him a chance to protest, she took his hand, led him to her office, and insisted he sit in the path of the oscillating fan that made the July day feel a bit more like May. "Now, can I get you some more water?"

He lifted his chin as the fan-powered air moved across his face. "Yah. If it is not too much trouble."

"It's not." She lowered herself to her desk chair, yanked open the bottom drawer, and fished out one of a half dozen water bottles it stowed. "Here you go."

"Thank you."

"I take it you've been working in your fields all day?" she asked.

"Yah. In Stutzman's fields, too."

She opened her mouth to question the increased workload, but closed it as reality sank in. It didn't matter how much work Benjamin had on his own plate; it was in his nature to help others, Amish or otherwise. All she had to do was look around her store and remember how close she'd been to losing everything to know that.

Because of Benjamin, she had the kind of bigger-ticket items that made a difference to Heavenly Treasures' bottom line. And because of that, she'd been able to stay in Heavenly, with the friends she adored and the man she envisioned spending the rest of her life with one day.

Jakob . . .

Forcing her thoughts back into the room, she waited for Benjamin to finish his latest gulp of water. "Did you know Wayne Stutzman well?"

He wiped the back of his hand across his mouth and recapped the bottle. "Yah."

"I'm sorry to hear of his death."

"Yah. He leaves behind his wife, Emma, and seven children."

She ran her finger along the edge of her desk and then glanced toward the shop's main room. "Annie is friends with the oldest boy, Henry."

"Henry will be a great help to Emma. He will look after the fields and help with his brothers and sisters. He is a hard worker."

"It's a shame he has to be," she murmured.

Benjamin drew back. "I do not understand."

Taking a deep breath, she tried to explain her words. "Henry is sixteen like Annie, yes?"

"Yah."

"He just got his first horse and is learning to drive a buggy just like Annie. And, because of the loss of his father, he will now have to move straight to adulthood."

Benjamin said nothing and, instead, looked around the room, taking in the calendar, the calculator, and finally, the framed photograph of Claire and Jakob on the swing outside Sleep Heavenly. He pointed at the picture. "Jakob will find the truth."

"About . . ."

"Wayne's death." Benjamin sat through one more swipe of cool air and then stood. "If he died by another man's hand, Jakob will know."

She swallowed around the sudden lump in her throat, the strides made between the two men over the past several months almost unfathomable. Six months earlier, the tension between the childhood friends had blanketed each and every space they inhabited together. Now, in the wake of a case that had necessitated conversation back in the early part of the year, there was a semblance of peace and mutual respect.

"So you believe Wayne Stutzman was murdered, too?" she said, her voice still raspy with emotion.

"I do not know what to think. But Eli makes good points."

"That's because your brother is a smart man . . . like you." She followed him back out into the hall and toward the door that would take him into the alley between Heavenly Treasures and his sister's bake shop. "It isn't any wonder why Ruth has not found the right man yet. Her yardstick is set quite high thanks to the two of you."

"Yardstick?" Benjamin repeated. "What yardstick?"

"Never mind." She rose up on the balls of her feet and planted a friendly kiss on the man's smooth-shaven skin. "Ruth will marry when she is ready."

He pushed open the screen door and stepped outside, his gaze flitting between Shoo Fly Bake Shoppe and Claire. "Mamm believes there will be a winter wedding."

"For *Ruth*?"

"Yah. She is courting."

She made a mental note to ask Ruth about her mystery man the next time they spoke and then looked up to find Benjamin studying her closely. "What?"

"Maybe she is not the only one who will have a wedding one day . . ."

More than anything, Claire hoped he was right—for himself as much as for her. Benjamin Miller was simply too special to continue living his life alone.

She was just getting ready to lock the front door when a familiar face waved to her through its glass panel.

"Mr. Naber, hello. Please, come in." Claire reopened the door, swept her arm toward the interior of the shop, and then closed the door behind her aunt's guest. "It seems we're always seeing each other in passing."

The balding man rocked back on his heels and nodded. "It does, indeed. But I've had both breakfast and dinner meetings the past two days. Of course, the people I've been in meetings with keep telling me all about the wonderful food I'm missing by not eating at the inn."

She laughed. "I wish I could put your mind at ease on that one, but I can't. You're missing out."

"Thank you for that." His brown eyes skittered across

the shop just before he plucked a notebook from his pocket. "You've done a nice job in here. It's quite warm and inviting."

"Thank you."

He paused his pen-holding hand above the notebook and smiled at Claire. "In fact, warm and inviting seems to be the prevalent feel throughout this entire town."

"I couldn't agree more. In fact, it's why I'm living here today."

"And it's certainly a feel that has its merit. One only has to look at the demographic stepping off the tour buses on a daily basis in this town to see that." Jim wandered over to the shop's large front window and the view of Lighted Way it afforded to the left and to the right. "It's the other demographics that need this town's attention now."

She came to stand beside him, her own gaze traveling up and down the road. "So how's it going with the mayor and the councilmen? Are you coming up with some interesting ways to advertise Heavenly?"

"We are. But we can't advertise to the younger demographic until we have something that appeals to them."

"Do you mean little kids?" she asked.

"No. I mean the twenty-somethings."

She turned her back to Lighted Way and focused on the man. "Why? They're not retired."

"Folks don't have to be retired to enjoy Heavenly. Open up a few bars, tweak a few of the countryside tours, and suddenly we have more than elderly folks walking the streets of Heavenly."

"But this isn't a bar town," Claire argued. "You bring

bars in here, and we'll lose the demographic that actually has real money to spend."

"Trust me, Claire. The twenty-somethings have money to spend. They just want to spend it in different ways."

She worked to steady her breathing, to remind herself that the man standing in front of her had merely been hired to make suggestions. "Besides bars, what else are you envisioning?"

"Countryside tours with a slightly different appeal than the ones being offered now."

"Oh?"

"Sure. The tour company could offer one or two runs a day that show tourists a different aspect of the Amish lifestyle."

"Different? Different, how?"

"That would be up to the tour bus companies, of course, but anything that shows another side to the Amish is a safe bet. I mean look at the shows on TV these days. People want to see—"

"Things that aren't true?" she finished.

"Does it really matter? It's captured interest. And that's all we want to do here—capture interest." Jim made his way over to a postcard display and gave the caddy a spin. When he found the one he wanted, he waved it toward the register, indicating he was ready to pay.

She wound her way around the counter, stopped in front of the register, and rang up the postcard. "People equate Heavenly with warmth and peace, Mr. Naber. You start changing that basic foundation and replacing it with something ugly and this town will be hiring you back to do damage control."

"You say that like it's a bad thing." He handed her the correct change, took the narrow paper sack containing the postcard in exchange, and headed back across the shop.

"You disagree?"

"Of course." When he reached the front door, he waved his paper bag in her direction. "A job is a job, Claire. You take one wherever you can get one."

Chapter 8

Claire peeked over the top edge of the paperback mystery she was reading, the amusement she felt mirrored on the face of the man seated in the single back chair to her right.

"Okay, Aunt Diane, it's time to let us in on whatever it is you're doing over there that has you so focused." She rested the book, spine-side up, on the armrest of the sofa and stretched. "Mr. Turner and I are jealous."

"*Hank*," the man reminded as he closed his book on marketing strategies for small businesses. Then, training his focus on the sixty-two-year-old woman hunched over the desktop computer in the corner of the parlor, he added, "Yes, Diane, please. Enlighten us. My book is proving to be a sleep tonic I don't particularly want or need at eight o'clock in the evening."

Diane removed her hand from the wireless mouse,

checked her wristwatch, and then swiveled her chair to the left, her cheeks reddening by the second. "I'm sorry. I didn't mean to waste so much time like this."

Waving her hands in protest, Claire stood and made her way over to the computer. "No one could ever accuse you of wasting time. Ever. We're just curious as to what you're"—she took in the full screen of print as she approached—"*reading* over here. It sounds fascinating."

"Fascinatingly sad, yes." Diane turned back to the computer, gesturing at the online article displayed on the monitor as she did. "This is a weekly bonus sent out to subscribers of *The Stable Life*. It usually includes puzzles and tidbits and photographs. Unfortunately, I'm not very good about staying up on them and I got to this one a few days late."

"Gee, I wonder why, Miss-I-Refuse-To-Stop-Moving-Until-My-Head-Hits-The-Pillow-At-Night," Claire joked as she rested her hand atop her aunt's shoulder and squeezed. "So what's so sad?"

"Carrot Thief is gone."

"Carrot Thief?" she repeated.

Diane looked up long enough to nod before filling in the gaps. "Carrot Thief was a Standardbred racer. She's been a trotter for a few years, although not necessarily a *race-winning* trotter. In last month's issue, her owner, Valerie Palermo, was the lead feature story. This woman owns a number of horses who win on a regular basis. And while that article was focused primarily on *those* horses, she talked about Carrot Thief, too. About the bond they have. It was a beautiful story."

"I take it the horse passed away?"

"It might have, but as of this most recent update to a

story that apparently broke two weeks ago, they still don't know." Diane pushed a strand of gray-streaked hair off her cheek and readjusted her bifocals. "I can only imagine how devastated Ms. Palermo must be right now. There was something mighty special about the two of them together."

"How could they not know whether the horse is dead or not?"

Diane closed out of the email, checked the rest of her inbox, and then signed off of her account with a rare and prolonged sigh. "I would imagine, after all the specifics they gave about the horse in this most recent update, if we don't hear anything positive in the report that should be due to post next week, the likelihood she's still alive is slim to none."

Hank's glass thumped against the coffee table as he placed it down on one of the coasters Claire had given Diane as a just-because present the previous month. The moment Jakob's sister, Martha, had brought the hand-painted set of eight into the shop, Claire knew they were destined to belong to her aunt. What she hadn't expected was the coaxing it would take to get Diane to use them.

"They're too pretty, Claire. I don't want water glass– stains on these pictures . . ."

"Did someone leave the horse's stall open?" Hank asked, returning Claire's attention to the subject at hand.

She followed Hank's gaze back to Diane and waited for the woman's answer.

"No. Carrot Thief was on her way to the farm between races and the van she was in overturned on a back road. The driver was killed."

Claire's gasp matched Hank's. "How awful!"

62

"Because it was a back road, the accident went unnoticed for hours. By the time it was discovered, Carrot Thief was gone."

"Wow."

Diane pushed her chair back from the desk and stood, the large plate glass window that overlooked the Amish countryside in the distance claiming her attention just as surely as news about the missing horse had done for the past twenty minutes. Whether the woman was actually seeing the farms or the cows or the crops, though, Claire couldn't be sure.

"I can't help but feel like the information they released in this most recent update might have been too much."

"How so?"

"Anyone who read last month's issue of *The Stable Life* knew Carrot Thief wasn't a great racer. Loveable, yes, but a racer, not so much . . ."

Claire joined her aunt at the window, but kept her body turned so as not to cut off Hank. "Okay . . ."

"The first email report that arrived after the accident was really just a breaking news piece—one that was especially moving on account of the magazine's subscriber base having just fallen in love with this particular horse two weeks earlier. Basic facts about the crash scene, the dead driver, etcetera, were provided, and a promise was issued to keep readers informed of any updates." Diane, suddenly aware of the fact she was standing still, pulled a cloth from her apron pocket and began flitting around the cozy parlor, dusting shelves, picture frames, and assorted knickknacks, her mouth moving as quickly as her hands. "Then, on Monday, they send out this latest update and it shows a snapshot of her sister. I'm not an expert on these matters by any means, but even *I* think that's information that was better left unshared."

"You lost me, Aunt Diane."

She watched her father's oldest sister move on to the mantel, her thoughts briefly visiting the many evenings spent in this very room in front of a roaring fire. "The wrong person comes across that horse and, well, she may never be returned."

"I'm still not following. You said something a minute ago about a sister. Is this the *owner's* sister?"

"No. Carrot Thief's sister, Idle Ruler."

She mulled her aunt's words over and came up with the only thing that made sense. "I take it Idle Ruler is someone special?"

"Idle Ruler is a champion trotter."

"So even if Carrot Thief isn't a good racer herself, her bloodlines are good, yes?" Hank posed from his chair.

"Exactly." Diane stopped dusting and turned, her eyes wide. "Hank, I'm sorry. I'm going on and on about some horse I've never seen while you're trying to relax and read."

"I could read through a natural disaster, Diane. I stopped reading because I was more interested in the conversation." Hank took a sip of his tea and then tapped the notebook that sat, opened, on his knee, a pen resting halfway down the page. "Hey, can I share a thought with the two of you?"

"Of course," Diane and Claire said in unison.

"I know this is taking my research for my business classes in a different direction, but I find it interesting how, at least with the Amish, the implementation of cottage industries has changed them."

Diane wandered over to the upholstered lounge chair she often selected for a rare evening of reading and sat down. "Changed them?"

"I guess I should amend that to say how I *think* it's changed them." Hank nodded at Claire as she made her way back to the sofa. "I mean, I'd always heard that the Amish kept to themselves. But the ones I've met while checking out some of their small businesses aren't that way at all. They ask questions, they answer questions, they even joke around a little on occasion."

"The increase in population and the lack of available farmland has made it so they have to turn to industries that put them in touch with the English on a daily basis. They've *had* to change." Diane folded her dust cloth and then slipped it back into her apron pocket. "Though, honestly, I've always found them to be delightful."

"Do they still put work aside on Sundays?" Hank asked, retrieving his pen and preparing to write.

Claire nodded, her gaze shifting between the book she knew she wasn't going to get back to and her aunt's handsome guest. "They do. Sunday is for church and family."

"Can you imagine the money they are missing out on by closing businesses that cater to tourists on a weekend? Amazing."

"They'll close on occasional Tuesdays and Thursdays during wedding season, too," Diane offered. "They do well, financially, but money is not the end goal for them as it so often is for the general population."

"They close up for funerals, too." Claire took in the clock and its advancing post-dinner hour and continued. "In fact, from what I'm hearing, many of the shops will be closed on Saturday for the funeral of Wayne Stutzman, a local Amish farmer who was found dead in his barn Tuesday night."

"Did he live next to a farm with a small engine repair shop out back?" Before Claire could respond, he added, "Because I saw a cop car parked outside that home on Wednesday afternoon and again earlier today, and that surprised me. I thought the Amish stayed away from the police."

"They do. But sometimes it's unavoidable."

"Why?"

Diane picked up the conversation, shaking her head slowly as she did. "The Amish, sadly, are easy targets. I wish that wasn't so, but it is."

Hank rested his pen atop the notebook and looked from Claire to Diane and back again. "Wait. I sort of remember reading something about the Amish keeping their money in their homes rather than banks. Is *that* why you say they're easy targets?"

"That's one of the reasons."

"Do they all do that?" Hank asked, wide-eyed.

"There are always a few exceptions to any rule, but I think it's safe to say that *most* do."

Claire pulled her book off the armrest of the sofa and inserted a bookmark into the place where she'd left off. "They're also easy targets because of their reluctance in seeking out police, as you mentioned a few moments ago."

"How do they keep track of that kind of money?" Hank asked, his eyes wide with intrigue. "I mean, if their business or their crops are even moderately successful, that could translate to a lot of cash sitting around their homes."

"They use paper and pencil." Diane returned to her feet, adjusted the throw pillow she'd dislodged by sitting, and made her way toward the hallway. "It works well for them."

"Maybe. But that's the one thing I would tell my students *not* to do. Money can't grow in a jar. It can only grow in a bank."

Diane paused at the door long enough to welcome Hayley and Jeremy all the way into the room and to address Hank's claim. "Oh, trust me, their money grows in those jars, and it grows well. But that's because of their choices and spending habits rather than interest and dividends. So maybe that *is* something your students should hear."

"Touché." Hank grinned at Claire as Diane disappeared into the hall. "Your aunt is one smart cookie."

"That she is." Claire scooted closer to the end of the sofa and smiled at the tall, lanky blonde and her dark-haired companion. "Hayley. Jeremy. Please. Come join us."

Hayley pushed a piece of hair behind her ear and strode over to Diane's chair, stopping short of actually sitting. Jeremy, on the other hand, took Claire's invitation.

"What smells so good?" the writer half of the blog duo asked, his gaze shifting around the room. "I haven't been able to think of anything else since that smell started pumping up the steps."

Claire laughed. "That, Jeremy, is the smell of my aunt's homemade chocolate chip cookies. They are, without a doubt, the best I've ever eaten."

"Well, that isn't making the wait any easier." Jeremy drummed the fingers of his left hand on the armrest and then sank back against the sofa.

"Busy day?" Hank asked.

"You could say that."

Hayley rolled her eyes, waving Jeremy's answer aside as she did. "My cohort, here, is struggling with the concept of work. To him, being busy is somehow bad. To me, it means getting the job done."

"So you're finding what you need here?" Claire asked.

"Not yet, but I will." Hayley made a face at Jeremy. "Assuming, of course, he gets off the couch and stops yammering on and on about nothing."

"I'm offended by what you said, Hayley. Deeply, deeply offended." Holding his hand to his wide chest, Jeremy feigned injury with such theatrics Claire and Hank both laughed. "First, I don't yammer—whatever that means. Second, contrary to what you have portrayed to these good people, I don't mind being busy. I simply want a chance to get some of these highly endorsed cookies before we're off and running again. Is that really too much to ask? *Sheesh*."

Claire met Hayley's baby blue eyes across the coffee table and smiled. "For what it's worth, Diane's cookies *are* worth the wait. I promise."

Chapter 9

It was, bar none, her favorite part of the evening and the one she looked forward to from the moment post-dinner cleanup was done. Yes, she treasured the time in between—time that included reading, cookies, and talking with Diane—but ending her day with Jakob had become something special, something both exhilarating and calming.

Settling her bare shoulders against the padded headrest of her bed, Claire plucked her phone off the nightstand and dialed the detective's number. Sure enough, before the first ring was complete, the man's warm voice came across the line.

"I was just about to call you," he said, his tone depicting the smile she imagined in her head. "How was your evening? Dinner? Time with Diane?"

"The evening was nice. I didn't read as much as normal, but that's because Hank, one of the guests, spent a chunk of the time with us."

"This is the college teacher, right?"

"Yes, and I suspect he's good at what he does. He really seems to love his subject matter, that's for sure. Couple that with an engaging personality and, well, I imagine his students learn a lot in his classes." Claire took a sip of water and then placed her glass back on the nightstand. "How was the rest of your day?"

"Whoa, whoa, whoa. Don't you go changing the subject just yet," Jakob teased. "You haven't told me what kind of cookie I missed."

Claire laughed and scooted down onto her pillow, her gaze landing on the ceiling. "I'm almost afraid to tell you."

A protracted pause was followed by a sigh. "She made chocolate chip, didn't she?"

"She did."

"I think it's time to lodge a formal complaint. No chocolate chip cookies unless I'm present."

"I'll see if Aunt Diane will take that under consideration. Though, knowing it's you making the complaint, I suspect she'll make the necessary changes." And it was true. Diane was in love with the idea of Claire and the detective being in love. In the beginning, it had been bothersome, maybe even a little bit annoying, but now, Claire couldn't agree more.

"Anyway, moving on from the cookies . . . How was *your* day?"

This time, when he sighed, there wasn't anything playful about it. Instead, the sound was laced with palpable exhaustion and frustration. "Well, I followed up your call about money missing from the Stutzman farm."

"And?"

"We're talking about several thousand dollars here."

"Several thousand?" she echoed, struggling back up onto her elbow. "Are you serious?"

"Trust me, it could have been a lot more."

"It's just gone?"

He nodded. "That's right. Poof! Gone!" Jakob cleared his throat and then continued, "Wayne kept it in an old milk can that sat in the corner of the kitchen. A large amount is still there, but it falls several thousand short of what's recorded in the victim's handwritten ledger."

"Maybe he'd simply fallen behind on his bookkeeping," she suggested.

"I thought the same thing until Henry showed me the updated total his father had logged the previous night. And considering Wayne was on the farm the entire day he died, and then at the dinner table with his family, there's nothing to suggest he spent that kind of money in twenty-four hours."

"Okay, so then what?"

"At first, I wasn't sure. I mean, the money could have disappeared at any time after Wayne made his final entry in his ledger. But while I was trying to piece together possible scenarios, one of Henry's younger sisters mentioned a man who'd stopped at the house to ask directions the same night Wayne was killed."

She sat up tall, hiking her knees against her chest as she did. "The killer?"

"Quite likely." A beat or two of silence was followed by a third sigh. "All I've really got, though, is a time frame that seems to work. This man stopped by and asked for directions after Wayne had already left for the barn. After

Henry gave them, the man asked for a drink of water. Henry took him into the house to oblige, but by the time he filled the glass, the man said he was no longer thirsty and needed to get on his way. My guess is he stuck his hand in the milk can while Henry was occupied at the sink, helped himself to a bundle or two of cash, and then thought it best to get out. Thirty minutes later, when Wayne didn't join his family on the side porch, Henry went looking for his dat in the barn."

"So you think this guy went into the barn after walking out of the house? Maybe looking for more cash or something else to steal, and killed Wayne in the process?"

"It's the only thing I've got at the moment."

"It's more than you had yesterday," she reminded him softly.

"In terms of motive, maybe. In terms of who, not so much."

"Can't a sketch artist help to fill in that blank?"

"That's the first thing I did." Jakob's voice softened as if in thought, only to resume its normal volume in short order. "It wasn't easy, I'll tell you that. At first, Emma refused the very idea of a sketch artist, but when I explained to her my belief that the missing cash is linked to Wayne's death, she relented under the condition the sketch artist came to them. So I obliged."

"And?"

"Henry described the man who'd stopped for directions while his father was in the barn, and the artist sketched him."

Claire hugged her free hand around her calves and took a slow, measured breath. "Okay . . . That's good, right?"

"It would be if we got something we could work with. A detail that we could put out to the community—freckles, bushy eyebrows, an identifying mark, eye color, something."

"I don't understand."

"Essentially all we've got is brown hair—similar to mine, no beard, and English."

"That's it?"

"That's it." A momentary pause gave way to a last-minute addendum. "Oh. And no hat."

"But that's more than half of the people we see on any given day," she summarized.

"Yep."

She released her hold on her legs and straightened them out once again, the seemingly insurmountable obstacle Jakob was facing almost depressing. "So now what?"

"I don't know."

As much as she wished she could be sitting on the couch in his living room having this conversation in person, she didn't need to see his face to know he was at a loss. "You'll figure this out, Jakob. I know it. And so does Ben."

"Ben?" he asked suddenly.

"He stopped by to say hello this afternoon, and Wayne's death came up. He, like Eli, is struggling to believe it was an accident. He also said he knows you'll find the truth."

"He said that?"

She nodded, and then, realizing her mistake, gave words to the unseen gesture. "He said that. And he meant it."

Silence blanketed the space between them for so long, Claire actually pulled the phone from her ear and checked the connection. When she was sure he was still there, she searched for something to say to draw him back into the conversation.

"Jakob? I . . . I hope you know I'm willing to help in any way I can. I know a case like this has to be difficult."

"Daunting is more like it," he said. "But thank you. That means more than you can know."

She opened her mouth to speak but closed it as he cleared his throat and moved on. "I'm sorry I'm not being a better conversationalist right now. It's not from lack of desire, I promise. It's just that feeling this directionless is tough. I want to figure out who did this to Wayne and bring him to justice. And while I know that rarely happens overnight in any case, this one is proving particularly tough."

"You've got a likely motive now. You didn't have that last night," she reminded. "And robbery takes the hate crime possibility out of the mix, right?"

"Technically, since Henry invited this guy into the house while he got the requested drink of water, it's larceny. *Grand* larceny because of the amount stolen."

"Okay . . ."

"Now as for whether that removes the hate crime possibility from the mix, it's too soon to tell. Maybe it does, maybe it doesn't."

"You have a picture now," she reminded him gently.

"One that could be half the males in this town."

More than anything, Claire wanted to slip her hands inside Jakob's and lean her head against his shoulder; instead, she had to hope that her words would provide the boost he obviously needed. "It's still more than you had yesterday. Maybe something will come in tomorrow, or the day after that."

"Wayne will be laid to rest Saturday."

"Maybe someone at the funeral will have seen this person of interest, too. Maybe they'll be able to provide more detail than Henry did."

"Maybe . . ."

Claire made her way around the empty seat to Hayley's left and quietly refilled Hank's orange juice glass, the conversation taking place around her no match for the one from the previous night that kept resurrecting itself in her thoughts.

She'd tried to be encouraging and optimistic, but once she and Jakob had called it quits for the night, she'd realized just how out of touch she'd been. With no workable sketch of the man who'd likely stolen the money from the Stutzman home, or witnesses to what happened to Wayne in the barn, finding the man's murderer was the proverbial needle in a haystack quandary.

For a man like Jakob, who'd sacrificed so much of himself in the name of justice, such a task had to be maddening, if not downright depressing.

"I never grow tired of looking at these pictures, Diane. They all tell a story if you're willing to take the time to see it." Judy Little pointed to the dining room wall and the framed black-and-white photographs that adorned it. "Like that one of the field. The horses resting off to the side of the partly plowed crop is so perfect. Then again, I'm still just as partial to the one of the Amish boy practicing his driving skills on the miniature horse with the heads of his siblings popping over the sides of the pull cart."

"When do Amish children start driving?" Hayley asked.

"When the parents feel they are capable of handling a full-sized horse and buggy." Diane placed a spoon inside a large bowl of fruit and set it down in the middle of the table. "Going to pick out a horse when they're a teenager is an exciting day. They'll actually take a horse out of the stall and test drive it prior to purchase just like we test drive a car. They want to know how the horse handles and how it responds to commands."

"Did you read the paper this morning?" Judy asked, switching gears. "The story about that Amish family who was robbed? I just can't wrap my head around the notion someone would steal from the *Amish*. I mean, *why*?"

Hayley lifted the pale yellow cloth napkin from her lap, wiped around her full lips, and then set it on the table next to her half-empty plate. "But what's to steal? It's not like they have expensive gadgets and jewelry."

"They have money," Hank stated between gulps of his juice. "You need to remember, Hayley, the Amish are incredibly resourceful when it comes to making a living and, since they don't believe in gadgetry and jewelry, they're not spending what they make."

"Wait a minute," Claire said, reengaging in the conversation. "Is this about the robbery at the Stutzman farm?"

"It was in the morning paper." Judy quietly requested that the syrup make its way back down the table to her spot and then took up where she left off. "At least one of them said something to the police this time. Although, looking at the picture of the suspect alongside the article, the cops are probably no better off with the picture than they'd be without one."

Claire wanted to argue, but she couldn't. After all, Jakob had essentially said the very same thing.

"There's a *picture*?" Hayley pushed her chair back from the table and rose to her feet, her gaze ricocheting between the clock on the wall and the faces of the people still actively eating. "I thought the Amish didn't *take* pictures."

Judy scrunched up her nose, shaking her head as she did. "It was a drawing. Done by one of those sketch artist people."

"And? It's not good?" Hayley prodded while simultaneously walking toward the doorway.

"My son was drawing more detailed pictures when he was in kindergarten." Judy propped her elbows on the edge of the table and leaned forward. "This sketch? It was essentially a round face with dark hair and dark eyes."

"I haven't seen it, myself, but I know that any lack of detail wasn't as a result of the sketch artist's ability," Claire volunteered just as Hayley's partner, Jeremy, came around the corner and skidded to a stop, his eyes wide.

"I'm not too late for breakfast, am I?" His eyes darted across the edible offerings stretched across the center of the table and swallowed in anticipation.

"No, of course—"

"Yes. Yes, you are." Hayley liberated her camera bag from its holding spot to the left of the buffet table and tapped her hand against its mesh side pocket. "Did you look outside your bedroom window like I told you to do when I knocked twenty minutes ago? Those are storm clouds,

Jeremy. We need to get some outdoor shots before any rain moves in."

"But I'm hungry," he protested.

Hayley shrugged and then hooked her thumb in the direction of the front hallway. "You should have thought of that when I first told you to come down. Now we don't have time for you to sit and eat."

"How about I put a few donuts into a paper sack for you and you can take them in the car?" Diane suggested. Without waiting for a reply, she disappeared into the hallway and the kitchen beyond, only to return moments later with a small bag. Thrusting it into Jeremy's hand, the woman smiled. "Here you go, young man. It's not a full breakfast, but it's something."

He took the bag, peeked inside, and smiled. "They look mighty good."

"Well you'll have to let me know if your stomach agrees when I see you again over dinner."

"C'mon, Jeremy. Please. We need to go. *Now.*"

"I'm not working through lunch, I'm telling you that right now." Jeremy reached into the bag, withdrew a donut, and winked at Diane. "And my parents wonder why I don't want to work . . ."

And then he was gone, the sound of his footsteps joining with Hayley's as they made their way down the hall, across the front foyer, and out the front door.

"Sounds like something I've heard in my own classroom a time or two." Hank helped himself to a second waffle and a handful of fresh strawberries before turning his attention to the sixty-something man on the opposite side of the table. "I would imagine, with you being a travel agent, Bill, folks who'd benefit from an increase in tourists must really try to pull out all the stops for you . . ."

Bill grinned around his bacon. "I'm treated well, yes."

"So what makes you decide to really push a particular location or to put together a group to go there?" Claire asked. "Are there certain criteria you look for?"

"Sure." Bill ate a couple of bites and then set the remaining piece back down on his plate. "But that criteria changes based on the group I'm targeting. If they're young, I look for nightlife, restaurants, shopping, that sort of thing. If they're families, I'm more concerned with available activities and cost. For the senior set, like I'm concentrating on for Heavenly, it's more about cost, restaurants, safety, pace, shopping, and an opportunity to learn something new."

Hank looked up from his waffle and smiled. "Sounds like Heavenly is a shoo-in."

"Cost-wise—it's good. Dining-wise—it's good. Pace-wise—it's good. Shopping-wise—it's good. But as far as safety—which is an important factor when it comes to seniors deciding where to go—the verdict is still out."

It was quick and partially stifled, but Claire still heard Diane's gasp. Although, based on the fact that everyone around them was looking at *Claire*, she suspected hers was louder. "But Heavenly *is* safe," she argued.

"A man was just killed not more than a mile or so from here. In the very heart of the area my clients will be most interested in visiting. That makes a trip here a bit harder to sell."

"But that's *one* incident."

"Add in the robbery and that's *two*." Bill poured some

cream into his tea and then added a spoonful of sugar. After a quick stir, he took a sip. "And that's not counting the murders that have occurred here over the past year."

Diane's shoulders demonstrated the defeat Claire shared. "Heavenly is a beautiful place—a beautiful, *peaceful* place."

"I agree. And that's the way I'll present it to potential clients. But seniors research things online these days now, too. They see enough articles about crime and, well, it could have an impact." Bill took a longer gulp, and then another, draining his teacup to the bottom. "The police need to get to the bottom of whatever happened here this week. The longer it takes, the worse it is for business. Unless, of course, you're Jim, here"—he swept his hand and Claire's gaze to the dark-haired, dark-eyed man seated on his right—"and your business hinges on problems that need to be fixed."

Chapter 10

Claire dropped the shop's key into her purse and followed Annie into the alley, the cessation of mouthwatering scents wafting from the windows of Shoo Fly Bake Shoppe her least favorite part of six o'clock.

"Five minutes ago, I was anxious for the workday to be over. Now, standing out here, all I can think about is wishing the day was still going so I could smell Ruth's apple pie or her cinnamon cookies." She caught up to Annie and matched her steps over to the hitching post behind the store. "Crazy, huh?"

"You could make such things at the inn. And then you could eat them, too." Annie ran her hand along the neck of the waiting horse and then rested her forehead against its taut skin. "Hello again, Katie."

The brown Standardbred horse seemed to melt against

Annie as if she were as glad to see Annie as Annie was to see her.

"I see you drank some water and ate the oats I brought you during my break," Annie said softly. "That is good." Then, pulling back, the teenager smiled at Claire and motioned toward the gray-topped buggy. "I would be happy to bring you home. It is not a pie like Ruth could give, but it is still good."

"Actually, it's perfect. Thank you."

Annie nodded, then pointed again at the buggy. "You may sit down. I will unhitch Katie and we will go."

The young girl unhitched the horse from the pole, nuzzled the animal's face with her own, and then climbed onto the bench seat beside Claire. A soft click of her tongue, combined with a firm pull on the reins, backed them into the alleyway. "Good girl, Katie. Good girl."

Claire couldn't help but smile at the animation on her employee's face. In fact, at that moment, it was hard to equate the girl sitting next to her with the one who'd first strode into her shop nearly five months earlier. *That* Annie had been standoffish, even a little surly. *That* Annie had been determined to use her Rumspringa to test the limits of her strict upbringing.

This Annie was more at peace—her determination to rebel weakening with each passing day thanks to better communication with her dat, and the ever-deepening bond with Claire. Katie was simply another plus in the positive column.

"You're really enjoying her, aren't you?" Claire asked as they headed down the alley and toward Lighted Way.

"Yah."

"I'm glad." She rocked side to side on the bench as the horse navigated the cobblestone road with the slow, easy steps Annie permitted. "How is Henry doing?"

Annie turned her head left as they approached the main road, but not before Claire picked up a hint of flushing on the young girl's face. At any other point in the conversation, she would have attributed such a reaction to the July heat, but considering its proximity to the mere mention of Henry Stutzman, she knew it was more.

"He wants to show that he is strong. For his mamm and his brothers and sisters. But he is still sad, still scared."

They turned left onto Lighted Way and immediately moved as close to the shoulder as possible to allow passenger cars the ability to pass if necessary. Claire watched a few go by, but, for the most part, no one seemed to be in any rush. "Scared? Of what?"

"That the person will come back."

"Person? What . . ." And then she knew. The person who killed his father.

"He does not want someone to come back and do that to him. He says his brothers are too young to take care of their mamm properly. That he needs to stay safe to take care of her." Annie loosened her hold on the reins and allowed Katie to slow even more. When they reached a place where they could safely stop, Annie turned to face Claire. "I do not want anything to happen to Henry."

"Oh, Annie, you have to know that Jakob will do everything in his power to find out who did this and make sure he never does it again. To anyone."

Annie's gaze dropped to the floor of the buggy, where it remained for several beats. Eventually, she looked at

Claire. "Do you think that is so? That he will not let this happen to Henry?"

Reaching across the narrow space between them, she covered Annie's hands with her own. "I do, Annie."

"I do not know much about Jakob. Only that he stops by the shop and is kind to you."

"He is that, but he's also a fine police detective." She returned her hands to her lap and her focus to the sidewalk. There, just two storefronts ahead, was a small group of Amish females Claire judged to be in their late teens and early twenties. They stood in a small circle, heads bent forward, each exhibiting the same rigid stance. "I wonder what's going on there."

Annie bobbed her head left and then right to afford a better view. "I do not know. But we will ask Ruth."

"Ruth? Where?"

Katie responded to the soft click of Annie's tongue and began to walk again, the side to side motion of the buggy a reflection of the terrain more than the budding skills of the young driver. When they were in line with Glorious Books, Annie again stopped the buggy. Like clockwork, four kapped heads turned as one.

"Hello, Annie. Hello, Claire." Ruth stepped forward and into the path of the sun. Using her long, slender hand as a shield, the bakery owner trained her ocean blue eyes on first Annie, and then Claire. "It was a good day today at the bake shop. Was it a good day for you, as well?"

"It was." More than anything Claire wanted to ask Ruth about the mystery man Benjamin had referenced the previous day, but she refrained. To do so in front of so many people would be unfair. Especially for someone as shy as Ruth.

Maybe tomorrow, if there was a lull in customers . . .

"Is everything alright?" Annie asked, looking from Ruth to the other women and back again. "You look worried."

Ruth peeked over her shoulder at her trio of friends but seemed to be addressing one in particular—a redhead with freckles across the bridge of her nose. "May I tell Claire? Perhaps she will have an idea that could help."

"But she is . . . *English*," the young woman whispered. "Maybe we should not say."

"Yah, she is English. But she is my friend." When she got the nod she was seeking, Ruth turned back to the buggy. "It happened to Rebecca as it happened to Emma."

Claire glanced at Annie to see if she was following the conversation, but she, too, looked perplexed. "Emma?"

"That is Henry's mamm." Annie leaned around Claire, her eyes wide with fear. "What has happened to Henry's mamm?"

"A man took the money. From her home."

Annie's shoulders relaxed just as Claire's stiffened. "Wait! Are you saying that money was stolen from Rebecca's house, too?"

"Yah," Ruth answered.

"When?" she snapped.

"It was today." The redhead dropped her hands to her sides and began to fiddle with her dress. Two pinched tugs to the left, two pinched tugs to the right . . . "Dat was in the field with my brothers, and Mamm was at Emma's house helping, when he knocked."

Claire swallowed over the lump now rising in her throat. *"He?"*

"An English man. He wanted to buy some furniture. I told him Dat did not make furniture to sell. He asked if I could draw a map to where he could buy furniture. I am not good at such drawings, but I found a piece of paper and a pencil with my sister's school books and tried. When I returned to show him, he was gone."

"And?"

"Money was missing from her dat's boot," Ruth supplied via a shaky voice.

Claire stepped down from the buggy seat and stood beside Ruth, her focus squarely on Rebecca. "Are you sure the money is missing?"

"Yah."

"And your father—I mean, dat? Is he okay?"

"Yah. He was still in the field when I left. He will not be happy when I tell him of the missing money."

"Did you tell the police?" Claire asked, pointing toward the station just two doors away.

"There is no need."

"No need?" she argued. "Of course there's a need. Someone stole money from your home! That's a crime, Rebecca—*a crime*. If you don't tell the police what happened, they can't help you . . . and they can't track down the money your dat earned with his hard work."

"He was a nice man. Kind."

Claire drew back, stunned. "You mean the man who came to your house?"

"Yah."

"Kind men don't—"

A strangled cry from inside the buggy brought Claire's attention back to Annie, the teenager's once-flushed face now ashen. "C-Claire?" Annie stammered. "C-could it be the same man? The same man who did this to Henry?"

Oh, how she wanted to say no. To assure the bishop's daughter, Benjamin and Eli's sister, and the other young Amish women that it was all simply a horrible coincidence. But as much as she wanted to, her gut knew better.

Someone was preying on the Amish . . .

Chapter 11

She saw the matching numbers on the dice, heard his triumphant cheer, and even semi-registered his discs being moved to his side of the board, but still Claire couldn't quite focus. She tried, of course, but every time she thought she'd left the encounter with Ruth and her friends back on Lighted Way, something stirred it back to the surface all over again.

First, it was the plate of brownies Jakob set down on the kitchen table next to the backgammon board. The treat, in and of itself, hadn't been the trigger, but his "I picked them up at Shoo Fly Bake Shoppe after lunch" had fit the bill.

Next, it was an offhand remark about money. For Jakob it had been about getting his paycheck; for Claire it had been an instant flashback to the fact that Rebecca's family had been robbed.

Jakob scooped up his dice and studied her across the table. "You do realize I'm beating you, don't you?"

On any other day, she'd be trying to distract him from smart moves with silly stories of her fellow shopkeepers or a litany of tantalizing dessert names until she pulled ahead again, but her mind was elsewhere. "I see that."

"What? No Harold Glick stories? No mouth-watering description of Diane's latest success in the kitchen?"

"I'm sorry," she said, shrugging.

His smile disappeared, replaced instead by concern. For her. "What's on your mind, Claire?"

Shaking her head, she straightened her shoulders, tossed her own dice onto the board, and then sank against the back of her chair, defeated. "I'm so sorry, Jakob. I'm trying to put it behind me and just enjoy this time with you. I really am. I've been looking forward to it all day. But now that it's here, I can't keep my mind in this room . . . or on this game."

"Is it something with the shop?"

"No. The shop is good. Great, even."

"Annie?"

"No. Annie is great, you know that. Letting Esther trick me into hiring Annie was one of my smarter decisions."

Jakob threw back his shoulders and puffed out his chest. "I thought *I* was one of your smarter decisions."

She laughed in spite of her mood. "You are. Maybe even my smartest."

"That's better." Winking, he reached for her hand across the top of the backgammon board and then gently tugged her to her feet. "C'mon. Let's go sit in the living room and talk."

Reluctantly she followed him across his kitchen and through its connecting door with the living room. When they reached the oversized couch, she fell into place beside him, the knot of tension at the base of her neck finally beginning to dissipate. The whole world could be topsy-turvy, yet when Jakob's arm was around her, she knew things would work out okay in the end.

He did that for her. And, she hoped, she did that for him.

"Okay, so what's going on?" he asked. "You have that look."

"That look?"

Jakob's chin bobbed up and down against the side of her head. "It means you're worried about something or someone. Is it Diane? One of her guests? Me? Because I can assure you I'm fine. And having you here with me right now elevates that fine to fantastic."

"I feel the same." She ducked the side of her face against his arm and took a long, deep breath. "I guess I just don't understand how you can handle this whole not-talking-to-you thing."

Gently, he guided her face away from his body until he could see her eyes. "Claire, I knew it was going to be like this when I came here, but I came anyway. At least here, I can see them. I knew the drill when I left."

"I'm not talking about you being shunned. I'm talking about the Amish not talking to the police in general. It's crazy. I mean, how are you supposed to help them and keep them safe if they won't talk to you? Don't they realize they're actually facilitating the problem?"

"Are we talking in general here or more specific?"

She felt her throat tightening and did her best to loosen it with a swallow or two. "More specific."

Raking his hand through his hair, he took in the ceiling briefly before giving her his full attention once again. "What happened now?"

"Money is missing from another Amish family."

His jaw hardened. "Who?"

"I didn't get the last name, but the daughter's name is Rebecca. She's a friend of Ruth's."

"Same age as Ruth?"

"I think so. Maybe a year younger . . ."

"Gingerich?"

"I don't know, Jakob. Maybe."

He paused as if trying to come up with any other last names that would fit her description and then moved on. "Is she sure it's missing?"

"Yes."

"Anything else?"

"You mean anything besides money? I don't think so. She didn't say." Claire widened the gap between them just enough to hike her calf onto the cushion and drape her arm across the back of the quilt-covered couch. "From what she said this evening, it sounds like someone—a man—came to her doorstep earlier today asking for directions. When Rebecca sketched them out and turned around to give them to him, he was gone."

"Along with some of their money," Jakob added in a voice that had become suddenly wooden.

"Yes, from her father's boot."

"Did she tell you anything about this man?"

"You mean other than the fact that he was kind?"

"Kind?" he echoed, only to wave off the note of sarcasm as quickly as it had come. "I shouldn't say that. It's the Amish way. They do not see the bad."

Her gaze wandered off his, skirted the mantel and its handful of framed photographs, and settled on the window and its view of Lighted Way. Few cars and even fewer buggies were on the road at this time of night, but still, she couldn't help but think about the people of Heavenly and the panic that would ensue if—

"Do you think it's the same person who asked for a drink from Henry Stutzman and walked out with some of his father's money?"

"That certainly stands to reason," Jakob said. "Similar MO, that's for sure."

"MO?"

"Modus operandi, or method of operation as it's more commonly known." He stood and wandered around the room, his words leaving his mouth in almost stream-of-consciousness type fashion. "The first time, he asks for a drink. While it's being secured, he peeks in Wayne's jar, sees the cash, and grabs a handful. The second time, he asks for directions. While they're being drawn, he looks around again. Gingerich's money was stuffed inside an old boot right there by the door. Our suspect obviously knows his target—at least in a general sense, and is going after them in the way he knows will work."

"Meaning?"

"Meaning, he knows the Amish will help. He knows they keep money in their homes and has figured out they tuck it away in plain sight. His request for something simple buys him a little alone time to look around. If he's lucky, he hits pay dirt. Easy in, easy out." He stopped in front of the stone fireplace and turned. "No one was hurt in conjunction with this incident?"

"No."

"Where were Rebecca's parents when this happened?"

She thought back over the conversation with the young woman and shared what she'd been told. "Her father was out in the fields with her brothers, working. Her mother was at the Stutzmans' farm helping Emma with the children."

"So, if he helped himself to something in the barn before or after he went up to the house, no one would have known."

Since Jakob's observation wasn't spoken in the form of a question, Claire remained silent. She still had much to learn about Jakob and his job, but one thing she knew was his tendency to talk himself through cases, as if speaking the words out loud helped clarify things.

"This certainly lends itself to the notion that Wayne was simply the casualty of a robbery gone wrong rather than some sort of intended target," he mused. "Doesn't make it any less important, but it does change the game a little bit."

"Do you think this person is done?" she asked.

"If he's still doing this even after he murdered someone, my guess is no. He's found a soft target and he likely intends to keep going. If he knows anything about the Amish, as it appears he does, then he's probably banking on the fact that they won't call me."

It wasn't what she wanted to hear, but empty reassurances weren't the answer, either. "So what do you do? Especially when we wouldn't even know about this latest incident if Annie and I hadn't stopped to say hello to Ruth and her friends after we closed the shop this evening?"

He walked to the window and stared out at the road, backgammon and spending time together clearly no longer in the forefront of his mind. "Well, for starters, we step up patrols out by the farms. The Stutzmans were robbed in the evening, and this latest one happened during daylight hours, so we don't have a targeted time, just a targeted group. I'll advise everyone in the department to keep their ears open around town for any rumblings of more incidents."

"I'll certainly do that, too."

He retraced his steps back to the couch and sat down. "I'm counting on that, Claire. And if you do hear something, I need you to encourage the person to speak to me. Remind them that providing us information is the only way we can possibly keep this from happening again."

"I know."

She felt the familiar thrill of his skin against hers as he sought her hand and held it tight. "I need every pair of eyes and every set of ears I can have out there on this case."

Dropping her foot back to the old-fashioned wood-planked floor, she reclaimed her spot in the crook of his arm. "I just wish they would come to you themselves. I mean, maybe Rebecca could describe this man with more details than Henry was able to do."

"I'm going to hope that's the case. In fact, if this Rebecca is who I think she is, I know her father. He was only a year or two older than I was in school."

"But he's Amish," she reminded him. "And you're not any longer. That changes everything, doesn't it?"

"He still may let his daughter speak to me. Especially when I explain the likely connection between what happened at his farm and what happened at Stutzman's. If he still won't after that, I'll solicit Ben's help."

Chapter 12

Claire tightened her hand around the trio of rocks she'd located along the southern bank of the pond and carried them back to Jakob and the red-checked blanket Diane had lent them for the day.

"How'd you do?" he asked as she joined him beneath the tree. "Did you get them good and flat?"

"Two of them are paper flat, and the other is pretty close. Considering the fact that rocks tend to be round, I think I did pretty good."

Grabbing hold of the underside of her hand with one of his, he used his free hand to gently pry back her fingers and take a peek. "Looks good to me. But let's wait on skipping them for a little while and just enjoy the sun. We've both spent too many days inside this week."

"Sounds good to me." She deposited the rocks onto a corner of the blanket and then stretched out beside him, the late afternoon's rays playing across their exposed arms and legs. "I'm sorry about putting such a damper on our time together last night."

He cupped the back of his head with his hands and gave her the dimpled smile she loved. "I needed to know about what happened at the Gingerich farm. So no apologies. Besides, I still beat you in two games of backgammon before that, and we're here together now."

"You sure this is okay?"

"What?"

"Spending this time together. I know you have a lot of work to do with the Stutzman case, and now, with what I told you last night, there's even more."

He silenced her words with the touch of his index finger. "It's late on a Saturday afternoon. I was at it early this morning, and will probably be back at it again this evening. But right now, I need *this*, too."

"I'm glad." She rolled onto her back and inventoried the clouds. Other than a few sporadic sightings, the sky was a brilliant blue. Still, as beautiful as the day was, and as wonderful as it was to spend some of it with Jakob, she couldn't help but juxtapose that moment against the one that saw the Stutzman family lay their beloved Wayne to rest earlier that morning. "I told Annie she didn't have to work this afternoon in light of the funeral, but she wanted to. She really likes being there and interacting with the customers."

"You've been good for her."

"For Annie?"

"It's like you've grounded her somehow, you know?"

She turned her head to the left and found him watching her, the intensity of his gaze making her shiver. "She's a good kid and a hard worker. Frankly, she's been every bit as good for me."

"And maybe that's true. But she was pretty lost and misguided when she showed up on your doorstep."

"I suppose." She blew a piece of hair away from her eyes and then sat up. "I can't imagine what it must be like for a girl to navigate the teenage years without a mom. And to have her dad be the bishop? Doubly hard."

"I suspect Henry Stutzman, in particular, is going to struggle without his dad. The younger boys, at least, will have Henry to look to for guidance." Jakob plucked a piece of grass from just beyond the blanket and played with it between his hands. "It's going to take someone like Ben to be a sounding board for that kid."

"Ben? Why Ben?"

"Because he's even, he's good-hearted, and he knows what it's like to suffer a loss, even if his loss is more in line with Emma's than Henry's."

She hadn't considered that aspect, but it made sense. "Maybe you could suggest to Ben that he be an ear for Henry. Especially if you do end up needing his help to get Rebecca in front of a sketch artist."

Pushing himself up onto his elbow, he dropped the blade of grass onto the blanket and reached for the picnic basket. "Ben is already on it."

"He is?"

"He was at Emma's this morning. Helping prepare for the funeral. He was his usual quiet self, but I think his presence was good for her and the kids." He flipped open the lid and peeked inside. "How did I know there would be cookies in here?"

With a gentle smack of his hand, she took charge of the basket and its contents. First came the paper plates. Next came the napkins. "Was everything okay out there? At Henry's?" she asked, moving on to the ham-and-cheese sandwiches and the grapes.

"As good as it can be, considering the circumstances. I guess I just wanted to see that they were all okay and check in with Henry to see if he remembered anything else about the man who wanted the drink of water."

"Did he?"

Jakob accepted the sandwich from her and took a bite. "No."

"I'm sorry."

"It is what it is," he said, shrugging. "But maybe, if Rebecca will work with the sketch artist, I'll get the break I need."

She settled in with her own sandwich and a handful of grapes. "Will she?"

"I don't know. I'll stop by tomorrow and ask."

"But tomorrow is Sunday. They'll all be busy with church."

He reached across his own plate, stole a grape from her hand, popped it into his mouth, and grinned. "Bishop Hershberger is at his other district this week."

"But they can still go to church in that other district if they want, can't they?" she asked.

"They can. And maybe Rebecca's family will do that. But I won't know if I don't try. If they aren't there tomorrow, I'll stop by on Monday."

Returning his smile with one of her own, she leaned across his plate and popped a second grape into his mouth. "So how was Henry? Is he holding up okay?"

"He feels bad. He can't shake the thought that his dat was checking on *his* horse when it happened. So, therefore, in his eyes, he's responsible for what happened to his dat." Jakob set his half-eaten sandwich down on his plate and stared out over the water hole he'd frequented as a child. "I've tried, many times, to tell him it wasn't his fault. *That* distinction belongs to the person who did this to his dat and no one else. But with the Amish, there is no blame. Only God's will."

"Then if there is no one to blame, why is Henry blaming himself?"

"Because the heart isn't always in sync with the head," Jakob said.

"Maybe it will help when you find the person who did it."

"*If* I find the person who did it." He shook his head, flashed a half smile at Claire, and got back to his sandwich and her grapes. "You know what? Let's not do this any-more. Let's just enjoy the rest of this time. We've earned it, you know?"

Claire slid her plate to the side and sidled up next to Jakob, the feel of his arm as it encircled her body making her smile. "You do have grapes on your own plate, you know . . ."

"I know. But yours taste better."

"Yeah . . . okay." She settled against his chest and allowed herself a moment to breathe, to really take in the beauty of their surroundings—the occasional croak of a frog, the flutter of a butterfly, the welcome shade of the tree at their backs, and the blessed privacy afforded by the grove of trees encircling the pond. It was, in a word, idyllic.

"I wish I could have seen you and Martha playing here as kids. It must have been so special."

"It was. And it's one of the main reasons why I wouldn't trade my childhood for anything."

They sat in silence for a while, enjoying their surroundings and each other. Eventually, though, Jakob pulled his arm from around Claire and pointed at the rocks she'd gathered. "So? Shall we see how accomplished you've gotten?"

At her nod, he rose to his feet and helped her onto hers. But just as he bent over to retrieve the rocks, the whinny of a horse made them both turn.

There, on the other side of the tree, making its way down the makeshift path worn into the ground from years of foot traffic, was Annie's buggy, with Katie dutifully leading the way.

"I thought she was at the shop," Claire said, stepping forward. "I hope there's nothing wrong."

Jakob pulled out his phone, checked the display, and shoved it back in his pocket. "It's five fifteen. And a Saturday. She's done for the day."

Together they approached the buggy. Annie pulled to a stop and smiled. "I am just here to tell you we had a good afternoon at the shop. We sold many, many things. I knew you would be pleased to know."

"And I am. Thank you." Claire hooked her thumb in the direction of the blanket. "We have some food left if you're hungry."

"That is kind of you, Claire, but I will not stay. I must get Katie home and in her stall before I am to make dinner. Dat will be late this evening, so that will help."

"I understand from Henry that you have been a good

friend to him," Jakob said, running his hand along the side of Annie's horse.

Annie's face reddened just before her barely perceptible nod.

"It is important that he tells me everything he can about the man who came to his house the night his father was killed. If he remembers something, please encourage him to speak to me." At Annie's obvious hesitation, he added, "Or tell Claire and she'll tell me."

Carefully avoiding direct conversation with the banned detective, Annie kept her eyes on Claire. "The man who stole from the Gingerich farm . . . is it the same man?"

Jakob gave Katie one last stroke and then stepped back. "I believe so, yes."

Annie's throat moved with a deep swallow, but she said nothing. Instead, she gathered Katie's reins in her hand and prepared to leave.

"Annie?"

Slowly, reluctantly, Annie looked at Jakob, a mixture of curiosity and fear dimming her normal sparkle.

"Be careful," he warned. "Don't let any strangers into the house when your dat is not home."

Chapter 13

Claire looked from the numbered tiles still left in her rack to the center of the table and waved her napkin in the air. "Okay, okay, so this isn't my game."

Diane tucked her crochet needle into her ball of unused yarn and scooted forward on the upholstered lounge chair she'd retreated to after losing to their returning guest one too many times. "See? I told you . . . Judy is a master of that game."

"Would you like to play again?" The seventy-year-old widow flashed a wide smile at both Claire and Hank. "I'll try to go a little easier on you this time."

Hank teed his hands in the air and then pushed his chair back from the card table. "Six losses are enough for me for one night, but maybe Jeremy or Bill would like to sit in for me."

"As tempting as it is, I'm going to decline," Bill said

from his spot in front of the parlor's large picture window and its view of Amish country. "I'm just kind of soaking everything up right now—this room, its vibe, this"—he gestured toward the farms in the distance—"whole place. It really has the kind of charm so many of my older clients are looking for."

Nodding, Judy bobbed her head to the left to address the dark-haired young man eating his way through one of the three cookie plates Diane had set around the room after dinner. "Jeremy? Would you like to play?"

"I can't," Jeremy said around what had to be his sixth or seventh cookie. "The slave driver over here doesn't believe in post-work fun."

Hayley lifted her gaze from the notepad on her lap, repositioned the almost empty plate of cookies just outside of Jeremy's reach, and then smiled at Judy. "My partner here doesn't realize that the concept of post-work fun only comes into play if you've actually worked."

"Hey! I'm *working*."

"Oh?"

"Yeah, I . . . I, uh, wrote my piece to go with today's picture . . ." A triumphant smile spread across Jeremy's face despite the eye roll he aimed at his coworker. "It's not my fault you need to plan out the next three days in one sitting. I mean, take it as it comes, you know?"

"Take it as it comes," Hayley repeated. "Oh yes, because that's worked so well for us in the past."

"I have to agree with Hayley on this, Jeremy," Hank said, rising to his feet and heading toward the sofa. "I see it with my students all the time. The ones who think ahead do better. The ones who don't tend to flounder a bit more."

"I guess. But you can only plan so much. Sometimes, you have to be able to operate without one, you know?"

"See, now I tend to lean more toward Jeremy on this one." Jim craned his head around the edge of his laptop. "Don't get me wrong, a lot of planning goes into my marketing ideas, but sometimes things go a different way, and you've got to be able to adjust."

Hayley pushed a strand of blonde hair off her face and waved a dismissive hand at Jeremy. "You want to play a game? Go ahead and play—"

A familiar television jingle cut the photographer's sentence off and had Judy scurrying for her purse. "Oh. My. That's my phone. I've been waiting on a call from a dear friend and I bet that's her now." The woman's face dipped from Claire's view just long enough to seek confirmation of her guess. "Oh yes, it's Greta. I'll have to take a rain check on that game, young man."

Jeremy shrugged and returned to the plate of cookies. "So, Hank, you teach college kids about owning their own business?"

"I do. And it's becoming more and more popular each semester."

Jim closed his laptop and stretched his legs across the oval-shaped hook rug in the center of the room. "Why is that?"

Hank eyed the cookie plate closest to the sofa but stopped short of actually taking one. "I'd like to say it's because of my teaching—and maybe for some, it is. But really, it's more a reflection of this generation. They're not really keen on answering to anyone, so they think that by owning their own business they can do things their own way all the time. They just don't realize, until we get into things, that being your own boss and therefore responsible for everything isn't all fun and games."

"I wouldn't mind owning my own business," Jeremy mused. "Though, what I'd do, I'm not exactly sure."

"You already own your own business, don't you, young man?"

Hayley's head popped up again, her gaze ricocheting between Jeremy and Jim before finally landing on Jeremy with a glare. "He doesn't seem to get that. If he did, he'd plan ahead a little better."

Jeremy's answering groan was drowned out by Hank and his passion for the topic at hand. "In a business like Hayley and Jeremy's, they need to always be thinking of ways to build readership, and thus, entice more advertisers to their site." Swiping at a spot on his left leg, Hank continued, "The key to success for any business—virtual or otherwise—is to grow. That doesn't mean locations, necessarily. Or even employees. But it does mean growing one's customer base."

"Are you hearing this, Jeremy?" Hayley snapped.

Jim began nodding before Jeremy could even respond. "That's exactly what I've been telling the mayor, the council members, and the handful of business owners I've been talking to these past few days. In order for Heavenly's tourism industry to grow, they have to start looking at ways to appeal to other demographics. The senior set is great—and it's served this town well. But expanding beyond that group will enable the revenue to grow across the board."

"I would imagine that's a fine line, though," Claire said, crossing the rug and perching at the bottom of Diane's chair. "The seniors flock to this town because of the peace and quiet that is Heavenly. It seems to me that if you start changing that draw in order to appeal to a different crowd, you risk losing the very group that put you on the map in the first place."

Bill left his post at the window and wandered over to the framed photographs of Heavenly. "Claire is right. You start opening up bars along Lighted Way and bringing in the kind of crowds that need that sort of entertainment, and, well, the seniors stop coming."

"But they're on a fixed income, right? How much money do they really have to spend, anyway?"

Claire and Diane turned, in unison, to look at Jeremy. *"Plenty."*

"And they come back, again and again," Diane added, swinging her focus back to Jim. "Sometimes they bring friends. Sometimes they just tell their friends. Either way, seniors are masterful at word-of-mouth advertising."

"And that word-of-mouth advertising works in both ways." Bill moved down the line of pictures, stopping as he reached Claire's favorite—a black-and-white shot of an Amish buggy meandering down a snow-covered country road. "They enjoy themselves, they tell people. They don't, they tell people that, too.

"This is a gorgeous photo, Diane. Did you take it?"

Diane's cheeks flushed red just before her shy nod. "Almost twenty years ago."

"I love the way you managed to capture the horse's breath on what was obviously a very cold day."

"See, Diane?" Judy said as she strode back into the room, her cell phone now closed inside her hand. "You really need to enter that photograph in a contest one day. It's spectacular."

Diane waved the suggestion aside. "Oh, I don't know. I'm sure Hayley, here, could take a far better picture than anything I've snapped over the years. And as it was, I had no idea I'd even captured that effect until after it was developed. All I was focused on at the time was trying to document the proud way in which she pulled that buggy despite the difficult weather conditions."

"You really do love horses, don't you, Diane?"

Dropping her hand to her aproned lap, Diane smiled at the man seated on the sofa opposite her own chair. "Oh, Hank, I've loved horses since I was a child. I remember hearing my folks saying I'd outgrow my fascination, but I never did."

"I'm like that with fire trucks." Hank took a sip of lemonade and then returned the glass to the coffee table between them. "Most people equate a fascination with fire trucks to children. But I'm coming up on forty-five and I still stop and stare anytime I see a fire truck go by."

Diane stood and made her way around the back of her lounge chair to stand beside Bill and the black-and-white photographs that had graced the wall of the parlor for as long as Claire could remember. "In the living room, I have a photograph of a Heavenly fire truck with an Amish farmer riding in the back. I didn't capture his face, of course, but the hat and the suspenders and the beard tell the story."

Hank, too, stood and made his way over to the pictures. "I knew I was coming here to gather research on small businesses, and I have. But one of the things I always tell my students is to become involved in their community. It grounds you. Makes you an integral part of a place and its people. I just hadn't expected to find that the Amish do that, too."

"No one offers assistance in times of trouble faster than the Amish." Claire gathered up the empty cookie plates and mugs from around the room and placed them onto the serving tray her aunt had used to pass them out. "You should see how quickly they can raise a barn after a fire. I saw it with my own two eyes at the end of winter, and it still boggles my mind."

"I've heard that." Hank gestured toward the photograph that had commanded Bill's attention. "So whatever happened with that horse you were telling Claire and me about the other day? Any luck finding him?"

"Carrot Thief is a girl, and no, as of the latest update that came out yesterday, there's still no word on the mare's fate. That poor woman is beside herself with grief."

"Poor woman?" Judy asked.

"Valerie Palermo. Carrot Thief's owner. They had a really special bond, the two of them, and not knowing what happened is obviously weighing on her. You could almost *hear* the tears in her answers to the reporter's many detailed questions about the horse. Heartbreaking, really."

Chapter 14

It didn't matter how many nights Claire spent looking out over the moonlit farms, she still felt an overwhelming need to pinch herself just to make sure she wasn't dreaming.

"I know I say it a lot, Aunt Diane, but moving here was truly the smartest thing I've ever done." She picked her foot up off the slatted floor and hiked it up onto the swing with her other one; the motion she'd managed to build up over the past ten minutes enough to keep her swaying for a little while, at least. "I mean, listen . . . It's just so utterly quiet and peaceful."

Hank shifted in his spot at the top of the short staircase and peered at Claire over his right shoulder. "Where did you live before this?"

"New York City."

"I can't picture you in the big city."

"That's because I never should have been there." She stretched her arm along the back of the bench swing and rested her face against the inside of her upper arm. "But then again, if I hadn't experienced that, maybe I wouldn't appreciate this quite as much as I do."

"What brought you to the city in the first place?" he asked.

"My then-husband. It's the only place he ever wanted to be."

He stretched his long arms above his head and then settled against the post at his back. "I'm sorry it didn't work out."

"Peter didn't realize what he had in Claire. But he will. One day." Diane lifted her face to the same breeze that rustled the trees along the driveway and smiled. "His loss was my gain. Detective Fisher's, too."

Claire yanked her head off her arm and shook it at the sixty-two-year-old. "Aunt Diane, *please*. Hank and anyone else who may be hearing this conversation from their open bedroom window doesn't need to hear the details of my love life."

"Diane didn't have to say a word," Hank said, laughing. "I've seen the detective with you in town. I'd have to be mighty blind not to know he's crazy about you."

There was no denying the heat infusing its way into her cheeks or the gratitude she felt for the dimmer switch her aunt had opted to have installed on the porch light. Still, she did her best to take the helm of their conversation and steer it in a very different direction. "So, Diane, what do you think of Jim's recommendation that Heavenly should start targeting the twenty- and thirty-something crowd as a way to increase our tourism revenue?"

"I think it's akin to you living in the Big Apple—it

doesn't fit." Diane brushed a piece of gray-streaked hair from her face and then took a sip of lemonade. "Heavenly is a tourist destination because of the Amish. People drawn to them are drawn to peace and quiet—to a simpler time when things weren't so hectic. Bars and movie theaters are part of today's landscape, not yesteryear's. That age demographic wants something very different than we can—or should want to—provide."

Claire took in everything her aunt said and found it to be a veritable match of her own thoughts on the subject. But maybe those feelings were simply a reflection of their own personal taste. Maybe other people could see it differently . . . "Hank? What about you? I mean, I know this is your first time here and that you came for work reasons, but as an outsider looking in, what do you think? Are we missing something in Jim's recommendation that we really ought to see?"

Hank extended his legs across the top step and pillowed the back of his head with his hands and the post. "Generally speaking, from a business standpoint, any opportunity to reach new customers is a good idea. But in this case, with this town and the *reason* it's an attraction, I think making some of the changes Jim is recommending would end up hurting the bottom line."

"My sentiments exactly." Diane lowered her lemonade glass to her lap and looked out across her property, a determined set to her jawline. "Which is why I will be setting up a meeting with the mayor this coming week . . ."

Claire couldn't help but chuckle at the polite fierceness behind the woman's words. "You're going to give him what-for, aren't you, Aunt Diane?"

"I'm certainly going to have my say. After twenty years of running this inn in this town, I've earned that right."

"If you want me to go along as the voice of another local business owner, I'll have Annie hold down the fort for however long it takes."

"I'll keep that in mind, dear." Diane dabbed at her thin lips with a napkin and then brushed the current subject off with a flick of her hand. "So, Hank, what are your plans for tomorrow? Anything special?"

"I thought I'd check out a few more in-home businesses. Someone at the coffee shop in town told me about a woman who sells homemade cookies to a tour group that comes through her property and a man who actually has turned his homemade birdhouse business into an online venture as well. With a full-color, glossy brochure to boot."

"Both worthwhile businesses to study, no doubt." Claire dropped her foot back down to the floor and used it to set the swing in motion once again. "But you'll have to wait on those until Monday."

"Oh?"

"Claire is right." Diane set her glass on the wicker table beside her chair and readjusted her glasses across the bridge of her nose. "Tomorrow is Sunday. The Amish don't work on Sunday. It is a day of rest and worship."

Hank pulled his right hand from behind his head and used it, instead, to smack his forehead. "I knew that . . . Or, at least I did earlier in the week . . . Wow. Now I have no idea what I'm going to do."

"The English-owned shops along Lighted Way will still be open. Many of us sell items made by the Amish," Claire reminded him. "So although the Amish themselves are either gathered at whichever home is hosting church that week or visiting with relatives on the off week, some of them are still earning an income through their partnership or consignment work with us."

"And how long is this church service?"

"About three and a half hours, right, Diane?" At her aunt's nod, Claire continued, "But then they remain at that particular home for lunch and sometimes even dinner."

"So they're there almost all day long," Hank mused.

Claire and Diane nodded in unison. "They are."

Hank swung his legs over the step and stood. "And they all go?"

"They all go," Diane confirmed quietly. "And in the evenings, the teenagers often go to a different home to socialize with one another via a hymn sing or a volleyball game."

"Hmmm. Okay, then I guess I better head inside and spend a little time rethinking my day." He headed toward the front door only to stop a few feet shy of his destination. "Thank you for a very nice evening, ladies. I'll miss this when I head home in a few days."

"Good night, Hank."

"Good night, Diane." He turned his head to take in the swing next. "Good night, Claire."

And then he was gone, the swath of light from the inn's front foyer disappearing from the porch as quickly as it had come. A few minutes later, a similar swath of light appeared on the front walkway as they heard Hank settle in to his second-floor quarters via the telltale creak of the desk chair through his open window. Somewhere to their left, a window slid closed and a different patch of walkway grew dark.

"He's a nice man," Diane said. "Very smart."

Claire nodded, her cheek finding the inside edge of her arm once again. "Esther is really starting to show now."

"I certainly hope so. She only has another, what? Two months to go?"

"Something like that."

"I imagine they're excited."

An image of Esther and Eli standing side by side in Claire's rearview mirror brought an instant smile to her lips. "They are. Eli is already planning ahead with a new horse he thinks will provide more reliable transportation for Esther and the baby. It's cute."

Sure enough, the mention of a horse had Diane's ears practically standing upright. "When will he be doing that?"

"He already did. Only the horse isn't fit for buggy duty just yet."

The woman's eyebrows perked upward as well. "Oh? Why not?"

"Esther said she has a strained tendon or something like that and Eli is nursing her back to health. Frankly, I was surprised he bought an injured horse, but I guess he thinks the issue is fixable and the horse solid."

"Eli has always been good with horses. I've heard Benjamin say that many times." Diane smoothed her hand down the front of her calf-length skirt then returned her hand to her lap. "What is her name?"

"You mean the horse?"

"Yes."

"Esther called her Carly. Said Eli got her at the same farm where Annie got her beloved Katie."

Diane nodded. "The Weaver farm. That's their business, you know—buying and selling horses. Retired Standardbred racehorses, mostly."

"Racehorses?" she echoed. "Why? Buggies and farm equipment move slow."

"These are mostly trotters. They are trained to pull things."

It made sense on some level, but still it surprised her. "Wouldn't a racehorse go for a lot of money?"

"Not always. Most owners just want their retiring horse to go to a good home."

"They don't keep them?"

"Some do, I suppose. But most of them are in the business of racing. Looking after retired horses is something else entirely." Diane reached over the arm of her chair for her lemonade glass and then rose to her feet, the approaching ten o'clock hour serving as some sort of internal alarm clock for the innkeeper. "On occasion, owners have been known to virtually give their horses away to make sure they go to good homes."

Intrigued, Claire leaned forward. "As opposed to what?"

"As opposed to them ending up with someone who has other plans."

"Like . . . ?"

"Selling them to a slaughterhouse."

Claire sucked in her breath. "Someone would really do that?"

"As long as there is a buck to be made, there will be someone looking to make it." Diane scanned the rest of the porch for any additional glasses that may have been left around during the course of the day and then inched her way toward the door. "That's why it does my heart good to see someone like Annie love a horse the way she loves Katie."

Shifting her focus from Diane's face to the darkened fields in the distance, Claire tried to pick out Annie's farm, but it was no use. The moonlight only cast a glow over so much . . . "She really does love that horse, doesn't she?"

"She does. But I'd also venture to say that Katie loves her as well. There is no mistaking the way that mare turned her head every time she heard Annie's voice out in the parking lot the other day." Diane stopped just shy of Claire's swing and looked off into the darkness. "It doesn't take an animal long to identify kindness and to develop a fondness for someone."

"You're thinking about that woman and her horse, aren't you?" Claire asked. "Carrot Thief, right?"

"I am. You only had to read two or three sentences of that original feature story on the two to know they were extremely close. I can only imagine how worried, and profoundly sad, Ms. Palermo must be."

"Maybe Carrot Thief will still turn up."

Diane's eyes, magnified behind her bifocal glasses, came to rest on Claire. "We can certainly hope. Well, dear, it's time I head off to bed. Tomorrow will be here before we know it. You probably should be thinking about sleep soon, too. I know you're on your own at the shop tomorrow."

"I'll head inside soon. I promise. I just want to enjoy this perfect night air for a few more minutes." She leaned her cheek forward to collect her aunt's kiss and then smiled up at the woman. "Sweet dreams, Aunt Diane. I love you."

Chapter 15

One glance at the line snaking its way up to the counter and Claire knew her chances of reaching the register and the hot chocolate she'd been craving since her feet hit the ground were slim. Still, she had to try.

Taking her place behind fellow shopkeeper Drew Styles, she allowed herself a moment to inhale the aroma wafting from the mugs of those customers who'd planned their morning better than she had.

"Ahhh, yes, the pitfalls of hitting that snooze button one too many times."

She opened her eyes to find Drew studying her with the same amusement she'd heard in his voice. "You say that as if you've done it yourself a time or two."

"I'm only one person in front of you, aren't I?" Drew joked. He let his eyes drift back to the front of the line long enough to shake his head in disgust at himself. "And

Sunday morning is not the time to gamble with the caffeine boost."

And he was right. Just as Claire employed Annie to help at Heavenly Treasures, Drew's second pair of hands around Glorious Books belonged to an Amish teenager as well—an Amish teenager who joined the rest of her Amish brethren in a day of worship or rest each and every Sunday.

"I tried to get up," she said. "I really did. But my bed seemed more comfortable than normal this morning."

"They always do on Sunday mornings, don't they, Al?"

At the mention of her landlord's name, Claire turned to see the owner of Gussman General Store ambling toward them, his still-tired eyes following the line up to the counter and back before settling on his wristwatch. "Ohhh . . . this isn't looking good."

"Good morning, Al," she said. "One too many snooze buttons for you, too?"

He flashed a quick smile at Claire just before it morphed into a yawn and disappeared behind his hand. "Oh. Wow. Excuse me. I didn't get much sleep last night. Too worried about the recommendations this Jim Naber is making to the council."

Drew stepped forward with the line and then turned back to Claire and Al. "I'm not familiar with that name."

"Jim Naber. He's the consultant the mayor was telling us about at the last business owners' meeting, remember?" Al replied. "The one who was hired to come up with ways to help increase the town's tourism revenue . . ."

"He's staying at the inn," Claire added, as much for Al as for Drew. "Nice enough man."

"You mean misguided—*grossly* misguided, to be even

more accurate." Al surveyed the dining area to their left and right and then stepped closer to the pair, dropping his voice to a near whisper as he did. "This guy thinks we need to attract someone who is looking to set up a bar in that vacant storefront next to the police station."

Drew stepped back as if he'd been slapped. "A bar?"

Again, Al moved forward. "Keep your voice down. I, for one, don't want any of the tourists in here getting wind of the fact Heavenly is even thinking of going that route. That gets out prematurely, and we'll disappear from every senior citizen travel blog out there."

"But a bar? On Lighted Way? Is this—this Naber guy *blind* or something?"

Claire motioned for Drew to move forward as a second barista opened another register and the line magically, mercifully, split. "He was hired to make recommendations. One of his recommendations is to target a younger demographic—a demographic who will want and need the kind of nightlife options we don't have in Heavenly at the present time."

"You think this is a good idea?" Drew asked.

"No. Of course not. But he's doing what he was hired to do."

"I would imagine Diane has argued the ludicrousness of this idea with this man, yes?" Al claimed the left line as Drew and Claire took the right.

"She's expressed her opinion, sure. But this man *is* her guest, too. She'll save her stronger protest for the mayor."

Al rubbed at his stubbled chin and then folded his arms across his broad chest. "Maybe what we need to do is sit down with the mayor as a group. Let him know that we think this idea is detrimental to everything that has made this town the draw that it is."

"Count me in," Drew said.

Claire nodded. "Me, too."

"My son is coming in to help at the store today. Maybe, if there's a lull in traffic at any point, I'll start making the rounds of everyone. To make sure they're all on board with this and to find a time that everyone can descend on the mayor's office this coming week—the sooner the better, if you ask me."

A quick jingle was followed by another as Howard Glick and Jakob entered the coffee shop within seconds of each other.

"*Howard*." Al nodded. "*Detective*."

The plump and bald proprietor of Glick's Tools 'n More veered toward Claire's line but changed course at the last minute and waved Jakob into that spot instead. "I imagine you'd like to stand with your girl, Detective."

"I would indeed. Thank you, Howard." Jakob slid his arm around Claire's back and pulled her in for a quick kiss. "I swung by the shop just now. When I didn't see you inside, I figured maybe you'd be here."

She nestled her face against his shoulder and used the strength and warmth she found there as the boost she needed. "For a while there, it was looking as if a morning jolt wasn't in any of our futures," she said, gesturing toward Drew in front of her and Al beside her. "But then they put another girl at the registers."

A flurry of movement in front of Drew put Claire and

Jakob second in line for their drinks. While Drew placed his order, Howard rocked back on his heels. "So who's ready to work like a dog today?"

"The day-trip bus is expected to arrive at noon," Al said. "My son is coming in at eleven thirty. So I'll be more than ready."

"Rub it in, why don't you?" Howard's laugh reached beyond the confines of their respective lines and earned him a few returning smiles from around the dining room. If he saw the smiles, he didn't let on, his focus still on the conversation at hand. "Every once in a while I think about hiring non-Amish, but then I remember how hard they work and I don't."

"You could always hire a Sunday-only employee," Claire suggested.

Howard followed behind Al as their line lurched forward. "My wife says that every Saturday evening when I'm moaning about the next day's workload. One of these days I probably should listen to the woman." He leaned across the gap between lines and pointed from Jakob to Claire and back again. "Here's some free advice for you, son. Don't wait so long to listen to this pretty lady right here. Otherwise you'll be old like me and knowin' you should listen, but too set in your ways to actually do it."

Jakob's laugh rumbled against her ear. "I'll keep that in mind, Howard, thank you."

"So who's hosting church this morning?" Al glanced up at the menu behind the counter as the person directly in front of him placed her order. "Anyone know?"

"The bishop is in his other district today." Jakob dropped his hand from Claire's shoulder to the small of her back and guided her into the spot Drew had just vacated. To the petite barista behind the register he said, "We'll take one large hot chocolate and one large coffee. Black."

Claire looked up at Jakob, her internal antennae instantly raised. "*Black?* Is everything okay?"

When the girl left to fill their order, he raked a hand through his hair and shrugged. "I talked to Luke last night."

"Luke?"

"Gingerich. Rebecca's father." Jakob reached into his back pocket, extracted his wallet, and handed the returning barista a ten-dollar bill. She gave him his change and the cups, and then turned her attention to Howard, who'd slipped into the empty spot behind them.

"So you were right on the family she belonged to?"

"I was."

"Well, good. I'm glad her father talked to you."

"Thanks to Ben, anyway." He motioned toward the front door and the workday that was now just minutes away from starting.

"Ben went with you?"

"Not at first, he didn't. But when Luke refused to talk to me, I went and got Ben. With Ben's help, Luke was finally willing to listen."

She bit back the frustration that always accompanied news of the cold shoulder imparted on Jakob by his former community and instead focused on the topic at hand. "Did he confirm money was missing? Did he see the man that Rebecca mentioned? Did he let Rebecca talk to you? Is she going to sit down with the sketch artist the way Henry did?"

They stepped onto the sidewalk outside the coffee shop and turned left into the path of the sun. "Yes. No. Yes. No."

She lowered her to-go cup and ducked her head. "Okay. That was a lot of questions at one time. Sorry about that."

"No worries. I followed them."

"I kind of forgot the order in which I asked them . . ."

He laughed. "Okay. Luke did, in fact, confirm that money was missing from the home. He was out in the fields at the time this man stopped by, so he didn't see anyone. He permitted Rebecca to speak to me. And no, she's not going to sit with a sketch artist."

When they reached the alley between Heavenly Treasures and Shoo Fly Bake Shoppe, she turned left. "But why not? I mean, if it helps you do your job, how can she not?" She reached her free hand into her purse and pulled out her key ring, her fingers instinctively finding the correct key and unlocking the back door.

Once inside, they parted ways—Claire toward the front door and Jakob to the main room's light switch. "I showed her the picture that was done with Henry."

"But it was lacking any real detail, wasn't it?" She flipped the window sign to its open designation and unlocked the front door.

"I was hoping she could add some, maybe dispute others."

"And?" she asked as she met him in the middle of the store.

"She took one look at the dark-haired Englisher and said, 'That's him.'" Jakob lifted his cup as if readying for a sip, but didn't take it. "I suggested she sit with the same person who drew Henry's picture and see if she could add anything. At first she didn't seem to understand, so I mentioned things like freckles, or bushy eyebrows, or a narrow jaw. When I finished, she just looked at the picture and said there was nothing else."

"How frustrating!"

"Tell me about it." He took a long pull of his coffee and then peeked over her shoulder toward the front window. "Think I could get another kiss before this place starts filling up with customers?"

She grinned and obliged. After a few moments, they reluctantly parted ways. "So what are your plans for the day?" she asked, wishing with everything she had that they could spend the day together.

"Well, I'm hoping that invitation to dinner at your place is still on. I've been dreaming about your aunt's shepherd pie all weekend . . ."

"Oh, that invitation still stands. In fact, when I was heading out this morning, Diane was asking me whether she should make her special homemade biscuits to go with it."

His eyes widened across the top of his to-go cup. "And? What did you tell her?"

"I told her no." She tried not to think about kissing him again as his mouth gaped open, and instead, gave him her best wink. "I'm kidding. I'm kidding."

"Give a guy a heart attack, why don't you," he said as he pulled her in for yet another hug. "Sheesh."

"And before that? Any special plans I can live vicariously through you while I'm chatting up customers and hopefully restocking the shelves they empty?"

His chin bobbed atop her head. "I'm going to whiteboard

what I've got from the Stutzman farm and this thing at Gingerich's place. See if something jumps out."

"I wish I could help." Then, realizing how her words sounded, she began to backpedal. "Not because I think you need me but because I find that to be kind of fun."

"I *do* need you, your help has proved *invaluable* in the past, and doing *anything* with you instantly makes whatever it is more fun. Including work." He pressed his lips to her temple and held them there for a long moment. "I've gotta find this guy, Claire. One way or the other."

Chapter 16

She felt him studying her as she moved around the now-empty table collecting dirty dessert plates and coffee cups.

"Would you like anything else?" Claire asked over the stack of plates. "Another piece of pie? More coffee?"

Jakob shook his head and forced a smile to his lips. "No, I'm good. Thank you, though."

"Then I'll be back in a few minutes."

"Wait." He pushed his chair back from the table and gathered up the half-dozen or so spoons and forks to his left and his right and then held out his arms. "Let me carry that stuff, Claire."

"I've got it, Jakob. Please. Sit. You're my guest. Guests don't have to help clean up from all the other guests."

He glanced down at the utensils in his hand and then

back up at Claire. "You do realize I don't want to be just a guest."

Something about the detective's voice sent off a wave of unease that started in her chest and rolled out to her limbs. "Jakob, I . . . I didn't mean to imply you're something less than you are to me. I just want to take care of this stuff as I would on any other given night, and then get back out here so you and I can resume our evening together. With fewer people this go-round."

"I don't want to be anyone's consolation prize, Claire. Especially when you deserve your top choice in everything that matters in life."

As if propelled by some sort of autopilot button, Claire made her way back to the table and the chair she'd inhabited throughout her aunt's traditional Sunday night dinner. Setting the stack of plates and smattering of mugs back atop the tablecloth, she sat and motioned for Jakob to do the same.

He did, reluctantly.

"Is this why you were so quiet all through dinner? Because you're doubting the way I feel about you?"

"No . . . Yes . . ." He deposited the utensils onto the top plate in the stack and then raked his fingers through his hair. "I sound like an idiot, don't I?"

"No. But I just don't understand where this is coming from. Did something happen today?" she asked.

"I didn't know it had been that serious." He stopped, swallowed, and then met her eyes with ones that were pained. "With you and Ben."

The unease turned to a chill that washed over her from head to toe. "M-me and Ben?"

"I mean, I know you two hit it off from the start, but . . ." He leaned back in his chair and released a sigh so loud it almost drowned out the roar in her head.

Almost.

More than anything she wanted to play dumb, to act as if she had no idea what he was talking about, but to do so would be just that—playing. And the last thing she wanted to do with Jakob was play games. She cared about him and the relationship they were building way too much for that.

She reached across the narrow divide between their chairs and took his hands in hers. "Jakob, when I moved here, I was lost. I never pictured myself a divorcée. Ever. I believed marriage was supposed to be forever. Heck, I *still* believe that. But it didn't work for me. Coming here, to Diane's, was difficult. Yes, I love her. And yes, this was exactly where I wanted to be in the aftermath of my failure. But it was still embarrassing. I mean, I wasn't a little kid or a teenager spending a week or two with my favorite aunt anymore. I was a grown woman who had nowhere else to go."

His face softened. "Your aunt loves having you here, Claire. Anyone with half a brain in their head can see that."

"And I love being here, too. But, initially, it still felt like I'd failed." She took a slow, measured inhale and then released it just as slowly. "For six months I almost never left this house. I helped her with the guests, of course, but I was too lost, too hurt to interact with life. Diane knew this and she tried to encourage me every moment of every day. Eventually, I realized she was right. I'd left Peter because I knew I deserved better, yet I wasn't treating myself any better than he had."

"He was a fool, Claire. A complete and utter fool."

"One day, Diane asked me what I wanted to do. And I said I wanted to own a gift shop."

The faintest hint of a smile inched the right corner of Jakob's mouth upward and he squeezed her hands. "I'm glad you did."

She claimed his full gaze and squeezed back. "I'm glad, too. Opening Heavenly Treasures has changed my life in more ways than I ever could have imagined at the time."

"In good ways, yes?"

"In *fabulous* ways," she corrected him before diving back into the reason behind their current conversation. "Suddenly, I had people to interact with—people who talked to me not because I was Diane's niece, but because I was me. I met Esther . . . and Eli . . . and Ruth . . . and Howard . . . and you . . ."

"And Ben."

At the unfamiliar rasp in his voice, she released his hands, stood, and began wandering around the room, the framed photographs and slightly askew chairs barely registering in her thoughts. "And Ben," she confirmed. "He was so chivalrous—carrying boxes into my shop, offering to take out the trash, always checking to see if I needed anything. It was . . . nice. Peter wasn't like that. He was always so lost in his own head that he saw nothing around him. Including me."

"So you *were* interested in Ben," he said.

She stopped when she reached the far side of the table, his words a near perfect match to a question she'd once asked herself a hundred times. A question she'd eventually been able to answer. "For five years I was married to someone who didn't listen, didn't *hear*. Ben heard. I needed that. I needed to share my thoughts—no matter what they were—with someone who would hear me. To suddenly have that . . . with a man, no less . . . it was mind-blowing to me. I mean, I'd actually convinced myself that the reason Peter was so disinterested in me was because of something *I* was lacking. Yet, here was this man, who not only seemed to like to listen to me, but *wanted* to listen to me, too.

"Jakob, I can't tell you what it was like to feel as if I was interesting to someone—especially a man. I was blinded by that. I really was. But, eventually, I was able to get a grasp on reality."

"And what was that?"

"That Ben, while an amazing listener, is my *friend*. The feelings I had were about me, not him. He helped me to like myself again. And for that, I'll be forever grateful, because it allowed me to get here—to this place. With you."

He drew back, surprised. "I don't understand."

"Ben helped me to heal. To stop seeing myself as dull. That puff of air, coupled with puffs from Diane and Esther and the rest of my new friends, helped me to believe in myself again. Which, in turn, helped me to be open to *you*. And"—she pointed between them—"*this*."

Silence filled the space between them, only to be broken by Jakob. "He was willing to leave the Amish for you. To build a life with you as his wife."

Instantly, she was back on the bench behind her store with Benjamin, talking about the life they could have and the life he was willing to forgo in order to have one with her. And, for the umpteenth time since that moment, she felt the prick of tears that always accompanied its memory.

"He was. And I'll never forget that. But doing that would have been a mistake. For both of us."

"How so?" Jakob asked.

"Ben would have lost everything that mattered to him. His parents. His siblings. His beliefs." Claire retraced her steps back to her chair and to Jakob. Slowly, she lowered herself down to her chair. "And I would have missed out on you."

She saw him swallow just before he pulled her against his chest and held her tight. "I'm sorry, Claire. I just had to know."

"I get it." And she did. No one wanted to be another person's consolation prize, as Jakob had said. "But how did you find out? About Ben's offer?"

He pulled back enough to see her face, but kept his arms around her. "Ben stopped by my office shortly before I came here. He wanted to see if I had anything new to report on Wayne's death or the robberies. He saw that picture of us that I have on my desk and the next thing I knew, he started telling me how he, too, had been willing to leave the Amish. For you."

"Is he . . . okay?" she asked.

"I think he's genuinely happy for us. I really do. But I also think he's wishing he could have something like this, too."

"I pray for him to find that nearly every day," she said honestly. "He's simply too special not to be someone's husband, and someone's father."

"I agree."

Four months earlier, those words never would have come out of Jakob's mouth—the decades'-old tension between the two men much too thick. But time had a way of healing all sorts of wounds, and she was glad.

"Knock knock." They turned toward the hallway and Diane's aproned form. "I'm sorry to interrupt, but Annie is outside and she is asking to speak with you. I invited her inside, of course, but she is quite reluctant to leave Katie."

Returning her gaze to Jakob, Claire knew the disappointment she saw in his face was mirrored on her own. "I'll keep this short, I promise," she whispered.

He leaned in, kissed her so softly it nearly took her breath away, and then stood, holding his hand out to her as he did. "As long as I'm spending the evening with you, it's all good."

They were barely through the side door when Annie started crying, her diminutive shoulders shaking beneath her lavender-colored dress.

Alarmed, Claire pulled her hand from Jakob's grasp and ran to the parking area, the detective close on her heels. "Annie? Annie? What's wrong, sweetie? Did something happen to your dat?"

Annie shook her head hard.

"Are you hurt?"

"N-no. I am not hurt." Wiping the back of her hand across her tear-soaked cheeks, Annie nuzzled her face against Katie's. "Dat is not hurt."

Claire glanced back at Jakob and saw the same confusion she felt. "Then I don't understand, sweetie. Why are you so upset? Is something wrong with Katie?"

At the mention of her beloved horse's name, Annie's tears turned into sobs.

"Annie, sweetie. Talk to me." Claire tugged the girl away

133

from the horse and held her close while Jakob began a long, slow walk around the animal and the buggy. "We can't help you if you don't tell us what's wrong."

Seconds turned to minutes as the girl's sobs lessened into sniffles before finally stopping completely. "I . . . I came home early from the hymn sing because it was not fun without Henry."

It was hard not to smile at the reason behind the tears. It was even harder not to smile at the deepening confusion on Jakob's face.

"Oh, Annie, Henry is dealing with a lot right now. I'm sure he'll be back at the hymn sings again before long. You just wait and see."

"I am not crying because of Henry. I know that he is helping his mamm." Annie backed herself out of Claire's arms and ran her hand along the side of Katie. "I am crying because I should be more careful. With Katie."

Jakob completed his inspection of the horse and came to stand beside Claire. "She looks fine to me, Annie."

"Yah. Because she was with me. But if I had ridden to church with Dat, she could be missing right now."

"Annie, I don't understand what you're talking about," Claire said. "What did or didn't you do in regard to Katie?"

"I did not latch her stall this morning, even when I am sure I did."

Jakob reached out, ran a soothing hand down the front of Katie's face, and then peered back at Annie. "You were probably just focused on getting her hitched to the buggy. We all get distracted sometimes, Annie. It happens."

"But what if one day, when she is inside, I am sure I latch it, but don't? I could lose her. She is curious."

"Do you think you'll do that?" Claire hooked a finger underneath Annie's chin and guided the teenager's gaze onto hers. "Because I don't. I see how careful you are at the store when you work. You always shut the register. You always make sure to remove your step stool the moment you are done using it so customers can't trip. You double-check the locks whenever you close. Not latching Katie's stall one time doesn't make you unfit to care for her, Annie."

"I agree with Claire," Jakob said as he dropped his hand to his side. "But if you're still worried, just make sure to double-check the door every time you—"

The familiar jingle of Jakob's phone cut his suggestion short and had him reaching into the front pocket of his khaki pants with a hurried hand. A glance at the illuminated screen was followed by a raised index finger. "I'm sorry, ladies, I've gotta take this. It's the station."

Jakob brought his phone to his ear and stepped off to the side as Claire tucked a strand of hair back inside Annie's kapp. "Jakob is right, sweetie. Mistakes happen. And I doubt you'd have left the stall unlatched if Katie had been inside. You're much too careful."

Annie opened her mouth to answer but closed it as Jakob returned. "Annie . . . Claire . . . I have to go."

"Is something wrong, Jakob?" Claire asked.

"That was the dispatcher. Ben called looking for me." Claire drew back. "Ben *called* you?"

Jakob nodded and then slipped his phone back into his pocket. "The Amish can use a telephone for business or emergency purposes. Considering what's been going on around here lately, he felt the call was warranted."

"There is a phone in a small shed at the bottom of the

Millers' property." Annie wrapped her arm around the underside of Katie's neck and gave the horse a hug. "Near the road. Ruth uses it to place orders for the bake shop."

"Okay . . ." Claire looked from Jakob to Annie and back again, a parade of questions filtering through her thoughts and out her mouth. "But why did Ben call you at the station? Is something wrong? Is he okay? Is his family okay?"

Jakob took Claire's hands in his and then pulled her forward for a hug. "My gut is that it's nothing serious. He didn't ask for assistance and he didn't ask for an ambulance. He simply asked that they locate me and that I stop by his farm this evening if possible."

"So it's probably nothing, right?" she said, her voice raspy.

"If Ben is using a phone to call me, I doubt it's nothing. But if it were something serious, I don't think he'd have wasted time asking for me."

The fear that took root in her heart the second she learned of Ben's phone call moved down her spine along with a chill. "He asked for you because he *trusts* you, Jakob."

Chapter 17

They were halfway to the Millers' when Jakob broke the silence that had settled between them like a third passenger. "I'm sure he's fine, Claire."

Turning her head, she found the closest thing she could to a smile and flashed it at the detective. "I'm sure you're right. Then again, in all fairness, I know you're worried, too."

"I'm trying not to be. Trying to rationalize Ben's call in all the same ways I did back at your aunt's just now."

"But . . ." she prodded.

"But I keep coming back to the same thing I think you're stuck on—Ben *called*."

Claire shifted the hem of her skirt across her knees and willed herself to think calmly. "You two have gotten closer again. I mean, look at the way he just helped you with Rebecca's father. Maybe his calling you on the phone has something to do with *that*. Maybe Rebecca remembered something, told Ben about it after church or wherever it is they may have been visiting today, and he's calling you because he knows it's something you need to know."

Yes, that sounds plausible . . .

"Maybe."

"Or maybe he heard something from someone else that he thinks is relevant to the case."

"Maybe," he repeated in the same skeptical voice.

Claire's gaze moved from his rigid jaw to his too-tight hold on the steering wheel and back again, whatever calm she'd managed to harness rapidly disappearing. "What aren't you saying, Jakob? Talk to me."

"Ben is about as relaxed as they come, you know?"

She did know. And it was why she was unable to brush off the man's call to his former Amish friend as no big deal. Still, if there had been a true emergency, surely he wouldn't have waited for Jakob to be located . . .

"But we'll find out soon enough." Jakob slowed as they reached the mailbox denoting the original Miller farm and turned into the driveway. The evening hour, coupled with the fact that it was a Sunday, had the tractors off to the side, and the horses tasked with pulling them safely in the large white barn visible through the passenger-side window. "The only trick now is figuring out whether we'll find him at his parents' house or his own."

She looked at the main house where Ruth lived with her younger siblings and her parents, and then toward the smaller house at the end of the driveway. For three short weeks more than a decade earlier, Ben had shared that house with his late wife, Elizabeth.

"I stopped by his house one evening last spring and I was struck by just how lonely he must be. I mean, to eat alone, night after night the way that he does." She released a breath she hadn't realized she was holding and slowly inventoried the windows on the first floor of Ben's home. "It made me sad."

"He doesn't eat with his parents and siblings?" Jakob asked as he pulled to a stop underneath a large willow tree and turned off the car.

"Maybe sometimes. But I don't think he does often." Movement behind a first-floor window caught her attention, and she pointed it out to Jakob. "I would imagine that's Ben right there."

Before he could respond, Ben's front door opened to reveal Ben himself. Nodding at Claire, Jakob exited the vehicle and waited for Claire to do the same. "Hey, Ben. I got the message that you called. Is everything okay?"

Ben glanced toward his parents' home and then waved Jakob and Claire onto the wide front porch he'd never truly gotten to enjoy with Elizabeth before her death. "Jakob. Claire . . ."

"I was visiting with Claire when the station called. I invited her along."

"I am glad." Then, turning his full attention onto Jakob, he gestured them inside. "If you have some time, I would like to talk. Inside. Where it is quiet."

She was about to make a comment about the entire Miller farm being cloaked in a blanket of peace and quiet, but thought better of it. Instead, she let Jakob guide her into Ben's home.

"Let us sit in the kitchen. There is candlelight when the

last of the day's light is gone." When they entered the clean, yet sterile, surroundings, Ben pointed toward the counter and a familiar bag. "Ruth brought dessert with my dinner as she always does. And, once again, there is too much for me to eat alone. Would you like some chicken? Or some cookies?"

Jakob waved the offer aside, then smiled at Claire. "Surely you're not going to pass up one of Ruth's cookies?"

She was glad for the low lighting ushered in by the end of another summer day, but it didn't really matter. Ben, too, knew her fondness for sweets and simply delivered a cookie to the table for Claire. "They are chocolate chip, Ruth says."

Claiming the spot next to Claire's, Jakob took control of the conversation. "So what do you want to talk about, Ben?"

"I think someone was here today. Looking for money."

Jakob's palm hit the edge of the table and Claire jumped. "Did you see someone?" he asked.

"No. I was at Eli's home. Visiting. So, too, was Dat, Mamm, Ruth, and the children." Ben fisted a hand at his mouth and exhaled. "But I am sure. Someone was here. In Dat's house and mine."

"Is there money missing?" Jakob reached for a shirt pocket he did not have and then looked around the room. When Claire realized what he was looking for, she reached into her purse and pulled out a small notebook and pen and set them down in front of Jakob.

Ben shook his head.

"Are you sure?"

"I am sure. But that is because it was moved."

She pushed her uneaten cookie off to the side and

leaned forward against the edge of the table. "What was moved, Ben?"

"My money. Dat's money, too. I did not want what happened at Stutzman's and Gingerich's to happen here."

"Where did you move it to?" Jakob asked, his pen poised and ready to record Ben's answer.

"Dat's money is now in his room. In an old pair of boots." As if in anticipation of the next question, Ben added, "It is still there. I have checked."

"And your money, Ben?"

"It is under my bed. It, too, is still there. Untouched."

Jakob took a few notes and then looked up at Ben. "Okay, so what makes you think someone was in your home and your dat's while you were at Eli's? Did someone tell you they saw someone?"

"There was no one to tell. Everyone was at Eli's." Ben let his hand drift back to the table, his eyes following suit. "It was the papers that told me."

"Papers?" Claire echoed. "What papers?"

"Dat's papers. My papers. They were not as they had been left."

Jakob stopped writing and pointed his pen at Ben. "So papers are missing? What kind of papers?"

"They are not missing."

Exhaling in frustration, Jakob looked from Ben to the notepad and back again. "I'm sorry, Ben, but I'm missing what you're saying."

"I keep papers on the things that I buy over there. In my desk." Ben's gaze traveled across the kitchen to a small alcove on the far side. "My dat used to keep papers on everything he bought—tractors, horses, buggies, cows, and the like. It is something I now do for the things I must buy."

"Okay . . ." Jakob prodded.

"I do not leave papers on the desk. They are in a drawer as they are in Dat's house." Turning his body toward his desk, Ben pushed off the wooden bench and stood. "But today, when I returned from Eli's, my papers were scattered across the desk and floor. Dat's, too."

"Do you have any idea why someone would do that?" Leaving the notebook and pen on the table, Jakob joined Ben in the middle of the room. "What they could be looking for?"

Ben's shoulders rose up beneath his suspenders in a shrug. "I do not know."

"Where are the papers now?" Jakob moved closer to the now-clean desk and looked back at Ben. "Did you move them?"

"Yah. I put them back in the drawer."

Claire could feel Jakob's disapproval from across the room and knew its origins. "Can you still get fingerprints?" she asked.

"We can try."

"Fingerprints?" Ben joined Jakob next to the desk, his confusion evident in everything from the lines around his eyes to the downward tilt of his eyebrows. "What does that mean?"

"Very often we can trace a criminal by his fingerprints. Assuming, of course, they're in the system."

"And this person left fingerprints behind?" Ben asked.

Jakob pulled his phone from his pocket but kept it down at his waist as he nodded at Ben. "If his fingers were bare, yes. They'll need to be isolated from yours and your dat's, but we should be able to pull some. But in order to do that, I need your permission to put a call into the station for one of my officers to come out here with a fingerprint kit. Is that okay?"

"Yah." Ben strode across the kitchen and retrieved a flashlight from the top of the refrigerator. "Perhaps there will be fingerprints in the barn, as well."

"The barn?" Jakob echoed.

"Yah. But there it is not because of papers." Ben hooked his thumb over his shoulder and then turned toward the door. "There, it is because of buckets. And feed."

Jakob met Claire at the kitchen doorway and guided her down the hallway and toward the front door. Back outside, they stepped off the porch and followed Ben across the driveway and into the barn.

"I was not happy when I saw the mess. Sometimes the younger boys are not always good about picking up after themselves. But then I remembered they were still with Dat and Mamm at Eli's. And they arrived at Eli's before I did, too. So it was not messy because of them." Ben led them over to the stalls that housed the family's horses and pointed into the first one. "That is one bucket that was knocked over. And that"—Ben pointed into the stall to their right—"one, too."

"Maybe the horse kicked it over," Claire suggested as Jakob stepped forward for a closer look. "They both look strong enough to be able to do that."

"Yah, but the buckets were *outside* the stalls when I left. And it is where I left them that they were knocked over."

Jakob's head snapped up. "And you're sure you were

the last one to leave here this morning and the first one back here this evening? There is no chance your dat came back at any point during the day?"

"I am sure." Ben walked to a third stall and pointed at a large draft horse. "And it is this one that was in the field."

Jakob tightened his grip on the still-unused phone in his hand and made his way over to Ben. "What do you mean?"

"It is a good thing he did not run. He is needed in the field tomorrow." Ben reached over the half wall and stroked the side of the sturdy animal. "It is as if he thought it was a workday."

"Are you saying this horse got out?" Jakob asked.

"Yah."

"How?"

"Someone left his stall open." Ben reached up under the front brim of his black hat and scratched along his hairline. "Perhaps it was him who knocked over the feed buckets."

Jakob nodded, his face deadpan. "Do you think one of your brothers forgot to latch the stall before church?"

"No. I checked on the horses before I left. The stall was latched."

"Are you certain?"

"Yah. I am certain"

"And, again, you are absolutely sure your dat did not return at some point during the day?"

"Yah. I am certain," Ben repeated.

Claire slapped a hand to her mouth in an effort to stifle the gasp that followed Ben's words, but it was too late. The sound earned the stare of both men, as well as the trio of horses closest to where she stood.

"Claire? Are you okay?"

She bypassed Ben's question and, instead, focused on Jakob. "Standing here, listening to Ben and everything he's saying, I can't help but feel like maybe Annie wasn't careless with Katie's stall door after all."

"I'm thinking the same thing. Only Annie didn't mention anything being wrong inside the house."

"Maybe she came straight to the inn after she found the stall door unlatched," she posed even as her thoughts jumped ahead to yet another possibility. "Or maybe, if it's a question of money being missing from inside her home, she simply hasn't noticed yet."

Jakob looked down at his phone, pressed a few buttons, and then held the device to his ear. Seconds later, he was barking out orders. "I need a patrol car out at the Miller farm ASAP. I also need Officer Latner out here with his fingerprint kit to do a sweep of both houses and the barn."

A few moments later, he lowered the phone to his side. "Once they get out here and I show them what I need them to do, I want to head over to Bishop Hershberger's place and check around. The fact that Katie's stall door was unlatched could be a coincidence or it could mean that the same person who was rooting around this farm was doing the same out at the bishop's place."

Chapter 18

For what had to be the hundredth time since the shop opened, Claire peeked at the clock on the back wall and noted the time in relation to Annie's expected arrival. Sure, the extra pair of hands on a relatively busy Monday would be nice, but more than that, she just wanted to know what, if anything, Jakob and his officers had discovered at the bishop's farm.

She'd stayed awake until the wee hours of the morning hoping Jakob would text or call when his work was done, but he hadn't, his concern for her need to sleep a likely reason. And that morning, on her way in to work, a peek at the parking lot behind the Heavenly Police Department yielded no sign of the detective's car. Whether that was because he was home sleeping or out in the field, she could only guess.

"Good afternoon, Claire."

Abandoning the display of painted spoons she wasn't really paying attention to anyway, Claire stepped off the footstool and took a moment to study her sixteen-year-old employee from head to toe. Dressed in a typical Amish dress and apron, Annie stood just inside the back entrance to the shop's main room, clutching a lunch pail in her hands. "Annie, you're early. I wasn't expecting you for another thirty minutes or so."

"Henry was coming to town and offered to give me a ride in his buggy." A hint of crimson crept across the girl's rounded cheeks just before she thrust the pail outward. "I brought you some chicken for lunch. An apple, too."

Claire crossed the room to Annie but stopped short of actually taking the pail. "Annie, you don't have to bring me lunch. You really don't."

"But I know how much you like the way Eva has taught me to bread the chicken. It is too much for just me and Dat to eat alone, anyway."

Feeling her stomach start to respond to the proximity of a meal she'd so far skipped, she took the pail and smiled at her young friend. "Thank you, Annie." Then, glancing over her shoulder at the front door, she carried the pail to the counter and removed the cloth cover. "We seem to be in a little bit of a lull at the moment, so maybe I will take a quick bite . . ."

"Why don't you sit down on the stool and eat. Or take it outside on the back stoop. I am here now. I will take care of any customers who come."

Again, she looked at the clock. "Are you sure? Technically you still have some more time to walk around with Henry if he is still nearby."

"Henry is not here to walk around," Annie said as she gazed down at the clipboard and the list of daily tasks Claire had yet to check off. "He is here to talk to your detective. I am here to work."

Claire let the chicken leg fall back into the pail and drifted back against the edge of the counter. "Henry is talking to Jakob right now?" At Annie's nod, she added, "Why? Do you know?"

"To see if the things that happened in our barn and the Millers' barn last night is what happened in Henry's barn."

"So Jakob thinks Katie's stall door being unlatched is connected to whatever went on at the Millers' house yesterday?"

Annie's dark eyes swung toward the front door and then back to rest on Claire. "I was to be in bed when the detective and the other policemen stopped by last night. But it was not hard to hear the things they said. Dat looked to see if his money was missing. But it was not."

"Was anything disturbed inside your house when you got home from your hymn sing yesterday?"

"I did not go into the house until after I came to see you at the inn, but when I got home Dat was there and everything was as it should be."

"Is he sure?" Claire asked.

Annie laughed. "That is the same question your detective asked. And just as Dat told him, yah, we are sure."

Claire reached, again, for the chicken and this time took a bite, her mind dissecting everything she knew so far. "But Jakob thinks someone was in your barn?"

"Yah. There was half a boot print in the earth that did not come from Dat or me."

"I wonder why this person didn't go into your home as they did Henry's, Rebecca's, and the Millers'." She took another bite of chicken and then slid the apple over to Annie. "I feel bad eating in front of you. Why don't you have the apple?"

"I already ate." Annie slid onto the stool next to Claire and lowered her voice despite the absence of any customers. "It is no surprise that this person did not go into my house. He could not get in."

She looked at Annie over her chicken leg and hoped any surprise depicted on her face didn't come off as judgmental. "You lock your doors?"

"No. But the doors stick. You must push in just the right place to make them open. The person in our barn did not know the right place."

"They didn't break any windows?"

Annie shook her head and then reached into the pail long enough to retrieve a pair of cookies Claire hadn't noticed underneath the napkin. "I brought cookies. They are from a recipe my mamm used to make. They are Dat's favorite."

"You are too good to me, Annie," she said honestly.

"*God* is good. It is He who has brought us to be friends. It is His will."

Claire reached her free hand across the space between them and patted Annie's knee. "I'm glad that it is," she said simply. And she was. Annie had been a godsend since the moment she started working at Heavenly Treasures, her presence and work ethic enabling Claire to reclaim a little bit of the personal life she'd lost when Esther left to marry Eli. The young girl's enthusiasm for the job and obvious admiration of Claire had simply been the icing on the cake.

Now, several months later, Claire considered Annie a friend despite the doubled age difference between them.

"So what time did Jakob leave your house? Do you know?" she asked as she finished the chicken and moved on to the apple and the cookies.

"It was ten when he left the barn. The others stayed, but he and Benjamin left."

"The others?"

"Policemen. They spent more time in the barn. Why, I do not know."

"They were probably lifting fingerprints. To see if the person who is doing this is the same as the person who was at the Millers' yesterday. If the person has a criminal record, it will show up in a special police database."

"If they do not?"

"Jakob will keep looking for the person behind everything that has happened this past week—the robberies, the trespassing, and most importantly, the death of Henry's dat."

Annie nibbled on her lower lip and then looked up at Claire, her voice barely more than a raspy whisper. "It is scary to think that someone may have been in our barn. What if Dat had been there? What if this person killed . . . *Dat*?"

"He didn't. That's all that matters right now, Annie." She wiped her hands on her napkin and then gathered Annie's hands inside her own. "Jakob will find the person responsible for all of this. I have absolutely no doubt about that. Jakob is very good at what he does."

Annie cleared her throat of any lingering fear and narrowed her dark eyes on Claire as if she was searching for something. "You care for him, yah? As someone much more than a friend?"

"I do." It was such a simplistic answer, but that didn't make it any less accurate. "Jakob is a good man. A kind, caring, generous man who wants nothing more than to make sure that everyone in this town is safe from harm. It's all he's ever wanted. Sadly, that calling has cost him dearly."

"He is happy with you. It is in his smile every time he sees you."

She considered likening Jakob's smile at seeing her to Annie's smile at the mere mention of Henry Stutzman, but thought better of it. At sixteen, such observations were almost invariably met with defensive words. Instead, she brought Henry back into the conversation via the topic at hand. "Do you think Henry has anything new to offer Jakob about what happened the night he found his father in the barn?"

Annie's head was already shaking before Claire had finished her sentence. "Henry was not in the barn when his dat died. He will not be able to help with that, but still he will try. Henry is like that. He likes to help."

The bells tasked with announcing the arrival of a customer jingled, prompting Annie to instinctively gather Claire's trash and stuff it into the wastebasket while Claire slipped off her stool and headed toward the door. "Good afternoon, welcome to Heavenly Treas— Oh, Hank! Hello."

The Midwestern college teacher's reply came via a broad smile, a quick wave, and a brief scan of his surroundings. "Hi, Claire. I've been spending so much time out at Amish home-based businesses, that I've neglected the shops here on Lighted Way. I figured it was time to change that."

"Well, we're glad you did, aren't we, Annie?" She glanced over her shoulder at Annie and motioned the girl over. "Annie, this is Hank Turner. He's staying at the inn while he researches small businesses for the college-level classes he teaches back in Wisconsin. And, Hank, this is Annie Hershberger, my trusty employee and friend."

At the word *friend*, Annie's cheeks, powered by her smile, rose nearly to her eyes while Hank stepped forward and extended his hand to the Amish teenager. "How long have you been working here with Claire, Annie?"

Annie's eyes drifted upward in thought, then back to Claire for confirmation. "Five months? Is that right?"

"It'll be five months next week." Claire slid her arm around Annie's shoulders and pulled the girl in for a quick side hug. "And she's been an absolute godsend, I'll tell you that much."

"Is it difficult to work for someone who is not Amish?" Hank asked Annie. "To adjust to their customs?"

"It is nice to work with Claire. I learn much from her." Annie crossed to the opposite side of the store and pointed at the wooden chests, footstools, and high chairs displayed there. "Claire gives many in our community a place to sell their handmade goods."

Hank followed the girl for a closer look at the items, even reaching out to run his hand across a chest and a high chair. "Why don't they just open their own shops and sell them on their own like Samuel Yoder does with his furniture store or Ruth Miller does next door with her bake shop? Surely someone who can make handcrafted furniture like this could survive on their own, couldn't they? Or would they not want to compete with one of their own?"

"The Amish who make the items you see here are

farmers first. Their jobs are in the fields or with the animals," Annie explained. "Claire's shop is a way to make money on things they build when they are not farming."

Claire ventured over to Martha's painted milk cans and the shelf containing Esther's Amish dolls and lifted one of the dolls into the air for Hank to see. "And items like these are ways for many Amish women to make money for their families as well."

"How do you work the whole social security tax aspect as an English employer with employees who aren't required to pay into the system?" Hank asked as he came closer to look at the variety of items displayed to the left and right of Claire.

"If they work for an English employer, they have to pay it." Claire took a moment to neaten a stack of handmade baby bibs and a pile of booties. "But even if they do, they still don't accept anything in return when they retire."

Nodding, Hank continued to take stock of her inventory, periodically stopping to touch something or hold it up for a closer look. When he reached a display of quilts, he pulled a pair of glasses from the front pocket of his trousers and slipped them into place across the bridge of his nose to allow a more thorough inspection of their detailed work. "The Amish really do quality work, don't they?"

"There's no question about that. Just ask Annie here."

Hank looked from Annie to the quilt and back again, his eyes widening. "*You* made this?"

"Yah."

"You do beautiful work, Annie. You must make a lot of money with a quilt like this."

Annie shrugged. "It goes to Dat to use as he sees fit."

"Do you ever think of opening your own shop one day?" Hank asked.

"No. One day I will have a husband and children. If I am to make money, it will be on quilts Claire sells here, or jams and jellies I sell from a stand."

"Amish women do not work outside the home once they are married." Claire took a moment to restack the selection of hand-sewn doilies, her thoughts flitting between the conversation with Hank and the tasks she still hoped to get done. "Their primary focus is on the family."

"So they're home all day, every day?" Hank asked. "Well, unless they have to run an errand or it's a church day?"

"Yah."

"Interesting." Hank rested his arms across his chest and leaned against a small stretch of wall between the shelf of dolls and the shelf of place mats and other table essentials. "So what happens to the bake shop next door when Ruth marries? Will it close down since she can't run it?"

That was a good question, and one Claire had never pondered until that moment. "Annie? Do you know?" she asked.

"Ruth will still bake, I'm sure. But perhaps her younger sister will run the shop." Annie bent over, repositioned one of the hand-carved footstools, and then straightened. "It will not be long before we know for sure."

Chapter 19

The guests were all there when Claire finally finished with the week's books and wandered into the parlor, their lighthearted voices and occasional bursts of laughter proving to be just the tonic she needed.

"If I'd known you were all having so much fun in here, I would have abandoned my calculator and pencil an hour ago." Claire instinctively lifted the half-empty tray of cookies from the table just inside the doorway and made the rounds of the guests. Jeremy, of course, took another, as did Hank and Bill.

"Then you'd be up until the wee hours of the night trying to finish what is now done." Diane leaned around her laptop computer and patted the bottom section of her lounge chair. "Put the tray down, dear, and come sit. You really need to see the photographs Hayley has been taking this past week. They're simply breathtaking."

"Let's not inflate her ego any more than necessary," Jeremy joked. "Hayley got lucky is all."

Diane peered at Jeremy across the top of her reading glasses, tsking playfully beneath her breath. "Now, Jeremy, is that any way to talk to your partner? Especially since it's *you* who handed the flash drive to me when I inquired about Hayley's work?" Then, without waiting for his answering banter, the woman hit play on the slideshow and handed the laptop to Claire. "Look at these. The one of the black horse through the branches of the tree is my favorite."

"You should see your face right now, Diane, it's glowing." Bill smiled at Claire's aunt from his seat beside the hearth. "Horses really do make you happy, don't they?"

"They're beautiful creatures." Diane looked from the pictures fading in and out on the screen in front of Claire to the photographer who'd captured the images. "Hayley, I have to imagine you feel the same way based on these photographs. I mean, there's almost a tangible reverence here."

Clearly uncomfortable being the center of attention, Hayley cleared her throat and volleyed the subject back to Diane. "Have you ever thought about purchasing a horse of your own? Your grounds are certainly large enough to accommodate one."

"I did. For a while. But if I purchased a horse, I would want to give it more time and attention than running this inn would allow me to do. So, instead, I enjoy seeing them pull buggies past my driveway, I enjoy seeing them in the fields of my Amish friends, and I enjoy visiting with each and every new horse that comes in for sale at the Weaver farm when my schedule allows."

Claire looked up from a photograph of a chocolate

brown–colored horse beside a pile of colored leaves and studied her aunt. "You go to the Weaver farm? I didn't know that."

"I don't do it all the time, dear. But I do it as often as I can. I love looking at them between worlds."

Hank lowered his pen to his notebook long enough to address Diane. "Between worlds?"

"Most of the horses that Mervin Weaver buys at auction are retired racehorses. The majority of their lives has been about racing. Once they're purchased by Amish farmers, their lives are very different. They're slower, for one thing. And their primary responsibility shifts from entertainment to transportation. It's just . . . different."

"Retired racehorses, eh? I wouldn't have guessed that."

"It actually makes perfect sense. Trotters are skilled at pulling a sulky. They're a natural fit for an Amish buggy."

Hank closed his notebook on his day's business notations and then stretched his arms above his head. "I'm telling you, the Amish are resourceful and incredibly smart."

"Yes, they are," Diane agreed.

Claire rewound the dialogue in her ear back to the part that had taken her by surprise. "But when do you go out to the farm and how did I not know this?"

"What am I going to say, dear? 'I spent a half hour introducing myself to a dozen or so horses I may never see again'? You'd think I'd gone mad." Diane wiggled her way past Claire on the chair and stood, her self-allotted time for rest clearly in her rearview mirror. "Which is what everyone must be thinking right about now, anyway."

"No. I . . . I'd think it was neat. And I'd want to hear more. Maybe even go with you to see them sometime."

Bill's nod was nothing short of emphatic. "I'd enjoy that as well."

"I could take pictures," Hayley chimed in. Then, poking an elbow into Jeremy's side, she added, "And maybe *you* could turn it into a blog when I got back."

Jeremy lifted his head off the back of the couch and forced his eyelids open. "Huh? What? What'd I miss?"

"Go upstairs and go to sleep," Hayley said, rolling her eyes as she did. "You're just taking up space on the couch that Claire could have right now."

Claire waved her hands back and forth above her computer-topped lap. "Hayley, I'm fine. There's plenty of room for Diane and me on this chair. Assuming, of course, my aunt would actually sit back down."

Diane readjusted her apron across her hips and then slowly looked from Claire, to Hayley, to Bill, and back again. "Would you really like to accompany me out to the Weavers' place?"

All three heads nodded in unison, followed by a raised index finger from Hank. "Don't forget me. I haven't visited a horse business yet."

"I've never done a—a . . . *field trip* before," Diane replied. "Are you sure?"

Claire took in the expressions on the faces around them and then looked up at her aunt. "Annie's on the schedule alone tomorrow morning . . ."

"I could do tomorrow morning." Hayley eyed her sleeping coworker and rolled her eyes again. "And he could just stay behind and sleep."

"Do you think they'll have a fresh shipment of horses ready to be sold off?" Hank asked.

"There's no guarantee what Mervin has on any given day, but it's more likely he'll have some horses than no horses." A slow smile erupted across Diane's face and traveled to her eyes. "I'm so pleased about this!"

Bill took a sip of coffee from the cup beside his chair and then rose to his feet to face Diane. "What time do you anticipate we'll head out?"

"How about nine o'clock? That will give me time to get the breakfast dishes cleaned up." At everyone's ready agreement, Diane took Bill's empty cup, added it to Hayley's and Hank's, and then ventured toward the parlor doorway. "You are all in for quite a treat. Mervin has a knack for finding the sweetest horses."

Claire had just settled her head against the pillow when her cell phone rang—the sound, coupled with her certainty as to the identity of the caller, propelling her up onto her elbow with a smile. Reaching over to the nightstand, she plucked the device from its resting spot, confirmed her suspicion, and then held it to her ear.

"Hi, Jakob."

"I didn't wake you, did I?"

"No, no. I hadn't even turned off the light yet. How are you? Busy day?"

"Busy enough that I didn't get to come and see you like I'd hoped." Jakob's voice faded off momentarily, only to return with a slight huskiness. "That's always my favorite part of any day, you know. Seeing you."

She felt her face warm in response to his words. "I feel the same." And she did.

"I'm glad."

Twisting her body to the side, she hiked her pillow upward against the headboard and then leaned back. "Annie told me that Henry spent some time with you this afternoon. Did anything come of that?"

"Nope. I keep hoping that Henry is suddenly going to remember some previously unshared detail that'll blow this whole case wide open, but so far it's a no-go."

"You'll find it, Jakob. With or without Henry."

His answering laugh was void of any humor. "I wish I could say your confidence is on target, Claire, but it's not. I mean, I know everything that's happened around here with the missing money and Wayne's death is all related somehow, but beyond that I've got nothing, and it's incredibly frustrating."

"So you really think someone was out at Annie's father's farm on Sunday?"

"I do. I think someone took advantage of the fact they were at church and used that as an opportunity to snoop around their farm."

"But nothing was missing or disturbed inside the house, right?"

"That's right. But that could be a result of an inability to figure out the door, or because this guy got spooked away before he could get inside."

She shivered in spite of the warm July evening. "Do you think Annie coming home could be what spooked him?"

"It's hard to say, Claire. Maybe. But that's just me trying to figure out why he found his way into all the other homes except the bishop's."

For a moment, she merely stared up at the ceiling, her

thoughts picking their way through everything Jakob had said and everything they knew at that point. "Jakob? Is there any way to know whether Henry's dat was killed before or after the man came to the house?"

"We're likely looking at a difference of ten minutes, so no. Not really. But I have to believe that someone isn't going to kill a person and then go up to that same person's home—where his family is playing games—and calmly ask for directions."

"Do we know it was calmly?" she asked.

"I actually asked Henry if the man seemed upset or winded, if he was sweating from exertion. Henry was insistent he was not. So my gut says he killed Wayne after having been in the house."

She considered Jakob's words and tacked on another layer. "So *after* he'd stolen the money, too . . ."

"Exactly."

"Okay. But then why go into the barn at all? It doesn't seem to me to be a place people would keep their money, you know?"

The momentary silence in her ear gave way to a grunt. "True."

"So maybe, in addition to money, he's looking for something else."

"Most of the truly big equipment is kept outside the barn. But even if it's not, it's not like anyone is going to be able to go unnoticed stealing something like that."

"Maybe it's not the tractors . . ."

"The only other thing of value would be the horses. But they're all still there."

"Some of them weren't there when our suspect was

rooting through the barns," she reminded. "Katie was with Annie, the bishop's horse was with the bishop, and I would imagine Ben's horse was with him."

"The buggy horses, anyway." Jakob grew silent save for the occasional noise that Claire tied to movement—pacing, perhaps?

"Then again," she mused, "the horses were in the stable at the Stutzmans', yes? And they're all still there . . ."

"That could be because our suspect was spooked off by killing Wayne . . ."

"What about the Gingerichs'?" she posed, following her thread outward. "Where were their horses?"

"Working in the fields."

"So maybe this person is interested in stealing horses, too."

Again, Jakob remained quiet for a while, his detective brain surely chewing on their conversation.

As she waited, she posed another question. "I imagine horses could go for a lot of money, yes?"

"Depends. Then again, a person hell-bent on stealing horses would have to have a way to get them off the property. Quickly. And neither Henry, nor Rebecca, mentioned anything about a horse trailer."

"Maybe they didn't make the connection."

"It's worth asking them, that's for sure. But something feels off about this."

"Well, is there anything else in a barn of value? A certain tool? An item used on the horses?"

"In some barns, sure." Jakob took a breath and then exhaled it slowly. "Saddles, mounts, anything made of copper that could be melted down . . . that sort of thing. But you'd be hard pressed to find that kind of stuff—or that kind of stuff with any worth—in an Amish barn. The simplicity of the Amish reaches into their barns, too."

"Maybe this person doesn't know this. Maybe he's just preying on the Amish because of the whole easy target thing." Now that she was going it was hard to stop. "They're not going to have security systems in their homes or barns, the men are in the fields during the day and the women, like their male counterparts, are passive people. In fact, I don't think you'd even have to be all that savvy about the Amish to know that."

"Hey, would you mind if we talked about something else for a little while? I think my brain needs a break."

Scooting her upper body off the headboard-propped pillow, Claire rolled onto her side and gazed at the scrap of moonlight poking its way around her window shade. "Of course. What do you want to talk about?"

"Tell me about your evening. What did Diane make for dinner?"

"A turkey roast."

"I love that."

"I know. That's why there's a small glass container with your name on it sitting on the top shelf of the refrigerator right now."

"Seriously?"

"Seriously." She smiled as she imagined the look on Jakob's face at that very moment. "I can bring it to you at the station tomorrow after we get back from Diane's first-ever field trip to the Weaver farm."

"The Weaver farm?"

"Uh-huh. Apparently, unbeknownst to me, Diane frequents the Weaver farm to check out all the new horses

163

before they're sold to the various Amish farms. She likes to introduce herself to them."

His laugh widened her smile still further. "I love your aunt."

"How could you not?" she joked, transferring her attention from the sliver of light around the window to the sliver of light beneath her door. "Just about everyone, except Jim . . . and maybe Jeremy, if he's still sleeping, is going along to see the farm. It should be fun."

"Jim?"

"The marketing consultant working with the mayor on ways to make Heavenly even more appealing to tourists . . ."

Jakob took what sounded like a sip of something and then released a tired sigh. "I hear he's talking about bars and things."

"He might be talking, but I can guarantee Diane, Harold, and Al are talking a whole lot louder."

This time his laughter was cut short by a yawn. "The chief, too. Heavenly doesn't need bars. That's not what this place is about."

"I couldn't agree more."

"Hasn't this Jim guy been at the inn a really long time?" Jakob asked around another, longer yawn.

"They've all been here for a while. I think Hayley and Jeremy are here for another two or three days, at least. Hank and Bill, too. Even Judy took advantage of a last-minute cancellation and extended her stay, although she wasn't around this evening. I think Diane said she was meeting up with friends in Breeze Point."

"That's nice. Hey . . . I saw Ben this afternoon."

"Oh?"

"He was out at Stutzman's again. Helping Emma with a few things."

"That doesn't surprise me."

"The fact that he was there doesn't surprise me, either. The lift to his step while he was there, however, did."

She rolled onto her back once again and imagined herself sitting on a couch with Jakob, his arm draped across her shoulder . . . "A lift to his step? I don't understand."

"It's the only way I can think to describe it. He seemed lighter. Happier."

"Ben likes to help people," she said.

"This was different."

Something about his words, his tone, brought her focus back into her bedroom and onto their conversation. "Different, how?"

"Like maybe, in time, he can finally move on."

"From?"

"From Elizabeth and on to someone else."

At the mention of Ben's late wife, she tightened her grip on the phone. "Someone else? You mean like Emma Stutzman? C'mon, Jakob, the woman's husband hasn't even been dead a full week yet."

"Oh, I'm not saying she sees Ben as anything other than a helpful friend . . . or that Ben has any ulterior motive. Because I'm not. I'm just saying I can almost picture them together. In the future."

She stared up at the ceiling and tried his words on for size . . .

Ben sitting on a buggy seat next to Emma Stutzman . . .

Ben eating dinner surrounded by family . . .

Ben guiding Henry and his brothers into adulthood . . .

Ben holding a child of his own one day . . .

Each new image that played in her thoughts made her happier than the one before.

She wanted that for Ben. She wanted him to be happy and in love again one day. Whether that happened with Emma Stutzman or someone else; it didn't matter. She just wanted Ben to know the same happiness she'd found with Jakob.

Chapter 20

Claire picked her way across the matching ruts that lined both sides of the Weavers' driveway, her last-minute decision to don sneakers rather than rain boots an unequivocal mistake.

"So much for the local forecast," she mumbled as her left foot sank into the mud and halted her forward motion with its sticky grip.

Extending his hand to her, Hank tugged her free. "They blow the forecast in Wisconsin all the time, too. Except in winter. *That* they seem to get right."

"It snows a lot in Wisconsin during the winter, doesn't it?"

"Yup." His hold loosened and then released completely as they reached the front side of the barn and a waiting Diane. "And to think, I'd actually started to believe it was always sunny in Heavenly . . ."

Diane nibbled back her smile just long enough to

respond. "If it was sunny all the time, Hank, crops wouldn't grow. And if crops didn't grow, many of the businesses you've been studying this past week would fail."

"True." Hank pointed at Claire's mud-caked left sneaker and shook his head. "Next time we have a field trip to a horse farm? Wear boots."

"I'll keep that in mind, Hank, thanks." She did her best to shake the mud loose, but gave up and addressed the lanky blonde standing next to her aunt instead. "Hayley, aren't you worried about your camera getting wet?"

Hayley glanced down at the camera bag slung across her shoulder and shrugged. "No. Not really. I've got tricks I can use if necessary."

"Do you know if this place is ever part of the country-side bus tours?" Bill surveyed the large white barn in front of them and then swung his gaze out toward the mud-soaked paddock beyond.

Diane tightened the strings of her hood, nodding as she did. "Sometimes. The tour bus operator likes to vary his stops often. He says it keeps the tour fresh and makes it so people want to come back again and again."

"He's right." Slipping his hand into his pocket, the travel agent extracted a notebook and pen and then hunched his shoulders forward just enough to protect it as he jotted down the information. When he was done, he returned both to his pocket and swept his hand toward the large door just off to their right. "Well? Shall we?"

"Yes." Diane stepped over one last remaining mud puddle, turned and pointed at it for Claire's benefit, and then led the way into the large cavernous barn and its stall-flanked center aisle.

Instantly, a dozen or more noses peeked out at them from the left and the right, with a few soft, whinnied greetings peppering the air. Diane stopped mid-step, reached into the pocket of her simple raincoat, and extracted a handful of peppermint candy. Spinning around, she opened up her palm and held it and the candies out for Claire and their guests.

"Everybody take two. When you find a horse that strikes your fancy, stick the candy in the center of your palm and hold it out, steady. Let's try to make sure they all get one, okay?"

Claire stepped back, waited until Bill, Hayley, and Hank each had their candies, and then took two as well, her focus skipping ahead three stalls to a dark gray horse staring intently back at her. "Hey there, little fella." She approached the horse with gentle, tentative steps, stopping just shy of the half wall that separated them from each other. "Are you looking at me because you know I have a treat in my hand? Or because I look like a drowned rat?"

"First of all, dear, he's a she. Second of all, she's as curious about you as you are about her." Diane paused just behind Claire's left shoulder and released a contented sigh. "She's a beauty, isn't she? She must have come in on a trailer yesterday, because she wasn't here on Sunday."

"You were here on Sunday?" she asked, pulling her gaze from the horse long enough to take in her aunt.

"I was."

"How often do you actually come out here?"

Diane looked past her at the horse, a tiny smile playing at the corners of her lips. "Once or twice a week, most weeks. Though I've missed a few weeks as of late on account of how busy we've been at the inn."

"And this is a recent thing? Your coming here once or twice a week?"

"If you call twenty years recent . . . then yes, it's a recent thing." Diane stepped around Claire and ran her non-candy-holding hand down the horse's neck, murmuring softly to the animal as she did.

Claire tried to make sense of the woman's words, but she came up empty. "I don't understand how I didn't know this. You're *always* at the inn."

"Around lunchtime, when the guests are off exploring Heavenly and you're either at the shop or working on something in your room, I head out. Sometimes I bring my lunch with me and sometimes I don't. I only stay for thirty minutes or so, but it's enough time to take a deep breath and recharge my batteries for the rest of the day."

Taking a moment to marvel at the way the horse nuzzled her face against Diane's, Claire collected her thoughts and posed another question. "So what do you do out here during those thirty minutes?"

"I give and receive a little love, I find the horses in need of a treat, and, sometimes, I grab a brush and help Mervin out a little." Diane parted company with the horse long enough to present it with a piece of peppermint candy. "It's the next best thing to having a horse-filled barn of my own."

Claire watched the candy disappear and then looked from the peppermints in her own hand to her aunt. "Does it make you sad when you connect with one like this and then it's gone the next time you come?"

Diane ran her hand down the horse's neck one last time and then stepped back to assess the stalls yet to be visited.

"No. Not really. It just means they've gone on to their new homes."

"Do you ever wish *you* could be one of those homes?" she asked.

"Sometimes, I suppose. But running the inn is a dream come true for me, dear. It truly is. The fact that I can do that in a community that relies so heavily on horses is simply a bonus."

Diane took three steps toward the next stall and then doubled back to a spotted white horse. "This one really is sweet, isn't she? She reminds me of a picture my father gave me when I was little. Same basic color, except that one had a plain white chest, whereas this one has markings there."

"Is that when you fell in love with horses? When grandpa gave you that picture?"

"It was. I used to study that picture every night before bed. Then, the next year, a new girl came into my class and she had a horse. Of her own. I'd listen to her stories at lunch and during recess and that was all I talked about when I got home from school each day." Diane whispered something in the horse's ear and then turned her attention back to Claire. "Everything was Sophie's horse this, Sophie's horse that. I don't know how Mom and Dad put up with me."

Claire wandered over to a wooden barrel, checked its stability, and then hiked herself up onto its lid, her legs dangling over the sides. "So why haven't you bought a horse of your own?"

"Because I'm an innkeeper, not a horse owner."

"Why can't you be both?"

Diane plucked a brush from a hook beside the stall and stepped inside. With gentle, careful strokes, she brushed the side of the horse, humming softly as she did. After several passes, she shrugged. "Your being here has wiped away any loneliness I may have had on occasion."

Claire pulled back, the sudden motion making the barrel rock. "Whoooaaa . . ."

"No worries, dear. It will hold you."

"And you know this how?"

"When there are several horses in need of attention at one time, I often sit on that same barrel and sing a song." Diane walked around the front of the horse and set to work on the other side. "For whatever reason, the horses don't seem to realize I'm tone deaf."

Claire laughed. "I've always loved your singing, too."

"That's because you grew up listening to my version of singing."

"There is no better version." And there wasn't. Visiting Diane as a little girl had been filled with perfect moments, singing included.

"You're biased, dear."

"No, I'm lucky." She scooted forward on the barrel and then jumped down onto her feet. "Well, I guess I better find some takers for my peppermints."

Slowly, she made her way down the aisle, passing Bill, then Hank, and finally Hayley, Claire's peppermints the only ones that had yet to be dispensed. About three stalls shy of the aisle's end, she found her first recipient—a jet black mare with long eyelashes and soulful eyes.

"Hey there, pretty lady, would you like a treat?"

The animal's answer came via a quick flick of her

tongue, followed by a snort of air on Claire's now empty palm. "Hmmm . . . I guess that was a yes, huh?"

Hank moved in beside her, laughing. "Peppermint is definitely a hit with this crew. The second horse I found actually stuck her nose in my pocket looking for a second helping. And boy was she persistent."

"Probably smelled the lingering scent from them having been in there in the first place." Bill stepped back from the stall he'd been visiting and gestured toward Hayley. "I imagine we've provided a few good shots for you. Unless"—he looked down at his hand and then wiped it on the only pair of jeans Claire had seen him wear all week—"saliva isn't what you're after."

Hayley disengaged the lens from the body of her camera and set both inside her bag. "It's not."

"I imagine it would be best to capture the ideal horse *outside* . . . on a sunny day, yes?" Hank asked.

"Outside, inside, makes no difference." Hayley zipped up her bag and then hiked it up and onto her shoulder. "I just need to find the right one, you know?"

Claire crossed to the opposite side of the aisle and the chestnut brown horse eyeing them closely. "This one is cute. Real wide-eyed and alert. Like she wants to have a conversation."

"I think it's more likely she's been watching all of her friends get treats and she knows it's her turn." Hank followed Claire and then leaned his head into the stall to address the horse. "That's it, isn't it? You know Claire has a peppermint, don't you?"

With a playful nudge, Claire pushed Hank out of the way and addressed the curious horse herself.

"Don't pay any attention to him. You've been waiting very patiently for your turn, haven't you?" Opening her fist, she held the red-and-white candy atop her palm and invited the horse to partake. Once again, her answer came via a tongue and a snort. Only this time, instead of retreating a few steps, the horse lowered her head once again and gently nuzzled Claire's empty hand.

"You're most welcome, sweetie."

Chapter 21

Carefully, with practiced hands, Claire set the glass-encased candle along the outer edge of the tissue paper and began to roll, the lavender scent she'd infused into the wax muting temporarily. When she was done, she placed it in the bag along with an Amish doll and a set of four place mats.

"My daughter is going to be so tickled when she sees those place mats. That shade of maroon is exactly the right color for her kitchen." The rounded woman who'd introduced herself as Margaret within moments of entering Heavenly Treasures held two twenty-dollar bills in Claire's direction, her pleasure over her purchases evident in everything from the tone of her voice to the giant grin that seemed to involve her entire face. "And that candle? I love its lavender scent. Especially as I'm drifting off to sleep."

Claire placed the money into the register and then

counted out the woman's change. "There has actually been some research done that shows a correlation between lavender oil and slow-wave sleep."

"Slow-wave sleep?"

"That's your really deep sleep. When your body is at its most relaxed." She transferred the change from her own hand to the customer's and then closed the register drawer. "Anyway, thanks for stopping by. I hope you enjoy the rest of your stay in Heavenly."

"I've loved every minute here." Margaret wrapped her wide fingers around the handles of the paper shopping bag and peeked inside. "I know the ladies in my tour group are going to think I'm crazy buying a doll when I don't have any grandbabies yet, but I couldn't resist. Even without faces, they're still the cutest things ever."

"I'll be sure to let my friend Esther know that. She'll be pleased."

Margaret's left eyebrow rose. "Did she make them?"

"She did."

"Is she Amish?"

Claire nodded. "She is."

"And you two can be friends?" Margaret asked.

"Of course." Claire came around the counter and walked with the woman to the door. "In fact, many of my friends are Amish, and—"

The shop's front door swung open, tripping its string of bells and alerting Claire to a customer. Only this time, instead of the sound ushering in a new face, she found herself smiling at one that was not only familiar, but a welcome sight as well.

"Oh, Martha, isn't this a wonderful surprise." Claire

reached for the loaded milk crate in the woman's hands and set it on the floor at her feet. "Margaret, this is my friend Martha King. Martha and her daughters, Esther and Hannah, make many of the things you see here in my shop, like the doll and the place mats you just bought for your daughter."

Her eyes widening, Margaret thrust her hand out and then in and then out again. "I'm sorry . . . um, do Amish people shake hands?"

Martha took the woman's hand in hers and shook it quickly. "We do."

"Wow. A real live Amish person. I mean, I've seen some of you from the windows of the tour bus, but . . . I didn't think I'd actually get to talk to one." Margaret returned her hand to the handle of her shopping bag and headed toward the door. "I can't wait to tell my friends. They just *had* to stop and get a cup of coffee before getting back on the bus . . ."

And then she was gone, her wide frame heading down the sidewalk toward Heavenly Brews, her shopping bag clutched firmly in her hand. When she was out of view, Claire turned her focus back on the forty-something woman clad in a muted blue aproned dress. "She sure was excited to meet you."

"I do not know why." Martha retrieved the milk crate from the floor and carried it over to the counter, her simple black lace-up boots making nary a sound against the part-tiled, part-carpeted floor. "I have brought some things for the store if you would like to display them."

"I'm sure I will." Claire joined Martha at the counter and watched as each new handcrafted item was plucked from the crate. "Your items are always huge—oh, Martha, that is precious . . ." She stared down at the hand-painted birdhouse in awe. "The windows . . . the flowering vines creeping around them . . . oh, Martha . . ."

"You would like to display it, then?"

Reluctantly, she pulled her gaze from the birdhouse and fixed it on Esther's mother. "How could I not? This is going to fly off the shelf. No pun intended."

"Then I will make more." Martha emptied the crate and then gestured toward the half dozen items in front of them. "Whatever you think is fair, of course."

Claire wound her way around the counter, pulled out her consignment ledger, and jotted down each new item in the section assigned to Martha. She was halfway through the list when the string of bells over the door jingled once again.

"Good afternoon. Welcome to Heavenly Treasures. I'll be right with—"

A quiet gasp at her elbow brought her attention off the ledger and onto the familiar face beaming back at her from the doorway. "Jakob! Hi . . ."

"Hi, yourself." He strode toward the counter only to stop mid-step as his gaze fell on his sister. "Martha, hello, I didn't see you standing there."

Claire hadn't realized she was holding her breath until Martha's whispered reply was followed by her own loud exhale.

"Hello, Jakob."

"How are you? How are the children?"

Martha removed the empty crate from the counter and held it in front of her torso like a shield. The fact that it was a shield between herself and her brother wasn't lost on Claire—or Jakob, if the momentary skitter of pain in his eyes was any indication.

The woman's reaction and its underlying reason was, without a doubt, the single biggest thing Claire didn't like about the Amish. How someone could be excommunicated for following a noble calling like police work was simply unfathomable to her.

"I am well. The children are well."

She supposed she should be grateful the woman was speaking to her brother at all, but it was hard to find solace in a reply that was so wooden.

"I need you to be careful when your husband is in the fields during the day. Do not let any strangers into your home. Make sure the children know the same thing."

Martha's grip on the milk crate softened. "I do not understand."

He came around the paneled upright and made his way over to the counter, his focus never leaving his sister's face. "You are aware of what happened to Wayne Stutzman, yes?"

Martha's nod was quick but sure.

"We have reason to believe he was murdered."

"I hope you are not right."

He stepped still closer, but stopped in his tracks the moment his sister stiffened. "We also have reason to believe the man responsible for Wayne's death is still in the area, possibly finding his way into people's homes and stealing their money."

"My husband said money is missing from the Gingerich farm."

"That is correct. Someone was also in Benjamin's home while he was at Esther and Eli's on Sunday."

"I was at Esther's on Sunday as well. She did not tell me money is missing from Benjamin's home."

"Because it isn't. Benjamin, knowing what's been going on around here, hid his money."

"How do you know someone was in his home if he was not there?"

"They went through his papers and left a mess." Jakob leaned against the counter, raking a hand through his hair as he did. "When people are home, this suspect is asking for directions and a drink of water. It is then that he—"

Martha's quick, yet audible intake of air brought Jakob's feet square with the floor and Claire around the counter.

"Martha? Is something wrong?"

"There was a man. He was just stepping onto the porch when I came from the barn. He asked if I knew where he could buy some fresh vegetables."

Something resembling restrained rage rolled across Jakob's face. "When?"

"Yesterday."

"He didn't touch you, did he?" Jakob barked.

"No."

"Did you let him in the house?"

"No. I pointed the way to the Lehmans' farm stand."

"And he left?"

Martha shook her head. "He asked for a glass of cold water. Hannah went inside and brought out a glass."

The relief that coursed through Claire's body at Martha's answer didn't cross over to Jakob. Instead, he widened his stance and fired off another question. "Then what?"

"He took many sips and asked many questions."

"About . . ."

Martha lowered the crate to her side and glanced down at the toes of her boots sticking out from beneath her dress. "He asked about the crops. He asked what we grew and when it would be harvested."

Jakob relaxed his pose somewhat but kept the questions flowing. "Did he say why he wanted to know?"

"He still does not know."

Claire glanced at Jakob and recognized the confusion he wore. "Doesn't know what, Martha?"

"What we grow and when it will be harvested."

"You didn't answer him?" Jakob asked.

"I answered. He did not listen." Martha reached her free hand onto the counter and straightened the stack of place mats she'd made. "He would point to the fields and ask his questions, but he would look at the barn."

"The barn?" Claire and Jakob said in unison.

"Yah. I wanted to invite him to see the horses, but he left before I could."

Jakob rested his hand atop his sister's and guided her focus back to his. "Why did he leave?"

"I am afraid he found me to be rude."

"Rude?" Claire echoed.

"Yah. I heard a funny noise and did not answer his question."

Jakob pulled his hand back to his side and leaned forward. "What kind of a noise?"

"I thought it was David with the dog. He claps when she does a new trick. But it was not David. He was not in the barn. He was in the field with his dat." Martha pulled the crate back against her chest and readied herself to leave. "I will bring more items by week's end, Claire."

LAURA BRADFORD

"Wait!" Jakob grabbed hold of his sister's upper arm, then pulled it away as she stepped back. "I'm sorry. I just need to know what happened after you thought you heard David."

"I turned to ask the man if he would like to see the horses, but he was walking down the driveway toward the road."

"He didn't have a car?" Jakob asked.

"No."

"Do you have any idea where he was going?"

"To buy vegetables."

It was hard not to crack a smile at the innocence of the Amish, who believed people did as they said. Yet, as quickly as the urge to smile came over Claire, it was gone, pushed to the side by reality.

Was it possible the man who'd been at Martha's farm had truly been looking for fresh vegetables? Maybe. But the likelihood of that being the case was slim. Very, very slim.

"Do you remember what he looked like?" Jakob asked as he secured a piece of paper and pen from beside Claire's register.

"Yah."

"What color hair did he have?"

"Brown."

"Eyes?"

"Brown."

"Any facial hair?"

"No."

"Any marks on his skin that you remember? Birth marks, moles, scars, tattoos, anything?"

"No."

Claire could sense Jakob's frustration building and

182

wished she could wipe it away. She hated seeing him stressed, hated knowing he was worried. The fact that his sister had been in such close proximity to a possible murder suspect only made things worse.

"How about his height?" Claire asked. "Or his build? Was he tall, short, medium? Skinny, heavy?"

Martha scrunched her nose in thought, releasing it along with the simplest of descriptions. "He was not tall like you"—she pointed at first to Jakob, and then Claire—"but he was bigger than you. He was not heavy, he was not thin."

Once again, they were left with a vision that could be half the Englishers in Heavenly, Pennsylvania, at that moment.

Jakob glanced down at Martha's description in his notebook and then laid it down on the counter, the smile he flashed at his sister showing signs of fatigue. "Thank you, Martha. For letting me know about this and for answering my questions."

Martha nodded once at Jakob, a second time at Claire, and then headed toward the door. When she reached it, she turned back to her brother. "We will be careful."

And then she was gone, the bells jingling softly in her wake.

"He was at my sister's house, Claire." Jakob's fist came down on the top of the counter with a thud. *"My sister's* house."

Closing the gap between them, she snaked her arm around his back and rested her cheek against his side. "You'll figure this out, Jakob. Soon."

Chapter 22

Claire climbed onto the step stool, moved Martha's birdhouse an inch to the right, and then climbed back down to gauge the change.

"Mamm was not sure if you would want a birdhouse in the shop, but I knew you would."

Whirling around, Claire fluttered her hand to her chest in surprise. "Esther! I . . . I didn't hear you come in."

"I'm sorry. I should have come in the front door like the customers." All color drained from the twenty-year-old's face as she stepped backward and hooked her thumb over her left shoulder. "I can do that now if you would like."

"Don't you dare." Claire crossed to her friend, took a moment to study her from head to toe, and then pulled her in for a quick hug. "This is exactly what I needed today."

"This?"

"A visit from you, silly."

"Is everything okay?" Esther surveyed the shop's main room and then narrowed her eyes on Claire.

"Of course. Why do you ask?"

Esther reached across the gap between them and gently touched Claire's forehead. "You were scrunching when I came in. You only scrunch when you are worried."

She opened her mouth to protest, but, in the end, she merely shrugged.

"Have there been customers today?" Esther asked.

"Yes. Quite a few, actually. Two of them bought your dolls."

If the continued popularity of her soft Amish dolls pleased her, Esther didn't let it show. Instead, the young woman simply narrowed her eyes more. "Are you not feeling well?"

"No, I'm fine."

"Is it your aunt?"

"No. Diane is fine."

Esther glanced back over her shoulder and then forward toward the shop's front window and Lighted Way. "Is my uncle okay?"

Realizing the questions would not stop without an explanation, Claire led the way to the counter and the pair of stools just beyond it. "Jakob is fine, Esther, I promise. In fact, if you'd been here with your mother about thirty minutes ago, you'd have been able to see that with your own two eyes."

Esther stopped mid-sit and stared back at Claire. "Did they speak?"

"A little." Granted, it wasn't the kind of warm and fuzzy conversation she'd like to see between the siblings, but considering the constraints put on them by the Ordnung and its unwritten rules governing the Amish, it was something. And something was better than nothing.

"I am glad."

Claire started to fill her friend in on the details of the conversation between Jakob and Esther's mother, but she changed her mind at the last minute. Esther was a sensitive soul, seven months pregnant or not. Her condition just amped up that fact. The last thing the young woman needed was to get worked up over something that had happened twenty-four hours earlier . . .

"Claire?"

Shaking her head, she mustered the closest thing to a smile she could. "Yes?"

"Your head is scrunching again."

She cast about for something to say to distract the mother-to-be from the scent of worry and, instead, flicked her hand toward the display of dolls on the other side of the store. "I'm getting low on the girl dolls. Is there any chance you might have some more by the end of the week?"

"Yah."

"Phew . . . That's a huge relief." She peeked back at Esther to see if her friend was buying her diversionary tactics. The look on Esther's face said no.

Hightailing it around the counter, Claire made a show of rummaging around on the same shelf where Esther had once housed her lunch pail during the workday. "You know something? My stomach has been acting up all day and now I finally know why . . . I haven't eaten since I got here at noon."

"Then you should be looking in your office. That is where you keep *your* lunch."

She snapped her fingers in the air. "Oh. That's right. Give me a second and I'll go grab that right now. Unless . . ." Claire took in the clock on the back wall and groaned. "Actually, I'll be closing in about thirty minutes and heading back to the inn, so maybe I should just wait. I've handled the unsettled stomach this long, I might as well just keep going, right? But don't worry, I'll try to make sure I don't do any scrunching if any customers come in between now and then."

"I do not think you are scrunching because—"

Claire placed a gentle hand on Esther's perfectly rounded stomach and grinned at the instant kick she received in response. "So how is our little kicker today?"

Immediately, Esther's gaze dropped to her stomach. "The baby is busy today. Mamm says that is good."

"Are you still feeling good?" Claire asked, pulling her hand back to her side.

"Yah. Eli insisted I sit down shortly after the noon meal and I fell asleep sitting in the chair! I have never done that before."

"Then you must have needed it, Esther. You *and* the baby."

"That is what Eli said when I woke up and went out to the barn to apologize."

"Apologize? For what?"

"For napping when there is work to be done."

Claire ventured back to the vacant stool beside Esther and leaned against the cushioned top. "When you are less than eight weeks from having a baby, napping *is* your work, Esther."

"That is what Eli says."

LAURA BRADFORD

"Your husband is a very smart man. You should listen to him."

The same smile she'd seen on Esther's face every time Eli used to show up in the alleyway between Heavenly Treasures and Shoo Fly Bake Shoppe tugged at her friend's mouth, and it warmed Claire from the outside in. Seven months into their marriage, it was obvious Esther was still very much smitten with her husband.

"That is what Eli says, too." Esther laughed and then turned her head to look out the side window to its view of the empty alleyway. "Has he been here today?"

"Who? Eli? Not that I know of. Then again, Annie was here alone this morning."

"No. I mean, was Samuel here? To see Ruth?"

She followed Esther's gaze out the window while simultaneously working to process her friend's words. "Samuel? Samuel Yoder?"

"Yah."

"I don't think so. Why?"

"Eli thinks they will marry this winter." Esther lifted her own hand to her stomach and cradled it lovingly. "Perhaps, next fall, when our baby is one, there will be a cousin."

Claire yanked her focus back to Esther. "Wait a minute. How long have they been courting and why have I not known this?"

"Because your eyes see only my uncle," Esther replied, grinning.

"No, but I—"

"Eli says Samuel stops by the bake shop every day for lunch."

"I know that. I've seen him myself, but—" Her sentence

died on her tongue as she traveled back to nearly every sighting she'd had of Samuel over the past six months.

The anticipation on the Amish man's face as he crossed in front of Claire's shop . . .

The contented smile he wore as he headed back toward his furniture shop some thirty minutes later . . .

"I thought he just really liked Ruth's food . . ." Bringing her palms to her cheeks, Claire shook her head at the startlingly clear reality that had somehow managed to escape her for months. How could she have been so blind?

"It is as I said. Your eyes are busy on Jakob."

Feeling her hands start to warm along with her cheeks, Claire pushed off her stool and wandered over to the window, her initial surprise over Ruth and Samuel's courting status bowing to pleasure. "I'm thrilled for her. Ruth is one of the sweetest people I've ever met, and she deserves to be happy."

"Yah."

"How is Eli taking this? I mean, he's always been so protective of his twin."

"Eli is pleased. He believes Samuel is a good man. That he will be a good husband to Ruth and a good father to the children they will have."

She watched a trio of tourists cross the mouth of the alley from the direction of Ruth's bake shop, the smiles on their faces, and the red-and-white-checked bags in their hands, shifting her thoughts from romance to business. "And the bake shop? What will happen to the bake shop when Ruth marries?"

"Ruth will still make her pies and her cakes. But it will be her younger sister who will run the shop."

Resting her forehead against the glass windowpane, Claire tried to imagine Lighted Way without Ruth's beautiful smile. She tried to imagine taking out the trash and seeing someone else's aproned form waving at her from the bake shop's back door.

"You are scrunching again, Claire."

"How do you know that? My head is against the glass."

"You do not just scrunch with your head. You scrunch with your whole body."

She wanted to argue, wanted to show that she was, indeed, happy, but she couldn't. Not at that moment, anyway. "I guess I'm just going to miss Ruth when she's gone. I keep getting attached to you Amish gals and then you up and get married on me and leave me all alone."

"I am still here. *See?*"

Parting company with the windowpane, Claire turned to find Esther pointing at herself. The silly sight made her laugh. "I see, Esther . . . I see."

"I am not far from here. You must visit more often. I will bake cookies and you can see Carly."

"Wait! You don't even know what the baby will be! How can you name it already?"

Esther slipped off her stool, giggling as she did. "Carly is the new horse, Claire! Not the baby!"

She matched Esther's laugh with one of her own and made her way back to the counter. "Oops. I knew that."

"Eli is taking good care of Carly and she is healing more and more each day. But she is a little bit of a sneak."

"A sneak?" Claire echoed.

"Yah. A food sneak."

Again she laughed, only this time it had everything to

do with Esther and the naked amusement she saw on her friend's makeup-free face. "A *food* sneak . . ."

"Yah. Cookies, cake, candy—she likes it all. But it is my sister Hannah's candy that she will push and push until she finds."

"I really do need to come out and see this horse sometime soon, don't I?"

"Yah. This evening would be nice."

She took in the clock and then glanced toward the front door. "Don't you still have to get home and cook dinner for Eli?"

"Yah. I can set another plate."

"Esther, I can't. Not for dinner, anyway. I promised Diane I'd be home to help get dinner on the table for the guests."

A flash of disappointment weighed on Esther's smile for just a moment, only to get pushed aside by the same determination she'd exhibited while working in the store alongside Claire. "Then come for dessert. I will make cookies. And cake."

"Cookies *and* cake?" she joked.

"Yah."

"You drive a hard bargain."

"I want you to come. To spend time with Eli and me. To see Carly. I have missed you, Claire."

She swallowed around the lump she felt forming in her throat and reached for her friend's hand. "I miss you, too, Esther. Every day."

"Then come. For dessert. Please."

"I will."

"When?" Esther asked.

"Would seven thirty be okay?"

Esther's smile rivaled that of any Christmas tree Claire had ever seen. "Yah."

"Then I'll be there."

Dropping her gaze to the floor, Esther's voice turned whisperlike. "Please bring Jakob."

Claire felt her mouth gape, and then shut, and then gape again. *"Bring Jakob?"*

"Yah."

"But you can't eat at a table with him . . ." she reminded her friend.

Esther peeked at the small mirror Claire had propped next to the register specifically for Esther's courting days with Eli and smoothed her hands over the top and sides of her kapp. When she was done, the young woman headed toward the doorway from which she'd come, stopping midway across the room. "We do not need a table for dessert."

Chapter 23

She was sitting on her aunt's front porch, looking out over the fields in the distance, when Jakob pulled up, the sound of his car, followed by the sight of him behind the wheel, igniting a nervous excitement in the pit of her stomach. Toeing the ground, she brought the swing to a stop and stood.

"Hey there, handsome." Claire crossed the porch to the steps and ventured down to the walkway. "Don't turn off the engine just yet, okay?"

Jakob poked his head through the open window. "Is something wrong?"

"No. No. Nothing like that." She came around the back of the car and then leaned in to look at him through the open passenger-side window. "I just thought maybe we could sit in here and talk for a few minutes. See if there's something we could, um, maybe go and do instead of just hanging around here."

Shrugging, he motioned her inside and then waited as she settled herself in her seat before leaning across the center console and kissing her gently on the lips. "Okay, yeah, that's what I needed."

She started to laugh but stopped as she noticed the tense set of his shoulders, the uncharacteristic frown lines around his mouth, and the lack of any discernable sparkle in his amber-flecked eyes. "Wait a minute. Are you okay? You look super stressed right now."

He pulled his hand from the back of her neck and leaned against the driver-side door. "So what you're telling me is that my plan to keep my foul mood back at the office is already showing signs of failing?" Resting his left forearm across the top of the steering wheel, he shook his head. "I'm sorry, Claire. I probably should have told you I couldn't come over when you called, but I had hoped being here, with you, could get my mind off things for a little while. Yet now that I'm here, I have a feeling I'm just going to end up ruining your evening if I stay."

"You could never ruin my evening, Jakob."

"Don't be so sure." He let his gaze drift to the left and to the tree and the scenery beyond before coming back to Claire. "Look, maybe a rain check would be wise."

She leaned forward, tugged his arm off the steering wheel, and entwined their fingers. "What's going on?"

For a moment, she wasn't sure he was going to answer, as his focus drifted through the windshield once again. But, eventually, he spoke, his words, his voice laced with agitation. "I know it happened yesterday. And I know she's fine—I saw that with my own two eyes. But I just can't shake the notion that the man who murdered Wayne Stutzman was talking to my sister yesterday afternoon. It—it's making me nuts just *thinking* about it."

"Hey . . . she's okay."

"The regular guy side of me knows this. But the other side of me—the one that's paid to know there isn't always a rhyme or reason to crime—keeps thinking about all the things that could have happened."

With the index finger of her free hand, she guided his chin until she was the center of his focus once again. "But they didn't, Jakob. *They didn't.*"

He tried to smile but he fell short. Instead, he glanced down at her hand in his. "Okay, so distract me. How was your day? I didn't get to ask you about it when I stopped by the shop this afternoon."

"It was good."

"Tell me about it."

Disengaging her hand from his, she reached across her right shoulder and secured the seat belt into place next to her left hip. "I'll tell you as we drive."

He looked from Claire to the seat belt and back again. "Oh? Where are we going?"

"To see Esther."

"Esther?"

"That's right."

Slowly, he set his hand on the gearshift and moved it into reverse, the tension he'd been hard pressed to shake off suddenly cloaked in disappointment. "Is there something you need to pick up there? Or are you wanting me to just drop you off?"

"Jakob Fisher," she admonished, "do you really think I'd invite you over this evening just so you could chauffeur me across town?"

He reversed the car, shifted into drive, and drove down the driveway toward the main road. "No, but—"

"There are no buts. I wouldn't do that." At the end of the lane, she pointed to the left as if he didn't know where he was going.

If he noticed, though, he didn't let on. "So does Esther have some new inventory for the shop or something?"

"Nope."

"Are you dropping off payment for things you've sold over the past week?"

"Nope." She braced herself for the transition from blacktop to cobblestone that was no more than a car-length away now, but it was unnecessary. Jakob's speed adjustment as they approached the entrance to Lighted Way made it so the transition was nearly flawless.

"Are we picking up something Eli has made?"

"We've been invited for dessert. And to see the new horse."

Jakob pulled the car to the right and slowed to a stop outside Heavenly Treasures. "Claire, what are you doing?"

"I'm not doing anything. This was Esther's idea."

"Claire, I get that you're trying to help, that you're trying to find opportunities for me to spend time with my niece and her husband, but—"

"It wasn't my idea, Jakob. It was Esther's."

He stared at her. "Esther's?"

"That's right."

Inhaling deeply, he raked his hand through his hair. "They can't sit at the table with me, Claire. You know this.

And while I might be able to handle sitting at a different table with everyone's back to me on a different day, I'm just not up for that right now. I'm sorry."

"We won't be sitting at the table."

"What are you talking about?"

"Esther said we wouldn't sit at the table. And when she mentioned me coming for dessert, she specifically requested that I bring you."

Jakob looked out the window, across the sidewalk, up at Claire's shop, and then finally back at Claire. "And Eli? He's okay with this, too?"

"You know Eli respects you."

"Claire, he has to follow the Ordnung."

"I won't tell if you won't tell . . ."

"It doesn't work like that, Claire."

She leaned forward until her nose was almost touching his and smiled. "Look, all I know is that we—as in the two of us—were invited to come for dessert. Can we just play this by ear and see what happens?"

For several long moments he said nothing, his thoughts as much a mystery to her as the way the evening would play out in the end, but eventually he spoke, his words accompanying them back into the flow of traffic and onto the gravel road on the far side of Lighted Way. "It would be nice to see the two of them. Besides, it'll give me a chance to pull Eli aside and let him know about the incident at Martha's yesterday."

She peeked at Jakob, rocking gently in the chair beside her, and allowed herself a moment to soak up the pure joy she saw on his face—a joy that had nothing to do with the pair of cookies on his lap and everything to do with the young couple sitting side by side on the other end of the porch. To an outsider looking in, she suspected his smile might be attributed to the warm summer night and the presence of loved ones. And, in some ways, they'd be right. But to truly appreciate the lightness he exuded and the smile that reached far beyond his mouth to his very being, one had to understand the magnitude behind the seemingly simple scene.

While normal in just about every home in America, the notion of visiting with family had been relegated to pipe-dream status the moment Jakob walked away from his Amish roots to become a police officer. In the blink of an eye, he lost his parents, his siblings, his friends, and his community. It was a fate he'd known and accepted eighteen years earlier, and a fate he'd lived every day since.

Yet, by the grace of God and the assistance of Esther's pure heart, Jakob was being given a moment of normalcy Claire knew he'd remember for the rest of his life . . .

"There are more cookies to be eaten," Esther said, rising to her feet. "Should I get them?"

Claire answered for Jakob by pointing to the cookies still in his hand. "Jakob is good, and I've had my fill, but thank you, Esther. They were delicious."

"They were." Jakob pitched his rocking chair forward to afford an uninhibited view of his pregnant niece. "If I'm not mistaken, I believe they were made from my mother's recipe?"

Esther's gaze dropped to the porch floor and then fluttered upward until it was trained on her husband's attentive face. "Yah."

If it bothered Jakob that Esther was avoiding eye contact, he didn't let it show. "They are just like Mamm's. I've missed them."

Unsure of what to say, Esther began to gather their plates and cups in her hands, only to set them back down at Eli's whispered direction. When she did as he asked, Eli turned back to Jakob and Claire. "Would you like to meet Carly?"

"Who's Carly?" Jakob asked.

"The new horse." Eli rose to his feet and motioned to Claire for them to follow. Step by step they made their way down the porch stairs, across the gravel driveway, and into the same barn that had once housed Harley Zook's prized cows.

"Whatever happened to Harley's cows?" she asked as she and Jakob shadowed Eli and Esther into the barn.

"I kept some. Stutzman and Lapp took the others."

Esther's finger guided their eyes to three cows lazily watching them from just outside the back door. "We still have Mary, Molly, and Maggie."

Jakob veered off from their path long enough to single out the cow in the center. "Well hello there, Mary, it's nice to see you again. Are you behaving yourself and sticking close to home these days or are you still gallivanting around town like you were back in the fall?"

"How on earth do you know which one is Mary? They all look exactly alike."

"They look nothing alike," Jakob protested, shaking his head at Claire in mock disdain. "Mary's swirls—for lack of a better word—are black trimmed in brown. Molly's are brown trimmed in black. And Maggie"—he stopped, craned his head over and around Mary—"she's got a little black mark halfway down the front of her chest that almost looks like a cat's paw print."

She sidestepped a water trough to look more closely at the cows and the minute differences between them as outlined by Jakob. Sure enough, Mary's black spots were outlined by brown, Molly's brown spots were outlined by black, and the spot on Maggie's chest did, indeed, resemble a paw print. "Wow. I could have looked at nothing else for hours and still not have noticed those details."

"That's because you didn't grow up on a farm." Jakob took Claire's hand and led her back to the center aisle and the Amish couple smiling at her in amusement. "Sometimes it's something as small as Maggie's faint paw print that can tell one farmer's animal from another's."

"Carly has such a spot on her chest, too. It is much harder to see on her, but it is there." Eli led the way toward the opposite end of the barn and the wide-eyed gray horse looking at them from across a waist-high wall. "She is heeling faster than I had hoped."

"What happened to her?" Jakob asked.

"Weaver did not know. Gingerich and Stutzman thought it was a mistake for me to buy an injured horse."

Jakob nodded along with Eli's words. "Why *did* you buy her?"

"Esther and the baby need a good, solid horse to pull the buggy. Carly will be that solid horse when she is well."

Looping her hand inside Claire's upper arm, Esther quickened their collective pace until they were standing directly in front of the half wall and Carly. "Hello, sweet girl. We have brought new friends for you to meet. I would tell you to be nice, but that is all you know."

Claire instinctively stepped back as the horse thrust her neck across the half wall and nuzzled her nose against Esther's forehead. Reaching around the base of the animal's neck, Esther's hands slid into the horse's coal black mane.

"Wow. They're really taken with each other, aren't they?" Claire whispered to Eli.

"Yah. I have been around horses my whole life and I have never seen such a thing."

"It's like I wasn't even standing there." Claire looked from the gray horse to Esther and back again. "All she saw was Esther."

"It is that way every time Esther is near."

"How long have you had her?" Jakob asked.

"It is ten days since I purchased her from Weaver." Eli guided their attention over the wall and toward the bandage wrapped around the mare's front left leg.

Jakob looked back at Eli. "May I?"

Eli's answer came via a slow nod.

Reaching around the wall, Jakob flipped open the latch and stepped into the recently cleaned stall. For just a moment, the horse turned to eye Jakob as he dropped into a squat beside her bandaged leg, but once she determined he meant no harm, she was back to nuzzling Esther. "My father's horse sprained his ankle once. Happened on the way home from church one day when I was about twelve, maybe thirteen. Dat was sure the aging horse would not recover. Martha was determined she would be well again and convinced me to help her make it so."

Intrigued, Claire propped her elbows atop the wall and leaned forward. "Did you?"

"Every day we unwrapped her bandage, iced her ankle, and bandaged her up again. Day after day we did this, for weeks, until, one day, while Martha was reading to her, she walked across her stall with complete ease. Martha was convinced it was her reading that made the horse well."

"Ten days ago, when I paid Weaver, I was certain I could help. The ice and the bandage have helped, yah, but that is not all that has helped. Esther's gentle ways have helped, too."

"Like mother, like daughter." Jakob ran his hand down the horse's bandaged leg and then stood. "She's a beauty, Eli. Real sturdy-looking."

"I love her fancy tail," Esther said, parting company with Carly's neck long enough to guide Claire and Jakob's attention to the back end of the horse. "I have never seen such a tail on a horse."

Sure enough, the straight, course hair Claire had always associated with a horse's tail was instead silky and sported a tightly wound curl that bordered on ringlet status. "Is—is that natural?"

Jakob's laugh filled the stall. "They're not using a curling iron on it if that's what you're asking."

She scrunched her face up at Jakob but abandoned it at the sound of Esther giggling. "You ate all of Hannah's special root beer candies this afternoon, sweet girl. That is why I tell you to slow down—to enjoy one candy before you start looking in Hannah's hands for more." Carly lowered her nose to Esther's hand and then reared back and shook her silky black mane. "I know, sweet girl. They are helping to make you well. I will get you more tomorrow."

"Hannah's candies are not making Carly well, Esther," Eli groused around the smile he was unsuccessful at hiding from Claire and Jakob. "The bandage, the ice, the rest, *and you* are making Carly well. The candies your sister brings will make her too big and lazy to pull you and the baby in the buggy."

Carly dipped her face back down to Esther's petting level and was quickly rewarded for her efforts by the unmistakable object of her affection. "Candies and cookies do not make *Claire* big and lazy!" Esther protested.

Jakob's laugh was so fast and so loud Carly reared her head back again. "Whoa there, Carly. I'm not laughing at you. I'm—I'm"—his face reddened in conjunction with a peek at Claire—"just, um, laughing, that's all . . ."

"At me." This time when Claire scrunched her face at Jakob, she stuck out her tongue, too. "Cookies and sweets do not guarantee laziness, *Detective Fisher*. They do, however, guarantee happiness."

Reaching into his pocket, Jakob extracted his trusty notepad and pen and made a show of readying both for recording purposes. "Candies and cookies guarantee happiness, you say?"

"Happiness and, if you're really lucky, maybe *forgiveness*, too."

Chapter 24

"Now, tell me I'm forgiven."

Claire slid her gaze from the mug of hot chocolate to the frosted chocolate brownie and finally onto the man seated on the opposite side of the two-person table. "Please tell me you know I was kidding about that . . ."

Clutching his hands to his chest, Jakob drew back in his chair. "You were *kidding*?"

"Of course I was kidding," she half whispered/half shrieked. "*You* were playing, *I* was playing—"

Dropping his hands to the table, he grabbed one of the two forks he'd set beside the plate and dug into the brownie, his dimples on full display. "Of course I know that. But you've got to admit, it gave me a ready-made excuse to bring you here instead of taking you straight back to the inn, now didn't it?"

She watched the piece of chocolate disappear into his

mouth and then shook her head in amusement. "You're too much, Detective."

"As long as I'm enough, we're good." He took a second forkful of the treat and held it out for her to try. "Ooohh, you're going to love this . . ."

Leaning forward, she opened her mouth and let him place the tip of the fork inside. Slowly, she closed her lips over the brownie, and backed away from the fork. "Oh. Wow. That *is* good."

"I told you." He studied her for a minute then swapped the fork for his coffee and took a sip. "Tonight was really fun. Thank you."

"Could they get in trouble for how they were with you tonight?" The second the question was out, she regretted asking it. They'd had a good night; why take a chance on ruining it? Waving her words away, she leaned forward and smiled. "Actually, you know what? Scratch that question, okay? It doesn't matter."

"No. It's a fair question." He took another, slightly longer, sip of his coffee and then set the cup back down on the table. "If Bishop Hershberger had pulled up when we were sitting on the porch, probably not. We were sitting in chairs facing out toward the driveway and you were seated between us. Had he walked into the barn when Eli and I were joking around, yes."

"Would they have been shunned at the next church service?"

His grip tightened ever so slightly around the handle of his mug, but it didn't last. "If Eli refused to acknowledge his mistake, yes. But I wouldn't have let it come to that."

Staring down into her own cup, she followed the swirls

of melting whipped cream with her eyes and tried not to let his reality sour her mood. But it was hard.

"Hey . . ." Jakob hooked his finger beneath her chin and gently lifted it until their attention was on nothing but each other. "No frowning, okay? It was a really nice evening."

"It was. I just"—she stopped, swallowed, and tried again—"love everything about the Amish except *that*. It's wrong."

"What *I* did was wrong, Claire."

"You didn't leave so you could gamble," she protested. "You didn't leave so you could bilk people of their money. You didn't leave so you could mock their beliefs and benefit from doing so. You left to protect and serve the community— *their* community."

"It's not like their reaction was a surprise, though. I knew, before I ever committed to baptism, that I was making a life choice. I'm the one who broke that, not them."

For what had to be the umpteenth time since she'd met Jakob, she couldn't help but marvel at his selflessness. It was, without a doubt, one of his most attractive qualities. "You really are something special. You know that, don't you?"

"If you think so, I'm honored. But really, the inability to have a relationship with my family if I left after baptism is something I knew before I walked away. I still walked." He extricated her hand from the side of her mug and entwined their fingers atop the table. "Do I miss being able to horse around with my sister at the lake? Sure. Do I miss teaching Isaac how to build a chicken coop or how to run the tractor? Sure. Do I miss being able to sit at the kitchen table with Martha and Isaac and my parents? Sure. But even if I'd stayed, those things wouldn't be happening. I'd be married just like Martha, and we'd be . . . adults."

"You'd still be able to sit at a table with them."

"I would. But then I wouldn't be sitting at one with you." He lifted her hand off the table and brought it to his lips. "Not like this, anyway."

"You wouldn't have known any different," she reminded him in a voice suddenly choked with emotion.

"God had a plan, Claire. I truly believe that."

She opened her mouth to say something, but closed it when she realized she was too moved to utter a word. Instead, she simply answered with her trembling smile.

"A year ago, when I came back here, I was prepared to watch my sister and my brother from afar. But now . . . largely because of you . . . I've had some special moments with both of them that carry me through the hard days. Because of you, I got to be present and watch my niece marry a really great guy. Because of you, I got to meet their new horse and enjoy a little lightness with my nephew-in-law. Because of you, I've finally come to grips with my misguided anger toward someone who was my best friend growing up."

"Shhhh . . . That's enough. You're making me sound way more important than I am." She held her index finger to his lips for a brief moment and then returned her hand to her mug, the warmth of the ceramic oddly comforting despite the July night. "Speaking of Benjamin, how is he? Is he still helping Emma Stutzman?"

He took another bite of brownie and then slid the rest of the dessert closer to Claire. "I don't know. I wasn't out there today. I'm really hoping the next time I stop out to see her, I'll be able to tell her I've arrested the man who murdered her husband."

"And you *will* be able to tell her that, Jakob. Soon. I'm sure of it."

He smiled at her across the top of his coffee cup. "You really do have a way of making me feel like Superman."

She popped another forkful of brownie into her mouth and shrugged. "If the shoe fits . . ."

A flash of light from just over Claire's shoulder bathed Jakob in a momentary glow, and he sat up tall, propping his arms on his hips. "Don't you mean the cape?" he teased.

Laughing, she peeked over her shoulder in an attempt to explain the fleeting source of light and found Daniel Lapp, a local Amish toy maker, staring at their table with a mixture of uncertainty and restrained agitation.

Jakob's chair scraped the empty one behind his as he stood. "Daniel? Is everything alright?"

Without lifting his eyes to Jakob, Daniel began to speak, his words, his tone flat. "I know I am not to be here, but I cannot forget what Miller has said."

"You mean, Benjamin?" Jakob asked.

"Yah. Benjamin." Daniel fidgeted with the ends of his beard and then slowly let his hand drift down his left suspender to the waist of his simple black pants. "He believes Wayne's death was not an accident."

"It wasn't."

"He says the man who killed him has been at many of our farms. That he has taken money at some."

Jakob crushed his napkin and then dropped it onto the table beside his nearly empty cup. "I can't say with absolute certainty that the two are related, but I haven't ruled it out, either."

"If it is not the same, I should not be here."

"Did something happen?" Claire stood, pulled an empty chair over to their table, and then motioned the hatted man to come closer.

Daniel's dark eyes left the center of the table and moved to Claire's face. "I was just getting into bed when I heard sounds."

Jakob stiffened. "What kind of sounds?"

"At first, I thought it was the wind rattling against the front door. But then I remembered there was no wind today." Daniel took two steps forward only to take one step back, the uncertainty he'd exhibited upon entering the coffee shop ratcheting up a few notches. "So I listened. The sounds changed, but there were still sounds."

Jakob, who seemed to have absorbed all of Daniel's agitation, clenched his teeth in time with his hands. "Go on . . ."

"At first, I did not know what it was. But then I knew it was footsteps."

"On the front porch?"

Daniel's focus flitted across the top of Claire's head and rested somewhere in the vicinity of Jakob. "No. Downstairs. In the front room. At first, I thought one of the boys did not stay in bed. But the footsteps, they were too heavy for young boys to make—especially young boys who do not wear shoes to bed."

"Did you go downstairs?" Jakob asked.

"I looked into the children's rooms first. All were sleeping."

Claire tried again to motion Daniel to sit, but the Amish man didn't budge. "Were you still hearing the footsteps downstairs?"

"I heard a quick clap of thunder in the distance and then more footsteps. But when I went downstairs there was no one."

"Was the door open?" Claire and Jakob asked in unison.

"No."

"Could it have been a neighbor?" Jakob stepped around the table and stopped next to the empty chair Claire had tugged over for Daniel. "Maybe Stoltzfus stopped by and then realized you were sleeping?"

Daniel's head began shaking before Jakob had even finished his question. "Stoltzfus would not take money without asking."

Claire gasped, but the sound was quickly drowned out by Jakob's fist hitting the top of the table. "Money is missing from your home?"

"Yah."

"Are you sure?"

This time, Daniel's assent was accompanied by an emphatic nod. "Five hundred dollars."

Jakob covered his mouth with his palm, only to let it slip down his face as he started firing off a parade of questions designed to get as much information as possible. "Did you see anyone? Did they leave anything behind—a footprint, a scrap of paper, anything? Did you see a car drive away? Headlights in the distance? Anything?"

"I did not."

"Did you look in the barn?"

Daniel's hand returned to his beard. "The barn?"

"Yes."

"I did not. I did not think to look in the barn. The foot-steps that I heard were in my house, not in my barn. I tried to go to sleep, to forget what I had heard, but Miller's words did not allow me to sleep."

"So you came straight here?"

"Yah. In case Miller is right. In case the man who took our money is the same man who brought harm to Stutzman. That is why I came. That is why I stopped here when I saw you through the window. I hope I did not make a mistake coming here."

"You did exactly what you should have done, Daniel. Thank you for that." Jakob grabbed their cups and plate and carried them over to the counter and the yawning twenty-something barista clearly counting the minutes until she could close up shop for the night. When he returned, he held his hand out to Claire and helped her to her feet. "I'm sorry, Claire, but I'm going to have to get you back to your aunt's now. I've got to rally a few of my officers and head out to Daniel's. See if we can find some-thing that will finally help us nab this guy."

She stepped into his arms to accept his hug and then grabbed her purse from its resting spot on the floor beside her chair. "Please, no apologies. And as for driving me to Diane's, it's not necessary. It's a nice night. I've made this same walk hundreds of times and I can make it again now. Go with Daniel and we can talk in the morning."

"You're not walking home by yourself at ten o'clock at night, Claire. It'll take me less than five minutes to get you to the inn and me back to the station." Reaching around Daniel, Jakob yanked open the front door of Heavenly Brews and waited for first Daniel, and then Claire to walk through. "Daniel, head back to your farm. If all goes well, I'll probably get there at about the same time you do. But if you beat me, don't touch anything, okay?"

Chapter 25

She was less than two steps from her room when she heard the telltale squeak of Diane's door across the hall.

"Claire?"

Glancing back over her shoulder, she couldn't help but smile at the sight of her aunt with a book in one hand and a mug of something in the other. "Why on earth are you still awake?" she whispered. "It's a good thirty minutes past your bedtime."

"You were still out, dear."

She released her hold on the doorknob and crossed the wood-planked hallway. "You don't have to wait up for me, Diane. I'm a big girl, and I promise I'd call if there was a problem."

"I know it's silly of me to worry, but I do." Diane waved Claire into her room and then kissed her on the forehead.

"This is probably why I never got married and had children. I would have worried myself into an early grave."

"Then I'm glad you didn't have kids, too, because I need you around for a long time to come."

Diane climbed into bed and then patted the empty spot by her feet for Claire. "Sit. Sit. Tell me about your evening. Did Jakob go with you to Esther and Eli's? Wait. You don't have to answer that. The way your eyes lit up just now is enough of a yes all on its own."

"Oh, Diane, I wish you could have been there to see him . . . and her . . . and even Eli. They were all so happy. The way it's *supposed* to be between family."

"They talked directly to Jakob?"

"It was more like everyone talked in a way that included everyone else. If Eli said something funny, or Jakob said something funny, it was kind of just out there for anyone to laugh about or respond to. And when they took us into the barn to meet Carly, it was just all so natural." She flopped onto her stomach next to her aunt and pillowed her cheek atop her hand. "It's actually kind of hard to explain, but somehow it just worked. And it was wonderful."

"They have common ground that connects them now because of you."

"They're family, Diane. They always have been."

"Yes, but that changed when Jakob left."

She felt her smile begin to slip away, and she forced it back into place. "Let's not talk about that right now."

"Why? Their common ground is you, dear. Esther loves you. Eli loves you. And Jakob loves you. Because of that, and because of you, there will be opportunities for that kind of general interaction again, provided it's done correctly."

She nodded her cheek against her hand at her aunt's overall sentiment, but it was one sentence in particular that had her peering up at her aunt, wide-eyed. "Do you really think that's true?"

"About you being a common ground for Jakob and Esther?"

"No. The part about Jakob loving me."

"I don't say things I think are untrue, dear." Diane smoothed a lock of Claire's auburn-colored hair to the side and then continued to gently stroke her head in much the same way she had when Claire was little. "Your hair is well past your shoulders now. It's really quite lovely."

Tilting her chin upward, she looked up at her aunt. "How do you do that?"

"Do what, dear?"

"Make me feel so . . . I don't know . . . *right*."

Diane paused her hand on the side of Claire's face. "I make you feel right?"

"Yes. Like I'm pretty and smart and someone worth"—she stopped, inhaled sharply, and added—"loving."

"Because you are. Anyone with even half a brain knows that."

"Peter didn't."

"Anyone who puts more into their career and their possessions than their spouse has no brain at all."

Soft yet rhythmic squeaking from the other side of Diane's closed door brought Claire back to a seated position. "Sounds like someone else is still awake."

Diane held her index finger upright and listened to the distinctively male-sounding footsteps that had clearly reached the top of the steps and were now making their way past her room. "If I'm right, that's probably Hank getting back from Heavenly Brews. Hayley and Jeremy were just getting back from their latest assignment when I came upstairs at nine thirty."

"I just came from Heavenly Brews and I didn't see Hank."

"Maybe he changed his mind and went somewhere else." Diane inched her upper body lower against the head-board until just her shoulders and head were propped above her pillow. "He's really working hard to put the informa-tion he's learned these past ten days or so into usable lesson plans for his students this fall."

"I have a feeling he's a really good teacher. Very animated."

Diane opened her mouth to answer, but yawned instead. "Oh, I'm sorry."

"No, I'm the one who should be sorry. I'm sitting here, chatting away with you, when it's past your bedtime as it is." Claire swiveled her legs until her feet were on the floor and then stood. "I'll make sure that whatever I do in my room is quiet."

"You're not going to sleep?"

Shrugging, she leaned across the side of the bed she'd just vacated and planted a kiss on her aunt's head. "I'm still way too keyed up from the day to fall asleep anytime soon, but I will. Eventually."

Diane pointed at her nightstand and the stack of paper-back novels that teetered precariously close to its edge.

"Take any one but the top one. I always find that reading in bed makes my eyes tired enough to sleep."

"If I try to read a book as I'm falling asleep—especially a murder mystery like one of those—I won't sleep at all because I'll have to keep reading and reading and reading to find out who did it and why." She stepped back from the bed and turned toward the door. "Do you want me to hit the overhead light as I'm leaving?"

"You don't have to read a book, dear. You could flip through a magazine instead. I have several over there on my desk."

Claire followed her aunt's gaze to the rolltop desk situated to the left of the curtained window. Sure enough, a half dozen or so magazines were stacked neatly on top. "I don't know, Diane, I think I'll be okay."

"You'll be more okay if you actually get some sleep—something you don't get enough of in my opinion, dear."

She walked around the bottom of her aunt's bed and stopped beside the desk. "Should I take this top one?"

"Take whichever one you want to, dear."

Shrugging, she lifted the stack of magazines into her arms and rifled through them one at a time.

Cooking Secrets . . .

Innkeepers Quarterly . . .

Bed & Breakfasts Around the World . . .

The Stable Life . . .

She stopped riffling and stared down at the cover and the black horse gliding over a rocky wall with breathless ease. Turning the magazine so her aunt could see it from her pillow, she said, "Mind if I take this one? You're always so up on the things that are important to me that it seems only right I take the time to do the same thing for you."

"You do enough for me already, dear. But if you'd like to read that until you fall asleep, that's fine. I just ask that I get it back when you're done with it."

She held on to the horse magazine and placed the rest back down on the desk. "Of course. You'll have it back first thing in the morning."

"There's no rush, Claire. Keep it for a day, a week, however long it takes you to read the articles that interest you most. I just ask that you bring it back to me when you're done as I like to keep that magazine more than any of the others I read."

"You got it." She tucked the magazine under her arm and made her way back to the door. "Good night, Aunt Diane. I love you."

"I love you, too, dear. Sweet dreams!"

Flipping the light switch, Claire closed Diane's door and headed across the dimly lit hallway to her own room. Once inside, she closed and locked her door, turned on her light, and flopped onto her bed.

She pulled the magazine out from under her arm and placed it on her stomach, scooting upward on her pillow as she did. Yet no matter how hard she tried to concentrate on the horse depicted on the cover, or the trio of faces watching him from a fence line in the background, all she could think about was Jakob.

Was he still at Daniel Lapp's?

Had he found something that could help in the investigation?

Had the man been in Daniel's barn like he had been at the Stutzmans', the Gingerichs', the Millers', and the Hershbergers'?

And, finally, was Diane right? Did Jakob *love* her?

Releasing her hold on the magazine, she covered her eyes with her hands and groaned even louder. What was she doing? Couldn't she just enjoy the moment with Jakob? Enjoy the romance that was brewing and see where it went?

After all, if his feelings were moving toward love as hers were, he'd say it, wouldn't he?

Then again, *she* hadn't said it yet . . .

She dropped her hands onto the bed and groaned. "Keep this up and you'll never go to sleep," she hissed at herself.

Swinging her feet back onto the ground, she set the magazine to the side and headed into the bathroom to prepare for bed. Once her teeth were brushed, her face washed, and her clothes exchanged for her favorite silky pair of summer pajamas, she returned to her pillow and the magazine.

Concentrate on the magazine . . .

Concentrate on the—

A quick vibration from the other side of the room had her scurrying back toward the bathroom and the tiny table just outside its door where she'd set her cell phone. Snatching it from its holding spot, she smiled down at the name displayed on the screen.

Jakob.

Pressing the message icon, she carried the phone back to her bed and settled against her pillow.

Hi. I probably shouldn't be sending this at this late hour, but I kind of feel like I got cheated out of a proper good night. I'm still out at Lapp's, but I wanted

> you to know I had a great time with you tonight at both
> Esther's and Brews. Thank you. I'll call you sometime
> tomorrow and we can talk.

"I can't wait," she whispered as her eyes immediately moved back to the beginning of the text and focused in on Jakob's words once again.

Finally, reluctantly, she relinquished the phone to her nightstand and the charge it needed in order to accommodate the phone call she was already looking forward to, like a child waiting for Christmas morning to arrive.

Still, she wasn't tired. If anything, she was even more awake than she'd been when she first entered her room. Groaning once again, she grabbed hold of her aunt's magazine, flipped open the cover to the first page, and promptly began to revisit her evening with Jakob—cookies on Esther's front porch, watching Carly shower Esther with genuine adoration, laughing at Jakob's playful banter, and continuing more of that same banter at the coffee shop when it was just the two of them, alone.

It had been, in a nutshell, a perfect evening. Right up until the moment Daniel Lapp came through the front door of Heavenly Brews, anyway . . .

She yawned up at the ceiling and then let her increasingly bleary eyes drop back down to the magazine and the cheerful welcome letter from the editor of *The Stable Life*.

Greetings, horse lovers! As I sit here, writing this, I am experiencing a wide range of emotions. Joy, anticipation, sadness . . .

Chapter 26

Turning her face toward the light, Claire stretched her arms above her head and slowly opened her eyes. The position of the sunlight peeking around the bottom edge of her window shade told her it was a little after seven o'clock and time to start the day.

Part of her wished she could roll over, bury her head under her pillow, and get back to the best sleep she'd had in a while, but she couldn't. Diane was counting on her to help get breakfast started for the guests, and Annie wasn't scheduled to come into the gift shop until lunch.

Slowly, she lowered her hands to her stomach, only to startle just a little when they touched something other than her body. "What on earth . . ." The words disappeared from her mouth as her gaze shifted from the window to the open magazine sprawled across her midsection.

"Maybe Diane was right," she mumbled. "Maybe I should read in bed more often."

She struggled up first onto one elbow, then two elbows, then up against the headboard. Once she was situated in a comfortably reclined position, she lifted the magazine off her stomach and smiled down at the horse depicted on page three. With its sleek gray head held high, the horse peered out at its photographer with nary a care in the world.

Moving on to the next picture, she couldn't help but register the white-haired woman who'd stolen the horse's focus from the photographer. If it was possible for a horse to show joy, this one did.

The last picture showed the horse from the side, the woman running a brush across its body and toward its black, curly tail . . .

"Perhaps *she* uses a curling iron, Detective." Chuckling to herself, Claire relinquished the magazine to the top of her nightstand and threw her feet over the edge of the bed and into her waiting slippers.

Twenty-five minutes later, showered and dressed, she stepped out of her room and let the scent of baking cinnamon guide her down to the main floor. At the bottom of the stairs, she started toward the kitchen, only to double back at the sound of hushed voices just inside the parlor door.

"Oh, good morning, Hayley. Good morning, Jeremy. You're both up early. Busy day ahead?"

Jeremy rested his head against the back of the floral couch, shaking it as he did. "You say that like it's an unusual occurrence."

"For you, it is," snapped Hayley. Then, looking up from the computer desk in the far corner of the room, Hayley found a smile for Claire. "Hey, your aunt said something about a book on Lancaster Amish. Do you happen to know *which* drawer she keeps it in? I thought she said the top drawer, but it's not in there."

"Middle drawer on the right."

"And while we're asking questions, do you happen to know exactly what your aunt is cooking in there that's making this place smell like heaven?" Jeremy asked. "Because I want whatever it is . . ."

"That is the smell of Diane's homemade cinnamon rolls again." Glancing back at Hayley, Claire confirmed the woman had found the requested book and then hooked her thumb over her shoulder. "Well, I better get in there with her now. Everything should be on the table by eight."

Jeremy hiked his feet onto the coffee table and lifted his chin to the morning sun streaming through the large front window. "I'll be there."

Pivoting on her toes, she resumed her original trek toward the kitchen, passing the staircase just as Hank appeared at the top. "Good morning, Hank. Breakfast will be ready in about fifteen minutes."

"Sounds good, but can I ask you something first?" He jogged down the steps and thrust his open notebook into her hands. "Could you give this a quick glance-over and see if I'm missing anything?"

She looked from the notebook to Hank and back again, the names and addresses of many of her fellow shopkeepers and local business owners listed down the center of the page. "What is this?"

"It's a list of the local Amish-owned businesses in the order in which I've visited them."

Slowly, she made her way down the list, her gaze registering a few unfamiliar names amid the many she knew and tried to support. "What do the different-colored marks next to them mean?"

"The ones with the red check next to them are the ones I've visited so far. The ones that also have a green check next to them are the ones that really embody everything I want my students to see in terms of growing a successful business."

About halfway down his list, she started mentally skipping ahead to names she'd yet to see.

Stoltzfus' Equipment Repair . . .

Fisher's Corn Maze . . .

Lapp's Toy Shop . . .

She opened her mouth to suggest those, but reversed course as she reached the last entry on the list. "Oh. You've got Lapp's on here."

"I got that one yesterday. Did you know he actually was in talks to make a line of wooden toys for the Karble company?"

"I did. It was kind of big news around here for a while." She considered filling him in on the details surrounding the offer and the rescinding of that offer, but opted, instead, to keep it light. If the subject was something he chose to research on his own, he could do that. Talking about deceit and murder so early in the morning wasn't her cup of tea. "You know, I better head in to help Diane. I kind of got Jeremy thinking about cinnamon rolls and it's probably best for business not to mess that up."

Hank's face fell, reminding her almost instantly of his initial request. "Oh, wait. I'm sorry, Hank. I got sidetracked thinking about the Karble deal and forgot what you asked me to do." She ran her index finger down the list, then tapped it on the empty space two lines below Lapp's. "I know it's not operating at the moment, but you still might want to talk to Mose Fisher if you get a chance."

"Oh?"

"Mose runs a seasonal business, and it pulls people from all over the county." She handed him back his notebook and waited as he added Jakob's father's name to the list. When he looked up, she continued. "He runs a corn maze during the last three weeks of October. His trails are quite intricate, with easy ones for kids and families, regular ones for most everyone else, and an expert course for people like me who love the challenge."

"Okay, yeah, that sounds mighty interesting." Hank tucked the notebook under his arm and leaned against the stair rail. "Does he make much money doing that? Do you know?"

"Considering the line of parked cars that goes on for nearly half a mile most Friday and Saturday nights throughout the fall, absolutely. He charges five dollars a head on weekdays and eight dollars a head on Friday and Saturday nights."

"How do people do the maze at night in Amish country? There aren't any lights."

She felt her smile before it even claimed her mouth. "Which is what makes it even more fun for a weirdo like me."

"You mean you do it in the dark?" Hank asked.

"*I* do, sure. But Mose also has flashlights for those who prefer a little light on their path."

"So the increased weekend admission helps offset the cost of batteries in the flashlights, I imagine?"

She shrugged. "I guess. I never really thought of that before, but it certainly makes sense. I just attributed it to the whole supply and demand thing."

Hank grinned. "I'm impressed. And yes, I imagine that's some of it, too. If I've learned one thing during my time here, it's that the Amish are extremely savvy when it comes to business."

"It's the English around them that seem to need a little help from what I can see."

Claire followed Hank's gaze over his shoulder and up the staircase. There, at the top of the steps fiddling with his tie, was the town's marketing consultant.

"I think that's a little harsh, Jim," Hank said by way of greeting.

"Doesn't make it any less true." Jim joined them at the bottom of the stairs and nodded at Claire. "You've seen it, Hank—the Amish are good at finding a niche market. They see a need, they fill it."

"And you don't think the English in Heavenly do that?" Claire did her best to control her tone, but it was hard. She loved Heavenly for all the same reasons Jim slighted it.

"Retirees aren't the only ones intrigued by the Amish. Yet they're the only ones this town seems to roll out the welcome mat for."

"I'm not sure what you're seeing, Jim, but I see families walking along Lighted Way all the time." And it was true. She did. In fact, from conversations she'd had with that demographic of customers, many were drawn to Heavenly because of its family-friendly values in a world where that was becoming harder and harder to find. "In fact, I challenge you to sit on one of the park benches next to Glorious Books or Glick's Tools 'n More and really look at who's walking around today. I suspect you'll be surprised to find that we're about fifty-fifty right now with retirees and families."

"During the summer, sure. Kids are off school and the climate in this area is far more tolerable than heading south to the theme parks. But there are nine more months in a calendar year, Claire. Nine more months to see the kind of revenue you do in the summer."

"The retiree traffic kicks up in the fall and spring, doesn't it?" Hank asked.

Claire nodded. "It does. Enough to offset the drop in families."

"Okay, now imagine what could happen if the powers-that-be in Heavenly cater to the other sect that is intrigued by the Amish, as well . . . Think that might just offset the dip in revenue you folks see around here in the dead of winter?"

"People who are intrigued by the Amish for who the Amish are already come, Jim. They don't stay away because we don't have bars. They come because they like the fact that we don't." She heard Diane's footsteps moving around the kitchen, cabinets opening and closing with nearly every other step. Yet, as sure as she was that her pair of hands was needed to finish the breakfast preparations, she also couldn't walk away from the topic at hand. Not yet, anyway. "The people you're talking about want a sensationalized version of the Amish—a version that is untrue. Why would we even think about catering to that? Don't you think any supposed business we'd gain from doing that would destroy the very thing that attracts the people here now? Because I do. And if we did that, the quiet winter months you refer to would be this place *all* the time."

Hank shifted his position against the rail and tugged his notebook out from under his arm. "Jim, I'm the first one to say I'm all about increasing business, but I have to agree with Claire on this one. I think any initial influx of additional customers Heavenly would see by catering to the twenty-somethings would ultimately drive its loyal base away—a base that supports the kind of tourism that's all around you here."

"I . . . second . . . Hank's . . . agreement." Bill came around the back side of the staircase in a pair of running shorts and sneakers, his words coming in stops and starts as he worked to catch his breath. "Heavenly is going after the right pockets. I have absolutely no doubt about that. And, based on what I've seen in the last week or so, it's money well spent. Heck, I stayed on nearly a week longer than I'd planned just because of how peaceful and relaxing this place is. I needed that way more than I realized."

It took everything in Claire's power not to lean around Jim to kiss Bill, but she resisted. Kissing the guests was never a good idea—even when they helped bring home a point that needed to be made.

Chapter 27

Annie hopped down off the step stool and spun around. "So? What do you think? Is it good?"

Looking up from the list of tasks she'd hurriedly written as the day's first customer was climbing the front steps, Claire tried her best to figure out what Annie was referencing but fell short. "I'm sorry, Annie, I was distracted by my atrocious handwriting and my inability to decipher line three."

"It says *birdhouse*."

"Birdhouse?" she murmured, glancing back down. "Oh, yeah, okay. I see it now."

"Do you like it?"

Again, Claire looked up, only this time Annie's outstretched finger guided her focus where it needed to go. "Oh. Wow. You did it already . . ."

Annie ran her hands down the sides of her simple pale

green dress and then lifted the step stool up off the ground. "I tried it on the shelf alone, but it looks better with the birds Benjamin has whittled, yah?"

"Yah—I mean, yes." She took a moment to really soak in the teenager's thoughtful arrangement of Martha's hand-painted birdhouse. Centered in the middle of a shelf in the section of the shop devoted to home, the wooden structure's whimsical touches stoked visions of baby birds peeking out through the center hole. The proximity of Ben's hand-carved birds only enhanced that imagery. "It's perfect!"

"What is next on the list?" Annie carried the step stool back to its hook just inside the back room and then returned to the counter.

Claire forced her attention off the new display and back onto the nearly illegible list at her elbow. Unable to make out her chicken scratch, she pushed the clipboard into the center of the counter and sank onto the closest stool instead. "I'm pretty sure it says *talk*."

"Talk? Are you sure?" Annie furrowed her brow and pulled the clipboard in her direction. "No, it says *prepare weekend sale items.*"

It took everything she had not to laugh out loud at the young Amish girl's literal innocence, but somehow she managed to refrain. Patting the stool next to her, Claire gestured toward the front door and the sporadic foot traffic on the sidewalk beyond. "Right now it's quiet in here. Let's take advantage of that and talk for a little bit. We can get to the sale prep when we're done."

"Are you sure?"

"I'm sure, Annie." Again, she patted the chair, adding

a smile of encouragement as she did. "Sit. Tell me how Katie is doing . . . And how Henry is doing, too. "

Like clockwork, Annie's face reddened at the mere mention of the eldest Stutzman son. "Henry is keeping a brave face. But he still hurts. I can see it in his eyes."

"I'm glad he has you to talk to, Annie. I'm sure that's a comfort."

Annie's brown eyes glinted with a rare burst of excitement she quickly covered with her hand. "Benjamin Miller has been helping Henry and his brothers with the farm."

"Ben is a good man."

"Yah."

"How is Katie?"

This time, when Annie's eyes brightened, she didn't hide them from view. "She is good. I am trying to teach her a trick." Leaning forward, Annie lowered her voice to a near whisper. "I want her to bounce her head when I hum a song. Like she is dancing."

"Is she doing it?"

"A little. If I have sweets to give." Annie hiked her simple black lace-up boots onto the bottom rung of the stool and leaned into the edge of the counter. "It is something I do when Dat is busy and my work is done."

"You're really enjoying her, aren't you?" Claire asked.

"Yah. I like having a horse of my own."

Claire peeked again at the sidewalk and the increasing number of pedestrians walking along Lighted Way. A look back at the clock over the register confirmed the waning lunch hour. Still, they probably had a few more minutes . . .

"My aunt loves horses, and so I'm trying to learn more

about them. In fact, I even spent a little time looking through a horse magazine last night—or, rather, this morning before I got out of bed."

"I have not seen such a magazine."

"I'll have to borrow one of hers to show you one day. Anyway, I didn't have much time to actually read any of the articles when I woke up, but I did look at a few pictures. One of the horses I saw looked just like Esther and Eli's horse, Carly. Have you seen her?" She grabbed hold of the clipboard, glanced at the list one more time, and then carried it around to the other side of the counter and the nail on which it normally hung. "That horse is completely enamored with Esther. It's really cute to watch."

"I saw her after lunch on Sunday. Her tail is so curly!"

"I couldn't believe that, either, but, after looking at that magazine this morning, I guess it's not as rare as I'd thought." Claire plucked a tiny scrap of paper off the top of the counter and then pointed toward the door with her chin. "Looks like we've got a customer coming in. I'll take this one if you want to move on to one of the next items on the list."

The door-mounted bells ushered in a familiar face and voice. "Claire? Are you here?"

Venturing out from behind the counter, Claire headed toward the travel agent. "Hello, Bill. Welcome to Heavenly Treasures."

Reaching up, Bill pulled his baseball cap off his head and smiled. "Hey, Claire. I'm on the way back to the inn now to get my stuff and head out, but I wanted to say goodbye and thank you before I left. It's been really nice getting to know you and your aunt and this fantastic little town."

"I'm so glad you did. It's been lovely having you at the

inn, and I know Diane and I both hope you'll be back again."

"Oh, I will be. I think Heavenly just moved to the top of my places-to-go-when-I'm-stressed list." He spun his cap around in his hands and then steadied it next to his side. "Actually, before I go, could you write down the name of Hayley and Jeremy's blog for me? I don't want to ask them again for fear of looking like a jerk for not listening the first time, but I thought, if I like it, that maybe I'll include that in some of my promotional pieces for a Heavenly trip. Some folks really like to read other people's thoughts and experiences on a particular place before they commit to going. "

"Of course I can. C'mon, I'll jot that down for you right now." Motioning for him to follow, Claire led the way back across the shop to the notepad and pen jar housed beside the register. "I'm pretty sure they said it's called Travel Time—Travel Time with Jeremy and Hayley."

She jotted down the name, added her cell phone underneath, and handed the paper to Bill. "I included my cell phone number in case you need anything when you're putting your flyers together."

Bill nodded down at the information and then tucked it into his back pocket. "Thank you, Claire. For everything."

"It's been my pleasure." She walked with him as he made his way back across the shop to the front door. "I hope you get a chance to see everyone one more time before you leave."

"I spoke with Hank briefly a little while ago when I was taking one last drive through the countryside. He was walking between farms with that notebook of his and a list of Amish businesses he wants to hit before he checks out on Friday. I saw Hayley and Jeremy at the coffee shop just now and, true to form, they were picking at each other the way they always do. And I just passed Jim on the way here, but other than a quick good-bye, I've not much to say to him. I think his ideas for this town are ludicrous, and I hope they fall on deaf ears."

"They will. And if they don't, Diane will rally the troops and make sure that they do."

Bill's laugh echoed around the shop and blended with the jingle of the door as he pulled it open. "Your aunt is a special lady, Claire. A special lady, indeed."

Something about the tone of the man's voice caught her by surprise, and she found herself studying him in a much different way than she had all week. Suddenly, the salt and pepper shade of his hair took him past "older" to "around the same age as Diane." And the smile he'd so easily worn whenever Diane shared a story now became more about Diane herself.

"Anyway, I better head out. I'm hoping maybe I can have a cup of tea with your aunt before I hit the road. Assuming she's not too busy, of course."

She made a mental note to call her aunt the second Bill was out of the store, and then held the door as he stepped out onto the front stoop. "Keep in touch."

"I will."

With the door still wide open to the afternoon heat, Claire watched Bill make his way down the stairs and across the sidewalk toward the simple navy-colored sedan parked on the opposite side of the street. A few moments later, when he was safely behind the steering wheel, she shut the door and turned to face Annie, her eyes wide. "I can't believe I've been so blind!"

Annie looked up from the sale signs she was making in a back corner of the main room and made a face. "Blind?"

"All this time, I just thought Bill was taken by everything Heavenly—the people, the food, the atmosphere. But that wasn't it at all."

"He did not like Heavenly?" Annie asked.

Claire waved the question aside with a flip of her hand. "No. No, I'm not saying that. I think he *did* like Heavenly . . . very much. But I think he liked my aunt even more."

Annie uncrossed her legs and rose onto her knees, her gaze skirting the tabletop display of candles for a direct view of Claire. "Does your aunt like him?"

"If you'd asked me that before Bill showed up here, I'd have said no way. Diane is far too busy with the inn to entertain a romantic relationship of any kind." She checked to see that Bill's car was no longer parked out front and then leaned her shoulder against the wall. "But we're talking about a woman who is so passionate about horses she spends an hour or so out at Weaver farm each week. And I didn't know that. So I guess it stands to reason she could have an interest in someone and I might have missed that, too."

"But you talk, yah?"

"All the time. And I mean, *all* the time." Claire tilted her head back against the wall and stared up at the ceiling. "On one hand, I have to wonder if our conversations have always been about me . . . but I know that's not the case. I know all sorts of things about Diane. I just didn't know about the horse thing."

"And the Bill thing?"

Pushing off the wall, she wandered from display to display across the shop, Amish dolls, Amish quilts, place mats, footstools, and painted milk cans barely registering in her thoughts. "I'm not sure there even *is* a Bill thing on Diane's end. It is possible she simply thought he was smiling at her stories the same way I did."

"And if she did not know?" Annie posed.

"I want her to know. I've always thought she was far too special to be alone all the time."

"She has many guests, yah?"

"Guests that come and go, sure." When she reached the candle display, she stopped, pulled her phone from her pocket, and looked down at the darkened screen. "I want Diane to have more."

Annie pushed the sale cards into a stack and then stood. "More?"

"I want her to have something special—like I have with Jakob."

Chapter 28

Claire took advantage of a momentary lull in customers to hijack a pretzel from the small snack bag she'd stowed away beneath the register. In hindsight, she probably should have taken Annie up on her offer to stay until closing rather than her scheduled three o'clock departure, but she'd really thought things would slow down.

They hadn't.

Looking around the shop, she conducted a quick visual inventory of the various shelves that were now either empty or severely lacking. If she did her mental math right, she'd sold close to a thousand dollars in merchandise since lunch. Granted, some of that fast intake of cash was due, largely, to the sale of two big-ticket items—a quilt and a blanket chest—but a number of smaller items had gone, too.

She finished one pretzel and moved on to a second, her gaze moving down the written list of items both she and

Annie had sold since the shop opened that morning. There was no doubt about it; they'd had a very good day.

"Good afternoon, Claire."

Startled, Claire dropped the next pretzel onto the counter and flew her hand to her chest. "Oh. Hannah. I . . . I didn't hear you come in."

The teenager's cheeks flamed red as her own hands—which Claire could now see were full—slowly lowered a few inches. "I did not mean to frighten you."

"No, it wasn't you." She stepped out from behind the counter and strode across the shop. "I should have heard the bell, but I was engrossed in something else."

"Something good, I hope?" Esther's younger sister cleared her throat and then glanced down at her hands. "Mamm asked me to bring you another birdhouse and this baby blanket she completed last night."

Claire took the birdhouse from Hannah and smiled down at the painted detail work surrounding the small round entrance hole. "I fell in love with the one your mother brought in for me yesterday and so, too, did one of my customers, as you can see." She waved her free hand toward the shelf the birdhouse had inhabited for all of about thirty minutes that afternoon and then looked back at Hannah. "Annie made this really cute display with the birdhouse and a few of Benjamin Miller's hand-carved birds and it sold in less than an hour."

"Perhaps you can put that one"—Hannah pointed at the house in Claire's hands—"in the same spot."

"And I will as soon as I record these new items in my book." She carried the birdhouse over to the counter, with Hannah close on her heels. Setting it down, she reached for the baby blanket and held it to her face. "Wow, this is so soft."

"Mamm does good work."

"She does, indeed." Claire lowered the blanket to the counter, plucked a pen from its holder, and flipped open the notebook tasked with keeping track of her inventory. Once the new items were recorded in the section set aside for Martha King, she closed the book and focused on the woman's second daughter.

Unlike Esther, who had soft brown hair, Hannah's coloring was lighter. Her hair, which was also parted neatly down the middle and secured beneath a white kapp, was more of a sandy blonde, like her uncle's, and her eyes leaned more toward a hazel than a true brown. Though, in just the right light, Claire could almost pick up the same hint of amber flecks that both Jakob and Esther sported in their eyes.

"I stopped at Esther's first, to see if she had any items she wanted me to bring to you, but she said she did not. She said you visited last night."

"We—" She felt the color drain from her face over her choice in pronoun and stopped speaking long enough to collect her thoughts. The last thing she wanted to do was rat out Esther's Ordnung infraction. If Esther chose to share details of her evening with their uncle, that was for Esther to do, not Claire. "*We* are running low on girl dolls at the moment, but Esther already knows about that and she's working on making more."

Nice save . . .

"Did you see Carly?"

Grateful for the change in topic, Claire jumped right

in. "I did! She's precious! And I hear she has a penchant for one of the hard candies you make."

Hannah's mouth spread wide with a smile just before the girl's hand disappeared inside the plain-colored satchel hanging from her shoulder. Seconds later, it reemerged with two small wrapped mounds in the center of her palm. "Here."

"Are these them?" she asked.

"Yah. Please. Have them."

Taking the candies from the girl's outstretched hand, Claire unwrapped one and popped it in her mouth, the instant burst of root beer flavoring on her tongue making her wish she'd inquired about the flavor before partaking.

"They are good, yah?"

She almost said something about her dislike of root beer but kept it to herself when she saw the hopeful expression on Hannah's young face. "Yes. Good."

"That is why I gave you two."

"And that is why I will save this second one for later." She slipped the wrapped candy into the front pocket of her summer slacks and tried not to give in to her natural gag reflex. Instead, in an effort to buy herself a little unnoticed time with a napkin, Claire directed Hannah's attention back to the shelf on which Martha's first birdhouse had been situated. The second the girl fell for her diversion, she rescued her taste buds from the offending candy and tossed it into the trash can with lightning speed. "Um . . . if your mother's new birdhouse sells as quickly as the first one did, I may be asking for more."

"I will let her know." Hannah turned back to Claire and flashed a smile nearly identical to one of Esther's. "The next time I am to bring items from Mamm, I will bring you *three* candies."

She felt her mouth begin to gape in horror, but managed to cover it with a quick shrug. "I don't want to take them away from you and Carly. I mean, from what Esther says, that horse is crazy about them."

"I can make more. I like to make candy."

"D-do you make other flavors?" she asked only to wince at the unmistakable note of hope she heard in her words.

"Yah." Hannah peeked out the window overlooking the alleyway and then headed toward the front door, glancing back at Claire as she walked. "Do you have a favorite one?"

"Butterscotch, cherry, strawberry . . . You know, anything like that."

"I gave a butterscotch candy to the man who asked Mamm for directions to the Lehmans' vegetable stand. He said it was very good."

It took a moment for the girl's words to register, but when they did, Claire sucked in a breath. "You mean the Englisher who was at your farm on Monday?"

Hannah stopped briefly to study the string of bells attached to the back of the door, then turned the knob and pulled. "I think it was Monday, yah."

"You gave him a candy?"

"Yah. When I brought him his drink of water. He said it was very good." Hannah stepped onto the front stoop and then turned to wave at Claire. "I will bring you a butterscotch next time. Perhaps you will think it is very good, too."

Chapter 29

Claire palmed the last bit of dough into a ball, placed it alongside the others, and then carried the baking sheet over to the preheated oven.

"Oh good, those are ready to go in now." Diane came around the center island and opened the oven door for Claire. "By the time they come out, the roast beef will be carved and ready for the guests."

She slid the sheet onto the top rack, then turned and smiled at her aproned aunt. "Now what?"

"You take a break." Diane lifted the egg timer off the counter and set it to twenty minutes. "And tell me about your day while we wait for the baked potatoes to finish baking."

"Sounds good to me. *After* I wash my hands, that is." Claire displayed her floured palms for Diane to see and then stopped at the sink.

A good thirty minutes had come and gone since she arrived home, yet, in all that time, she'd only *entertained* the notion of asking about Bill. Somehow, every single time she found a way to inquire without sounding too nosy, she chickened out.

She suspected some of that was because she'd opted not to call Diane after her conversation with Bill at the store. At the time, she'd rationalized her last-minute decision with her aunt's age and not wanting to be a meddling niece. Yet as the afternoon wore on, she'd second-guessed herself for not calling.

"Bill told me he stopped by the shop and said good-bye to you this afternoon," Diane said.

"So you were here when he left, then?" Hearing the shrillness of her voice, Claire forced herself to act casual. She could mull over her aunt's mind-reading ability later, when she was alone.

"I was. We had some tea and cake together before he headed out."

Claire shut off the water, grabbed the hand towel from its rack under the sink, and used the time it took to dry her hands to try to decipher whether the change in her aunt's tone was tied to the act of carving or talk of Bill's departure. When her hands were bone dry, she turned and made her way over to the counter, the sight of the first piece of cut beef reminding her of her minimal lunch and the hunger she'd failed to abate with a handful of pretzels.

"That's nice." Claire pulled a stool out from under the counter's eave and cozied up within arm's reach of the cutting board. "That looks really, *really* good, Aunt Diane."

Pointing the tip of her knife alongside the first piece, the woman scooted it across the board to Claire. "Here. Nosh on this."

"You don't have to tell me twice," she quipped. With clean fingers, she extracted the piece of beef from the board and took a bite, the flavors her aunt was so gifted at enhancing popping inside her mouth. "Oh. Wow. That's even better than it looks."

Diane brought the knife to the top of the roast again and began to cut, her focus moving between the meat and Claire. "You skipped lunch again, didn't you?"

"Not intentionally. We were just really busy. I did eat a few pretzels, though."

"Pretzels aren't a meal, dear."

"I beg to differ." Then, holding up her hands in surrender, she brought the conversation back to Diane . . . and Bill. "So how was tea?"

"It was quite lovely. Bill is a very interesting man. He really loves pairing people up with the vacation destination that's best for them."

"Maybe he could pair you up with one."

"Oh, he tried, dear. He thinks I'd love Paris since I enjoy cooking so much. He said it would be a chance to let others cook for me." Diane paused her knife above the roast and looked at Claire over the top of her glasses. "He asked me if that was something I thought I'd enjoy, and I honestly don't know. I love being the cook. I love being the innkeeper."

"I wonder what *Bill's* ideal place would be."

"I asked him that."

"And?"

"He said Paris. He said he finds it magical."

She couldn't help but grin at the notion of her aunt being squired across the ocean by a man who put stock in magic.

Diane pointed the tip of her knife at Claire. "You're smiling . . ."

Uh-oh.

"I guess I like the idea of you taking some time off and going somewhere special." She guided her aunt's focus back to the meat and then smiled even wider as another tiny scrap was pushed in her direction. "You never do anything special for yourself."

"Meeting all these lovely people *is* something special," Diane protested. "I love what I do, Claire. You know that."

"I do. But everyone needs a vacation once in a while. Even people who love what they do."

"I can't just shut the inn down, dear."

She stopped chewing and brought her hands to her hips in dramatic indignation. "I'm fully capable of running this place for a week."

Diane resumed her cutting and then placed the slices onto a waiting platter. "You have your own business to run."

"And a very capable employee to cover for me."

Reaching down to the waistband of her apron, Diane pulled out a towel, wiped her hands, and glanced toward the egg timer. "Looks like the rolls will be done in about five minutes. Can you pull the potatoes out and get those ready to go?"

"Sure." Claire slid off her stool and crossed to the oven. "But, just so we're clear, we're not changing topics. You really ought to think about a vacation. Maybe even Paris, like Bill said."

"I'm not going to go by *myself.*"

"Go with Bill." More than anything, she wanted to peek over her shoulder and gauge her aunt's reaction, but to do so might look too obvious. Besides, she had potatoes to rescue from the oven . . .

"Good heavens, Claire, I can't just go gallivanting to Paris with a man I've only known for a little over a week!"

Holding the now-filled bowl of potatoes against her side, she closed the oven door and headed straight for the plate of butter and the salt and pepper shakers. "I don't think Bill would mind."

"Claire!"

She slit open each of the potatoes and shook a smidge of salt and pepper into each one. When she was done, she set the shakers down and met her aunt's widened eyes. "You don't think it's curious that he suggested you go to Paris, and then told you that's where *he* would go, too?"

"No. He was making conversation, dear."

"You don't think it's curious he wanted to have tea with you before he checked out?"

"He's a nice man."

"He's a nice man who just happens to be interested in *you*, Aunt Diane."

Diane's mouth opened, closed, and opened again. But no words, no sound came out.

"I take it you didn't pick up on it, either?"

The egg timer chirped and sent Diane scurrying for the oven. "It's time to focus on dinner."

"But—"

"Please, Claire." Diane pulled the golden rolls from the oven, covered each with a slice of butter, and then carried them over to the waiting bread basket. As she transferred them from the pan to the basket, she took control of the conversation once again. "Hank and Jim are both leaving Friday morning. Hayley and Jeremy are still up in the air as to when exactly they're checking out."

Looking up from the potatoes now stretched across a wide serving plate, Claire watched her aunt for several long moments. Diane was, without a doubt, the happiest, most cheerful person Claire had ever known. As a little girl, it had never really registered with her that her aunt wasn't married. All she knew was that this wonderful woman she got to visit a few times a year fawned all over her as if she was something special. As a teenager, it registered on occasion, but she never thought to ask. Then, as a newly divorced adult who'd sought solace in the woman's arms, she'd simply accepted her aunt's "too late" admission every time the concept of marriage had come up.

But was it too late?

Diane was only sixty-two.

Maybe, instead of "too late," her aunt's never-married status was simply a case of not having found the right man . . .

"I'm going to bring the rolls and the potatoes out now. I'll be back in a moment." Diane's voice snapped Claire back into the present in time to see the woman exit the kitchen through the open doorway leading to the dining room.

Shaking herself back into the here and now, Claire readied the vegetables and the meat platter and carried them out to the table and the four guests eagerly waiting for their meal. Like the well-oiled machine that they were, Claire and Diane moved around the table serving the meal, filling water and wine glasses, and answering any questions that popped up.

Once everyone was situated and happily eating their meal, the pair retreated back to the kitchen and the assorted cooking pans and utensils that represented the next part of their evening. "Shall I wash, dear?"

"I can wash if you'd—" She startled as her hand came down against her pocket and the odd little mound it housed. Reaching inside, she slowly pulled out the item and winced. "Oh. Yuck. I almost forgot about this thing."

Diane leaned forward. "It looks like a homemade candy."

"It is. Esther's sister, Hannah, made it."

"I take it it's not very good?"

She looked down at the dark candy and felt a wave of guilt wash over her from head to toe. "It would be unfair of me to say, either way, on account of the fact it's root beer, and you know how I feel about root beer."

"Let me try, dear."

Guilt morphed into relief and she handed the candy to her aunt. "Be my guest . . ."

Diane unwrapped the candy and popped it into her mouth. Seconds later, the woman closed her eyes and moaned. "Oh, Claire, it's definitely you. This is delightful!"

She watched in amusement as her aunt abandoned the notion of washing dishes and, instead, took a rare break against a nearby counter. "It's that good, huh?" she teased.

"To a root beer fan such as myself, yes, it's that good." Diane ran her hand along the top of the counter and then followed the motion with a dish towel. "You know who would have loved this candy?"

Claire carried the pots and pans over to the counter beside the sink and then turned back to her aunt. "Who?"

"Carrot Thief."

"Is that the horse who went missing after the trailer accident?" she asked.

"Yes." Diane spotted a saucepan on the stove and brought that over to the counter, too. "Didn't you read about her in the magazine you borrowed last night?"

"No. I started to read it last night, but, just as you predicted, I fell asleep. Hard." She stepped up to the sink, retrieved the dish soap and strainer from the cabinet below, and turned on the faucet. "It was still on my stomach when I woke up this morning."

"Good. You need your sleep."

"I did look at a few of the pictures near the front."

"Then you saw Carrot Thief. She was the main feature in that particular—"

Claire sucked in her breath so hard and so loud, all background chatter from the dining room ceased, along with the rest of Diane's sentence.

The majestic gray coat . . .

The beautiful black mane . . .

The black curly tail . . .

The penchant for root beer . . .

"Claire? Is everything—"

Spinning around, she covered her cheeks with her wet hands. "Diane! I think I know where Carrot Thief is!"

"What are you talking about, dear?"

"I think Carly is Carrot Thief!"

Diane grabbed hold of Claire's hands and guided them away from her face. "Slow down, dear. Take a deep breath."

She tried to do as she was told, but all she could think about was Esther . . .

"Claire? Who is Carly?"

Slowly, she made herself focus on her aunt and the answer she didn't want to give.

"Claire? Who is Carly?" Diane repeated.

Breathe . . .

Answer . . .

"She's Esther and Eli's new horse."

Chapter 30

Claire took the steps two at a time up to her room and shut the door. She'd tried to convince herself she could put Carly's true identity on the back burner of her thoughts until after the kitchen was cleaned, but she couldn't. Her only hope now was that she'd persuaded Diane to wait on contacting the magazine until after Claire had a chance to talk to Jakob and Esther.

Esther . . .

The pure joy on both Esther's and Carly's faces when they were around each other was unmistakable. Knowing she was about to strip that away from both of them was making Claire's head pound.

Still, it had to be done. Carly didn't belong to Esther. She belonged to a woman named Valerie Palermo—a woman who'd been searching for her racehorse for nearly two weeks. The good news, of course, was that the horse

LAURA BRADFORD

was fine, save for a sprained tendon in her leg. The bad news was that Esther had grown attached to the animal.

Flopping onto her back, Claire removed her cell phone from the nightstand and held it above her face. More than anything, she wished she'd never looked at Diane's magazine, that she hadn't seen the picture of Carrot Thief, that she hadn't handed Hannah's root beer candy to a woman who devoured every line in every issue of *The Stable Life*.

But she had.

To ignore it all away now would be akin to lying.

Releasing a pent-up groan, she scrolled through her contacts and stopped on Jakob. Maybe he'd be too busy to pick up. Maybe he'd be too busy to say anything more than hello. And, for the first time since they'd taken the leap from friends to more, she actually found herself hoping that would be the case. Not because she didn't want to talk to him, but simply because she wanted to buy Esther a little more time with her beloved Carly.

Two rings later, the sound of Jakob's voice in her ear changed everything. She wanted to tell him what she suspected and what was upsetting her so he could make it right. After all, that's what Jakob did, wasn't it? He made things right.

"Claire? Are you there?"

She closed her eyes tightly and mustered the smile he deserved. "I'm sorry, Jakob, yes, I'm here. How are you?"

"Crazy busy. Crazy frustrated. Same as yesterday," he laughed.

"Then I'll just call back later . . ." She parted her eyelashes and gazed up at the ceiling, her emotions a jumble of relief and disappointment. "Or maybe tomorrow."

"No! I actually could use the break. Especially if it means getting to talk to you for a little while."

"Oh. O-okay." She caught the falter in her voice and braced herself for the veritable certainty that he had, too.

"You alright, Claire? You sound funny."

Releasing her breath, she rolled onto her side and caught a glimpse of her aunt's magazine on the vanity bench. "Not really."

Any fatigue she may have heard in his tone when he answered her call disappeared in favor of worry. "Talk to me, Claire. What's going on?"

"It's Esther." Then, realizing how that could be taken, she rushed on. "I discovered something this evening that is going to make her very, very sad. And I don't know how to tell her."

"What is it?"

"She's not going to be able to keep Carly."

A long, low whistle filled her ear, and she could imagine Jakob leaning back in his desk chair, eyes closed. "Oh no, did the horse reinjure her leg?"

"No."

"Then why wouldn't she be able to keep the horse? They're clearly crazy about each other."

Crazy about each other . . .

She felt a telltale prick of heat in the corners of her eyes and squeezed them shut. "The horse isn't hers."

A faint squeak from Jakob's end of the line let her know she'd been a beat or two premature on the leaning-back-in-his-chair part. "What do you mean it isn't hers? Eli bought it out at Weaver's, didn't he?"

"That's a whole different aspect I haven't even thought about yet."

"Claire. Please. I'm not following any of this," Jakob protested. "Take it from the top."

"A few weeks back, a racehorse from New York went missing after the trailer it was riding in was involved in an accident on a back road somewhere along the New Jersey–Pennsylvania border."

"Yeah, yeah, I heard about this. The driver was killed, right? And the accident wasn't found until a few hours after the fact, yes?"

"Correct."

"I saw something about it on a database we have, but that was it. I figured the horse would eventually turn up."

She felt the lump rising up her throat but managed to eke out her reply anyway. "It has."

"That's good news, right?" he prodded.

"For the horse's owner? Yes. For Esther and Eli? Not so much."

"Wait a minute. What do Esther and Eli have to do with this race—"

She could almost hear his brain connecting the two horses together. And, sure enough, it did . . .

"Wait. Are you saying that Carly is this missing horse?"

Oh, how she wanted to say no, to tell him she was playing a trick on him. But she couldn't. "Yes."

"Did someone see Carly?"

"*I* did."

"Claire, please."

Jakob was right. She needed to just spell everything out and let the chips fall where they may. "I saw a picture in one of Diane's magazines this morning, and although I didn't read the article that went with it, I remember thinking in the back of my head that this horse—Carrot Thief is its name—looked just like Carly. Right down to the same shade of gray and the curly black tail."

"Go on . . ."

"Since I don't know much about horses, I figured that wasn't unusual. I mean, really, there are only so many colors a horse can be, right? Black, white, brown, gray. Surely it's not unusual to find horses that look alike."

"But this one had the black curly tail?"

"Yes. And a penchant for root beer candy."

"Excuse me?"

She sat up on the edge of the bed, reached across the divide between herself and the vanity bench, and pulled the magazine onto her lap. With a flip of her hand, she found herself staring down at the exact same trio of pictures that had claimed her attention that morning. Only instead of a passing glance, she took a moment to really study the horse depicted in each one. Suddenly, the similarities that had tickled at her subconscious that morning turned into full fledge smacks.

"What's this about root beer candy?" Jakob clarified.

"Apparently Carrot Thief has a thing for root beer candies. Carly loves them, too. You remember what Esther told us about this, don't you? That Carly is always looking to see if Hannah has more."

Silence gave way to a strange sound in her ear.

"Jakob?"

"That's right. I remember now." Jakob's sigh matched hers, and she knew he was finally getting the enormity of what this meant for his niece. And, just like Claire had done in the kitchen, he tried to find a way around it. "Okay, so Carly has a black curly tail and likes the same unusual flavor of candy. That doesn't necessarily mean it's this Carrot Thief horse."

"Carly has an injured leg."

"So . . ."

"It kind of makes sense if the animal was in an accident and then left to fend for itself in the woods."

"How did Weaver end up with her?" Jakob asked.

"Good question. And one that definitely needs to be asked." She leaned forward as a small, soft gray mark on Carrot Thief's upper chest caught her eye from the bottom right picture. "Jakob?"

"Yes?"

"Do you remember seeing a little mark on Carly's chest?"

"Yeah. It looked like a paw print."

"And the color?"

"A slightly darker shade of gray than Carly herself."

She sank back against the bed. "Carrot Thief has the same mark . . . in the same place."

When Jakob said nothing, she filled in the empty space with the part that made her want to scream. "How do we tell her, Jakob? How do we tell Esther that she can't keep Carly? She's going to be crushed."

His second, longer sigh let her know she wasn't alone in her frustration. But after several long moments, he took control of the conversation and her fears. "Look, I promise we'll find a way to break this to her gently. But can we put it on the back burner for just a little while? I've got to focus on what's going on in Heavenly right now. I don't want any more people being victimized by this larcenist. And it appears as if he's moving down the street in a semi-orderly fashion."

"If you know that, why don't you just stake out the next house on the street? You know, wait for him to show up there and then nab him. I mean, I know that Henry Stutzman and that Gingerich girl, Rebecca, weren't able to give the sketch artist much of a description, but surely, if you put the person in front of them, they could identify him. Especially now that we know your sister saw this guy, too."

"I thought about that. And I still might do it. But my gut is telling me that all that will do is spook him off—maybe straight out of Heavenly. The sight of a cop car in a driveway, or a cop sitting on a front porch, has a way of deterring crime. A good thing the majority of the time, but not what we're going for in this circumstance, you know?"

She took in the pictures of Carrot Thief one more time and then chucked the magazine across her room. Jakob was right. He had way too much on his plate right now to worry about a horse.

Breaking Esther's heart in two was up to Claire, and Claire alone.

Chapter 31

Slowly, inch by inch, Claire maneuvered Diane's car between the trailer ruts that lined Weaver's driveway, each miscalculation on her part making her head ache all the more. Her being there was probably futile. Mervin Weaver wasn't going to be able to tell her anything about Carly's true identity that she didn't already know.

Carrot Thief and Carly were one and the same horse. Of that, she had no doubt.

But it was the how and the why behind that reality that had made it impossible for Claire to sleep. Well, that and the knowledge that she was about to hurt Esther.

When she reached the parking area, she shifted the car into park and studied the weathered building off to her left. Long and squatty compared to the majority of barns in Amish country, the Weaver barn was strictly about horses. Some stalls, from what she'd learned while visiting with Diane, were rented by Englishers looking to board their personal horses. A few stalls housed Weaver's own team. But most of the stalls served as temporary housing for the horses Mervin bought at auction and then sold to local Amish.

Somehow, some way, Carrot Thief had been one of those horses. And, because of that, Esther had grown attached to a horse that wasn't hers to love.

Releasing a pent-up burst of air from deep inside her chest, Claire reached for the door handle, only to pull her hand back in favor of reaching for her phone and giving in to the sudden and overwhelming need to delay the inevitable. Seven digits later, she started counting rings . . .

One.

Two.

"Heavenly Treasures. How may I help you?"

"Hi, Annie, it's me."

"Hello, Claire."

She closed her eyes in an effort to savor Annie's telephone voice and everything it represented. In it, she could sense an excitement that so many of Annie's English counterparts would never know. To them, a phone was routine, normal. To Annie, it was like visiting a foreign land.

"Claire?"

"I'm here, I'm here." Forcing herself to get to the point, Claire began firing off the same spate of questions she always asked if Annie was in the shop alone. "Any issues opening? Do you have enough money in the drawer to start the day? Any problems I should know about?"

"All is well, Claire. I have made two sales already this morning."

Claire glanced at the dashboard clock. "Okay, that's good news."

"Yah. But now my shelf is empty."

"Your shelf?"

"I sold Martha's birdhouse and Ben's birds."

"Wow. Two birdhouses in less than twenty-four hours. Martha will be pleased."

"Yah."

She turned her head to the left and gazed out at the stable once again, a handful of horses now visible through open exterior panels. Annie was fine. Keeping her on the phone any longer was really more about Claire stalling the inevitable than anything else. "Thanks, Annie, for going it alone this morning. I promise I'll get there as quickly as I can."

"There is no hurry. I am fine."

"I know you are." And she did. Annie had proven that many times over in the handful of months they'd been working together. "Don't worry about the shelf. We can always figure that out later . . . when I get back."

A faint jingle in the background of her call let her know a customer had just entered the shop. Stall-time was over. "I hear you have a customer, so I'll let you go. Call me if you need anything."

"I will."

Dropping the phone back into her purse, she pulled the keys from the ignition and stepped out onto the same driveway that, days earlier, had been one big puddled mess. She stepped across the first rut, now dry and firm, and then headed toward the second, her resignation slowly but surely dissipating.

No, she wasn't suddenly okay with hurting Esther. She'd

never be okay with that. But the sooner she got her answers, the sooner they could get through the bad and focus on the good.

Like the impending arrival of Esther's first child.

She stopped so suddenly, she nearly twisted her ankle inside the second rut. "I know!" she said. "We could have a baby shower!"

A head popped out of a panel midway down the side of the barn. "Well hello there! Welcome to Weaver—wait! I know you! You are Miss Weatherly's kin . . ."

Picking her way across the rest of the driveway, Claire walked over to the window panel and smiled up at the hatted man with the long, gray beard and infectious smile. "Good morning, Mervin."

"Tell me what your name is again."

"Claire. Claire Weatherly. I'm Diane Weatherly's niece."

He dipped his head ever so slightly and then gazed across the top of her head to the parking lot. "Is Miss Weatherly with you?"

"No. I'm here alone."

"You like horses, too?"

"I don't know much about them," she said, shrugging. "But I know they're beautiful, and they sure make my aunt happy."

"I keep telling her she should buy one for herself. I would give her a fair price and I would even board it here in my stable for free. Least I could do for all them tasty treats she brings me when she visits, and all that grooming she does on the horses even though I insist it is not her job to do."

"When my aunt makes her mind up about something, there's no dissuading her, that's for sure." She smiled at the image of her aunt, hands on hips, holding her ground with Mervin the way she did with Claire. "Besides, she loves horses."

"So what brings you to my farm on this fine summer day?"

Her smile slipped away as Mervin's question dropped reality at her feet once again. "I . . . I was hoping I could ask you a few questions about a horse you recently sold."

"I sell a lot of horses, but I can sure try to help." Mervin waved his calloused hand toward the end of the barn. "Why don't you come on inside and we can talk while I look after the horses. I need them to be ready come Saturday."

"Saturday?"

"Most of my neighbors come to buy horses on Saturday. I have a few this week that will go quickly." Again he waved Claire toward the end of the barn. "Now come on around and I will see to the horses and your questions."

Following along the exterior wall of the barn, she headed in the general vicinity in which she'd come. Save for the sound of rain pounding on the roof, the sights and smells that greeted her as she stepped inside the barn were the same as they'd been two days earlier.

Mervin Weaver strode down the center aisle and stopped. "If I remember correctly, your aunt told me you took a good long time deciding who to give candy to when you were last here."

She smiled at the memory and then slipped her hands in and out of her front pockets. "No candy this time. Sorry."

Tucking his thumb inside his suspender strap, he made a quick face. "Just as well if you ask me. All that candy makes them mighty picky about the food I give them. I tried to tell that to Eli Miller when he stopped by with a report on his horse the other day."

Eli . . .

"Seems that horse likes root beer candy." Mervin pulled his thumb out and hooked it in the direction from which he'd come. Then, turning on the soles of his worn boots, he led the way back down the aisle. "So what horse are you asking about today?"

"Eli's."

If that surprised Mervin, he didn't let on. Instead, he stopped alongside a stall inhabited by a sleek brown horse and pulled a brush off a hook just outside its door. "My son has been that way since he was a young boy."

Confused, she leaned against the stable's half wall and watched as Mervin began to brush the side of the horse. "Your son?"

"Then again, Eli is mighty pleased with that horse. Says she's coming along nicely."

She tried to follow what the man was saying, but it was no use. The moment he mentioned his son in relation to Eli and Carly, she was lost. "I don't understand what your son has to do with Eli's horse."

"Willis purchased that horse from a trailer that was passing by. When I came home from auction that day and I saw the horse was injured, I could not understand why. Injured horses don't bring as much money. But Eli bought her that next Saturday, anyway. Seems he saw the same thing in her that Willis saw."

"Is your son around?" she asked. "Could I speak to him?"

"He left to go back to his farm in New York before I could even tell him the horse sold. But that's okay. Gives me something to tell him the next time I write a letter to him and his wife."

She smacked her hand against the weathered wall, earning her a startled look from the horse and from Mervin. "I'm sorry. It's just that . . . Do you know *anything* about the person who sold him that horse?"

Mervin stopped brushing and studied her closely. "I know it was an Englisher. About the same age as Willis."

She stopped herself, mid-sigh, and stepped back. She'd wasted enough time. How Carrot Thief ended up in Mervin's stable really wasn't the issue. How to tell Esther was.

"Well, I guess I better head out. Thanks for your time." She saw the question in the Amish man's eyes but let it go. After all, she didn't have any answers, either.

"Say hello to Miss Weatherly for me." Mervin straightened to a full stand and waved his brush. "And be sure to tell her there's a horse or two out here I think she might like to meet."

Mustering a smile she really didn't feel, Claire nodded and returned his wave. "I will. And thanks again."

"So how did it go, dear? Was Mervin able to shed light on how he ended up with Carrot Thief?"

Claire pulled onto the shoulder just beyond the Weaver farm and gave into the breath she'd been holding for entirely too long. "Mervin's son, Willis, purchased Carrot Thief. From a passing trailer, to use Mervin's words."

"But Willis left to go back to New York two weeks ago," Diane countered.

"Exactly. Which means I know nothing more than I did

when I woke up this morning." She let her head drop back against the headrest. "Why can't the Amish have phones? Did they not get the memo about their usefulness?"

Diane's soft laugh in her ear brought a smile, albeit a fleeting one, to her own lips as well.

"Do I really need to answer that, dear?"

"No. I'm just frustrated, is all."

"I know you like to have answers, Claire. You've been that way since you were a little girl. But maybe the only answer that really matters in all of this is that Carrot Thief is alive and well. And she didn't fall into the wrong hands."

She closed her eyes momentarily and waited for Diane's positive thinking to rub off on her, but it simply wasn't happening. "Meaning?"

"Remember what I told you a while back? About Carrot Thief's sister? Her name is Idle Ruler and she's a pretty famous racehorse. Lineage like that makes Carrot Thief worth a lot of money."

"Money means nothing to Esther. Carly, however, does."

"And I empathize, dear. I really do. But you need to remember that Carly was Carrot Thief first. And Valerie Palermo loves her every bit as much as Esther does." A beat of silence was soon followed by Diane's voice again—a voice that had grown quieter but no less determined. "We have to get word to this woman as soon as possible, dear. She's been worried sick about this horse. Telling her that her beloved Carrot Thief is safe and sound is the right thing to do."

Diane was right. She knew that.

"I assure you this Valerie woman will be called. I just want to tell Esther first. That, too, is the right thing to do."

Chapter 32

In the nearly twelve months since Claire had officially opened Heavenly Treasures, no two days had ever been exactly the same. Customers were different, questions were different, and requests—while often similar—always seemed to have a slightly different twist.

But the one constant, throughout all seasons, was the lack of customers during the lunch hour. Senior citizens, as she'd come to learn, liked to eat at the same time every day—a fact that attributed to a burst in sales for Heavenly Brews and Taste Of Heaven(ly) during the same hour that all the other shopkeepers on Lighted Way got a breather. Most, like Harold Glick and Drew Styles, used that breather to grab a bite while sitting quietly behind their own registers just in case. It was, after all, the smart thing to do. Why she failed to do the same thing was a question to dissect at another time. Especially when she was already trying to weigh the pros and cons between heading inside the shop the way she should and hightailing it across the street to the police station to get a hug from Jakob like she wanted to . . .

A peek inside the front window of her shop confirmed a lack of customers and freed her heart, at least momentarily, of any guilt that might have otherwise been associated with stepping down off the curb, picking her way across the uneven cobblestones, and finally stepping up onto the curb on the other side. If she kept her visit with Jakob to the exact time it took to get a hug, and possibly a kiss, she could be back in the shop before Annie finished her apple.

Sidestepping the stream of customers still heading into Taste of Heaven(ly), Claire turned left, her quickened pace making short work of the storefronts situated between the restaurant and the police department. Housed in the same simple quaint white clapboard-style building as its neighbors to the left and right, the Heavenly Police Department blended into the landscape for the average tourist. But those with a sharp eye quickly realized it was the one building on the entire street that had no Amish foot traffic going in or out.

She stopped outside the station's front door and took a deep breath, her angst over Esther and Carly showing little to no sign of letting up. With any luck, a few moments with Jakob would help.

Pulling open the door, she stepped inside the bright and airy waiting room and headed straight for the day-shift dispatcher. "Good afternoon, Curt. Do you happen to know if Jakob is around?"

"He sure is. Should I tell him you're here?"

"If he's not too busy."

Flashing a knowing smile at her over the top of the half wall that separated the waiting room from the station's inner sanctum, the balding and always good-natured dispatcher rolled his chair over to the intercom and paused with his finger above a button on the top right. "I'm quite sure he'll make an exception for you, regardless."

"Thank you, Curt."

"My pleasure." He pressed the button and leaned forward a smidge. "Detective Fisher? Claire Weatherly is out here to see you."

"Thanks, Curt. You can send her back."

Releasing the button, Curt rolled himself back to his desk and the button on its underside that would unlatch the door to his left. Two short beeps were quickly followed by a beckoning motion of his hand. "That's your cue."

She stepped through the door and into the hallway beyond. Then, mindful of the ticking clock in her head, she made a beeline for the open door at the hall's halfway point. Ignoring the black-lettered name plate she didn't need, Claire poked her head around the corner to find Jakob standing just inside the doorway, waiting.

"Okay, confess. Did the chief call you and beg you to stop by so I would stop being such a grouch?"

"No. But are you? Being a grouch, I mean?"

"Yes!" bellowed a voice from an open doorway farther down the hall.

"See?" He rolled his eyes toward the ceiling and then opened his arms wide, wrapping them around her as she happily stepped inside. "Oh, yeah, this is exactly what I needed."

"Me, too," she whispered in a voice suddenly choked with emotion.

Guiding her back a step, he tipped her chin up with the fingers of his right hand until she was looking him straight in the eye. "You sound upset."

"No, I'm okay—or I will be after I get a little bit more of that hug."

He obliged, adding a kiss on the top of her head and then another on her lips before stepping back once again. "Can you sit for a few minutes?"

Oh, how she wanted to say yes, to sink into the folding chair across from his desk and lose herself in his warmth for as long as possible. But she couldn't. Annie had been on her own long enough. "I really can't. I was supposed to open with Annie this morning and I called her at the last minute and told her I'd be a little late. If I stay here any longer, I'll really be pushing it."

He quieted her words with a gentle finger and then guided her over to the chair. "It's lunchtime. She'll be fine."

She opened her mouth to protest but, in the end, her own best interests won out and she sat. "So how are things around here? Busy morning so far?"

Leaning against the edge of the desk closest to Claire, he folded his arms across his wide chest and shook his head at her question. "Oh no, you don't. Ladies first. What did *you* have going on this morning that you had Annie opening alone?"

Resting her left forearm on the empty stretch of desk

in front of her, she traced her finger along a faint scratch. "I went out to the Weaver farm."

"Thinking about buying a horse?" he teased.

She stopped tracing and let her hand fall back into her lap. "I went to ask about Carrot Thief and how she ended up at Esther's."

His dimples rescinded and he braced his hands on the edge of the desk. "And?"

"Mervin Weaver's son, Willis, is the one who bought Carrot Thief. From someone who just showed up at the farm with a trailer and a horse to sell." She cleared her throat of the fogginess she felt building and continued. "Mervin said it wasn't unusual for his son to have a soft spot for an injured animal so it didn't really surprise him that Willis had bought a horse with a sprained tendon."

"So I guess this person who sold the horse to Willis probably came across Carrot Thief wandering around after the accident and had no idea what he'd happened upon. So he sold her to Weaver. Probably made a few hundred bucks, maybe less on account of the injury," Jakob speculated.

She shrugged and moved on. "Mervin was surprised by just how quickly the horse sold."

"To Eli . . ."

"To Eli," she confirmed. "A man who apparently has a lot in common with Willis Weaver."

A vibration at her feet momentarily sidelined her thoughts and she reached into her purse. Pulling out her phone, she checked the screen and then held it up for Jakob to see. "It's a text from Diane. Do you mind if I check it real quick?"

"Of course not, go ahead."

She pressed two buttons and began to read . . .

I found my magazine in the parlor where you left it for me. Thank you!

Confused, she reread the words one more time and then looked up at Jakob. "Okay, that's weird."

"What?"

"Diane lent me a magazine to read the other night—the one that was about Carrot Thief, actually, and she's texting to thank me for leaving it in the parlor for her."

"Okay, so what's weird about that?"

"I didn't leave it in the parlor. It's in my room—right where I left it when I threw it across the floor last night." She shook her head, read the message a third time, and then dropped the phone back into her purse. "Whatever. She has it now."

"Anyway, about what you were saying . . . I thought Willis Weaver lived in upstate New York," Jakob mused.

"He does. He was visiting. Mervin was at auction when Carrot Thief—aka Carly—came in." She paused as Jakob's remark sparked a question of her own. "Do you know this Willis guy?"

"Not really. Not the man he is now, anyway."

"What do you mean?" she asked.

"Willis was probably all of about ten when I left."

She did a little mental math based on what she knew about Jakob's past and put a number to her calculation. "Making him about twenty-seven now, yes?"

"Yeah, why?"

"I don't know. Just trying to think of something other than Esther and Carly, I guess." Looking up, she did her best to smile at Jakob. "Now it's your turn. What's going on around here?"

"I've been looking through my notes, drawing a time-line of everything that has happened around here the past week or so." He pointed to the whiteboard on the wall next to his desk, various colors and words filling the surface from top to bottom. "Even drew a map, as you can see."

Pushing off the chair, she wandered over to the white-board, her gaze riveted on the series of boxes representing the farms that had been robbed or almost robbed. Off to the side of the map, tacked to the wall, was the composite of the suspect.

Nondescript didn't even do the drawing justice . . .

"Wow." She looked from the drawing to Jakob and back again before returning her focus to the map and the pair of underscored question marks near the end of the one-dimensional road. "Wait a minute. Is this second question mark there supposed to be Esther and Eli's house?"

His mouth tightened just before he granted her a quick nod.

Fear gripped her insides and she stumbled backward against the desk. "Please tell me he didn't go there."

Jakob took her hands in his and squeezed them. "He hasn't. Not yet, anyway."

"Yet?" she repeated, her voice shrill.

"Yet."

"Does that mean you think he's going to?"

He pulled his hands back and raked them through his

hair, exhaling through pursed lips as he did. "I do. Which is why I have a few uniforms out there right now."

She sagged against him in relief. "Good."

"Good because it keeps Esther and Eli safe, yes. But bad, because our officers being there, and so visible, means this guy isn't going to show up."

"And if he doesn't show up, you can't catch him," she mused.

"Exactly. But there aren't enough bodies in the department to patrol *and* go undercover on an ongoing basis. So uniforms are there, but they're also ready to respond elsewhere if needed. It's all I can do right now. I can't risk anything happening to her, Claire. I just can't."

She glanced toward the whiteboard and followed the suspect's progression down Jakob's makeshift map. When she reached Esther and Eli's house, she sucked in her breath.

"Claire?"

Esther with her kapp and simple dress could be anyone . . .

"Claire?"

She stepped around the corner of the desk and turned to face him, her mind made up. "Let me be Esther."

His left eyebrow rose. "Excuse me?"

Now that the idea had formed, she simply couldn't shake it. "Dress me up as Esther and put me in her house. Give me a walkie-talkie or whatever it is you do for undercover officers and move your guys out where they can't be seen. When he shows up, I'll let you know and you can nab him in action!"

For a moment, she wasn't sure he'd heard her, based on

his blank stare. But when first surprise, and then out-and-out refusal paraded across his face, she knew he had.

"Come on, Jakob. This makes all the sense in the world."

He pushed off the edge of his desk and began pacing, the angst in his steps matched only by the angst in his response. "Using you as a decoy makes zero sense, Claire. *Zero.*"

"Yes it does," she argued. "Think about it, Jakob. You don't have any female officers in your department. Using one of your guys, or even *you,* as a decoy might scare him off. But an Amish woman alone in the house? That'll make him comfortable, maybe even draw him in!"

"No!"

"Slow down there, Jakob." Their heads turned as one toward Jakob's still-open door and the former-military-man-turned-police-chief staring back at them. "Claire might be onto something here."

Jakob thumped his fist down on the top of his desk. "No, Chief. No."

"She'd be wired . . . You'd be on the grounds . . ."

"Chief—"

Chief Martin stepped all the way into Jakob's office and stopped in front of Claire. "You sure you want to do this, Claire?"

She reached around the chief and captured Jakob's hand in hers, her eyes trained on his even while her answer was directed at the chief. "Yes, Chief. I'm sure."

Chapter 33

She stared at her reflection in the handheld mirror, the hushed gasp from her own mouth drowned out by the louder one from Jakob's.

"It's me, but . . . it's not," she whispered. "I . . . I really look Amish."

Turning slightly to the left and then the right, she took in the hint of auburn hair peeking around the edges of her kapp, its severe middle part making her forehead appear flatter somehow. Her blue-green eyes peered back between lashes that were bare, and her skin, which saw little sun throughout the workday, wasn't far removed from the term *milky white* . . .

"Let's hope our guy thinks the same thing." Jakob pitched forward on the kitchen bench, dropping his forearms onto his thighs. "I'm really not liking this whole setup, Claire."

Slowly, she lowered the mirror to the kitchen table and swiveled herself around to face Jakob. "I can do this, Jakob. I won't let you down."

His head popped up, his eyes wide. "No one said anything about you letting me down. I'm worried about your *safety*, Claire!"

"You're going to be on the other side of the trees, aren't you?

He nodded.

"Then there's nothing to worry about. If something goes wrong, you're here in what? Less than a minute? I'll be fine."

He closed his eyes in time with an inhale and then opened them again with such reluctance, it tore at her heart. "I love you, Claire. I don't want anything to happen to you."

She blinked against the instant burn in her eyes and the tears she knew were mere seconds away. "Y-you . . . love me?" she whispered.

Reaching across the corner of Eli and Esther's kitchen table, he gathered her hands in his and held them tightly. "It's not necessarily the way I wanted to say it the first time, but I also didn't think I'd be sitting here, letting you do . . . *this*."

For a long moment, she said nothing. She simply gave herself time to breathe, to work past the lump of emotion now lodged in her throat, and to savor everything about their surroundings and the man looking at her with tangible affection. Finally, when she was sure she could speak without sobbing, she met his amber-flecked eyes with a smile that started from deep inside her being. "I love you, too, Jakob. You brighten my life in ways I never thought possible, and for that and so many other things, I am truly grateful."

He leaned forward, brushed a kiss against her left temple, and then squeezed her hands once, twice. "I probably shouldn't say this, but you asked me once if I regretted leaving the Amish, remember?"

"Yes."

"Do you remember my answer?"

She looked down at her hands inside his and swallowed. "You said no."

"I did. And I meant it. But if I'd seen"—he tugged his right hand free and used it to gesture at Claire—"*this* you back then, I wouldn't have left. Not for any badge in the world."

"Ha, ha," she joked as she lifted the mirror from the table and peered at herself again. "I look—"

"*Beautiful.* Just like you always do, Claire. But now it's time to hand that over to me. Amish women don't peer at themselves in mirrors." He took the pink-trimmed mirror from her hand and carried it over to Esther's utensil drawer. Pulling the drawer open, he tucked the mirror inside and then turned back to Claire, pointing at her purse as he did. "If I could hear that vibration just now, so could our guy. Find a place to put your purse."

"Can I just check that message first? I'll do it really quick."

"Yeah, okay. It'll give me a chance to make sure my guys are in position."

She reached down to the floor, pulled out her phone from inside her purse, and opened the message from Diane.

My mistake. That was actually Hayley's magazine. I'll have to get mine from you when you get home tonight. Unless you're still reading?

She started to type her reply, but stopped when Jakob returned from the front room. "If we don't do this now, I'm calling it off."

Dropping the phone back into her purse, she, too, stood. "I'm going to be okay. I promise. I'm smart."

"I know that. Now let's just make sure you've got everything down, okay?" He guided her away from the table and then pointed at her ear. "In about thirty seconds, one of my officers is going to say something in your earpiece. Nod the second you hear his voice so we know if the kapp impedes your hearing in any way."

She tried her best to lighten Jakob's mood with a smile, but it was no use. He was worried. Plain and simple. "I'm going to be— I hear that!"

"What did he say?" Jakob asked.

"He said he likes pickles."

"Very good." Jakob pointed at her pale blue dress and the tiny mic hidden beneath the fabric. "Say something back."

She lowered her chin to answer but lifted it again at the sound of Jakob's snap. "What?"

"Keep your chin up. Talk normally. You don't want to give this guy any reason to think something is up."

Nodding, she kept her eyes trained on Jakob and said, "I prefer chocolate."

Jakob shifted his mouth to the right and spoke into his shoulder mic. "Did you get that?"

"Got it, Detective."

He turned his attention back on Claire and sighed. "Okay. Looks like we're ready."

"Can't you hear me in your earpiece?" she asked, pointing at the black object tucked around his ear.

"I can. But since I'm standing here with you, I had to make sure you're truly transmitting."

"Oh. Okay. That makes sense."

Jakob looked around the room and noted the open windows, the makeshift cooking project Claire had planned, and the position of the sun as it peeked its way around the partially raised dark green shade. "Just keep yourself busy. Read. Bake. Whatever. Just remember you're Amish. Play the part."

"I'm Amish," she repeated as she stepped forward and kissed Jakob. "And I'm in love. With a really cute guy."

When the kiss ended, he stepped back, cleared his throat, and pointed at Claire. "If you get scared or you change your mind, let me know."

"I will. But I won't." She waved him toward the back door and then accompanied him over to it. "I'll be fine. I promise."

"I'm holding you to that."

And then he was gone, his broad back and long legs making short work of the side yard before disappearing behind the line of trees that separated Esther and Eli's farm from the English housing development on the other side.

When she was sure she couldn't see him any longer, Claire closed the door and turned back toward the kitchen, her pace quickening at the telltale jingle of an incoming call.

"Claire, silence your phone."

She started to dip her chin to her chest again but held it steady. "I'm sorry, Jakob. Let me just answer this one time and then I'll shut it off and hide it inside the drawer with the mirror."

Realizing she'd never moved her purse, either, Claire grabbed it off the ground, fished inside for her phone, and stared down at the unfamiliar number on the screen. "I don't know who this is."

"Then silence the call or get them off the line."

"I'll get them off." She raised the phone to her left ear and took a quick breath. "Hello?"

"Is this Claire?"

At a loss for a name to go with the male voice in her ear, she nodded. "It is. Who is this?"

"Claire, it's Bill. Bill Brockman. I stayed at your aunt's place this past week and—"

"Of course. What can I do for you?"

"I was wondering if you could double-check the name of Hayley and Jeremy's blog and get back to me as soon as possible. I'd really like to include it in my travel flyers on Heavenly."

"Did you lose the paper I wrote it down on?" she asked.

"Nope. Have that in my hand right now. You wrote your number on the back."

"The address didn't work?"

"It sure didn't."

"Did you do a search on the blog's name?"

"I did."

"And?"

"Claire . . . I really need you to wrap this up," Jakob said in her right ear.

"One minute. Please."

"Oh, that'll be great, Claire. I really appreciate you checking on that for me."

Realizing Bill thought she was requesting a moment from him rather than Jakob, she tightened her grip on the phone. "Actually, I'm a little tied up right now, but I'll be sure to ask Hayley about that tonight at dinner."

"You won't be making dinner tonight," Jakob reminded.

She rushed to make the adjustment for the man in her left ear. "Or tomorrow over breakfast. Either way, I'll get that information to you as soon as possible. Though I'm really surprised a basic search of the blog's name turned up nothing."

"The blog's name . . . Hayley's name . . . Jeremy's name. I checked them all. And I got nothing."

Hmmm. Weird.

"Maybe I misunderstood and they're just getting it up off the ground," she posed.

"Maybe. Anyway, thanks for your help."

"My pleasure, Bill."

She started to pull the phone away from her ear but stopped as she heard the man's voice once again. "Say hello to your aunt for me, will you?"

She'd just popped the bread out of the oven and set it on the cooling rack next to the chocolate chip cookies she'd made when she heard the knock.

"Someone is here," she whispered.

A beat of silence, followed by chatter in her ear, finally morphed into Jakob's singular voice. "Steve says he didn't notice anyone, but he apparently got out of his car to check out a stray cat. Proceed with caution. Keep me in the loop the way we practiced."

"I will." Feeling her hands begin to shake, she steadied them at her sides and sent up a silent prayer of thanks that Diane had no idea what she was doing at that moment. When she was sure she was ready, she headed down the hallway and toward the familiar face peeking through the glass door. "False alarm. I know this guy. He's a guest at the inn."

"Hold your cover. If he doesn't know it's you, let it go. It'll be good practice."

"Roger that," she joked. "Get it? Roger that?"

"Focus, Claire. Please."

She whispered her pledge to do as Jakob asked and then opened the door, the familiar face peering back at her with nary a clue to her true identity. "Hello."

"Yes, do you happen to sell vegetables?"

"No." Then realizing she sounded too curt, she added, "I do not."

"Can you direct me to one of your Amish neighbors who do?"

She started to say she wasn't sure, but stopped herself as a name popped into her thoughts. "The Lehmans do."

"Where can I find their place?"

"Take a right at the end of our driveway and it's no more than six farms down on the—"

Jeremy stepped forward while simultaneously looking over his shoulder toward the driveway. "Would you mind writing it down for me? I'm not good about remembering details."

A strange chill slithered down her spine as Martha's voice echoed in her head.

"I pointed the way to the Lehmans' farm stand."

"It's really not difficult—a straight shot, actually." She silently cursed the wooden quality to her voice and willed herself to relax. This was Jeremy. The fact that he was asking for a vegetable stand was a coincidence . . .

"Oh. Okay. Thanks." Jeremy started to turn, but stopped himself and gestured into the house, his gaze darting around the front room. "I hate to ask this, but would it be possible to get a glass of water? I'm not feeling too good right now. I think it's the heat. It's bordering on brutal, you know?"

No it wasn't. In fact it's kind of nice—

She took in the distracted face of the man who'd sat at her aunt's table for dinner over the past eleven days or so—his clean-shaven skin, his plain brown eyes and hair, his—

"Let him inside, Claire."

She opened her mouth to argue, to point out Jeremy's regular-joe looks and the way his requests were eerily similar to the victims' accounts, but closed it as she realized Jakob was hearing everything Claire was hearing.

Jakob wasn't telling her to let him inside to be nice. He was telling her to let him in so they could trap the twenty-something with his hand inside Eli's money jar.

Swallowing back the bile that rose up the back of her

throat, she stepped to the left and waved him inside, hoping and praying as she did that he didn't notice the way her hand trembled with rage. So far, he hadn't given her more than a passing glance. If that changed, she could be in trouble.

Two steps into the front room, he stopped, and cocked his ear toward the still-open front door. Confused, she glanced outside and then froze as she heard a rapid sound coming from the direction of the barn.

A sound that wasn't much different than a clap . . .

Only it didn't stop.

"Oh. Wow. You know what? I'm not thirsty anymore."

She swung her attention back to Jeremy and then froze as Martha's words flooded her thoughts once again.

"I heard a funny noise and did not answer his question . . ."

"I thought it was David with the dog. He claps when she does a new trick. But it was not David. He was not in the barn."

And then she knew.

There was someone else.

Bracing her hands against Jeremy's chest, she shoved him backward so hard he tripped over a thigh-high table and fell onto his back, knocking a Bible and a songbook onto the ground beside him.

"Claire? What was that?" Jakob barked in her ear.

"Jeremy. Come get him," she yelled as she ran through the door, onto the porch, and across the driveway as the clapping finally subsided. But it didn't matter. She knew who was responsible for that sound just as surely as she knew why.

Rounding the corner, she ran into the barn and stopped, her gaze traveling down the center aisle to the familiar blonde now leading a not-so-happy Carly from her stall. "Stop!" she shouted.

Hayley's head snapped upward and into the path of the late afternoon sun streaming in through Carly's open window. Dropping her hold on the mare's lead, she swapped it for a metal rake and stepped forward. "You better turn around slowly and go right back to your farmhouse if you know what's good for you."

Claire stepped closer instead, fisting her hands at her side as she did. "It was the two of you all along, wasn't it? He was sent to distract, while you searched the barns for"—she pointed at the wide-eyed horse standing behind the woman—"her."

"You're pretty smart for an Amish chick," Hayley snorted. "Pretty smart *and* pretty dumb."

"And you, Hayley Wright, are a murderer."

"Claire? Where are you?" Jakob shouted in her ear.

Hayley tried to shield the sun from her eyes but wasn't entirely successful. Instead, she stepped forward and blinked. "How do you know my name?"

Reaching upward, Claire pulled off her kapp and dropped it at her feet, the earpiece Jakob had attached to its inside landing on the top of her right boot.

"*Claire?*" Hayley hissed through clenched teeth.

"That's right."

"If a shovel can get the job done, so can this." Lifting the rake above her head, Hayley charged forward so fast and so forcefully, Claire banged into the side of a stall in her haste to escape. Steadying herself against the slatted wall, she looked back in time to see the metal rake coming at her head.

"No! Please!"

She closed her eyes and ducked, the quick move sending the metal rake crashing into the wall where Claire's head had been. Looking up, she saw Haylcy rear back for a second strike only to drop to the ground under the weight of Jakob's body.

Chapter 34

(TWO DAYS LATER)

Claire pulled Jakob's arms more tightly around her midsection and silently willed the warmth of his chest against her back to permeate the chill she'd been unable to shed since sharing Carly's true identity with Esther.

There had been shock at first, followed by tears, but in the end Esther had accepted reality, just as Claire had known she would. Still, standing there, beside Carly's stall, watching Esther's face as her beloved horse nuzzled Valerie, Claire couldn't get past the ache in her heart.

Yes, calling Valerie had been the right thing to do.

No, she wouldn't have kept Carrot Thief's whereabouts a secret even if she could.

But doing the right thing didn't always come without

pain. Anyone standing in Eli's barn at that moment, with a clear view of Esther's face, would know that to be true. Hannah's quiet cries from the other side of the barn only made things worse.

"So this Hayley person came across Carrot Thief where?" Valerie ran a hand down the side of her horse and then turned to face the people responsible for reuniting her with the animal.

Jakob's chin left its resting spot atop Claire's head. "Jeremy is actually the one who found your horse. His house isn't too far from the crash scene, and he found her limping around his yard the next day. He called his old high school chum, Hayley, and asked what he should do. She knew enough about horses to know they could turn a fast buck or two and so, after a little research, she steered him toward Weaver with the understanding she'd get fifty percent of whatever they offered."

"So *that's* why Hayley had no problem going on Diane's field trip to Weaver's place . . . Because it was *Jeremy* who'd handled the actual sale and therefore she was in no danger of being recognized," Claire mused, as much for herself as anyone else.

"That's right." Jakob loosened his hold on Claire and came around, instead, to her side. "Shortly after that, Hayley got one of those between-issue email updates from a horse magazine she subscribes to."

"*The Stable Life*," Claire and Valerie said in unison.

Jakob nodded. "Sounds right. Anyway, Hayley realized that the horse Jeremy had found in his yard was Carrot Thief and that she was far more valuable—because of her lineage—than what they'd gotten from Weaver. So they went back."

"Only Carrot Thief had been bought by Eli and had become Carly." She glanced toward Esther in time to see a ripple of pain shoot across the young woman's face. "And so their hunt began."

"And a man died?" Valerie asked.

"Wayne Stutzman." Jakob cupped his hand across his mouth, then let it slip slowly down to his chin. "Near as we can figure, based on the timing, Wayne must have come across Hayley in the barn while Jeremy was keeping the rest of the family busy in the house. He probably questioned her and she, feeling threatened, picked up a shovel and hit him. Sadly, it was a fatal blow."

Valerie pressed her fingers to her own chin and closed her eyes briefly. "How awful! Did he have children?"

"Seven."

"Seven?" Valerie echoed. "How will they manage?"

Eli unlatched the stall door and stepped inside with Carly. "My brother, Benjamin, is lending a hand. He'll see that Wayne's wife, Emma, and the children are well taken care of. It is his way."

"Eli is right," Jakob agreed. "As for Hayley, she was so set on finding Carrot Thief and so confident she hadn't been spotted she continued staying at Sleep Heavenly, the bed and breakfast owned by Claire's aunt, Diane Weatherly. Taking care not to raise too much attention, she hit one farm a day—sometimes two, using her camera as her ruse for moving around town. A camera she didn't even seem to know how to use, based on what one of my officers said."

"But I saw her pictures!" Claire protested.

"You saw pictures she'd saved onto a flash drive to make it *look* like she was working. And it worked. No one was any the wiser." Jakob turned back to Valerie and finished the story. "Unfortunately for Hayley, her chosen partner got a little greedy and started stealing money during his assigned post as lookout man. Chasing him down brought us—or rather, *Claire*, here—to Hayley."

Valerie closed the gap between them to address Claire. "I can't thank you enough for everything you've done to bring Carrot Thief back to me. I had all but given up hope on ever seeing her again."

Aware of the sudden weight of everyone's eyes, Claire did her best to acknowledge the woman's words with the closest thing to a smile she could offer at that moment. After all, none of this was Valerie's fault—she was as much a victim in this whole mess as Esther. "I . . . I take it your Carrot Thief is a good racer?"

Valerie laughed. "No. Not really. In fact, Carrot Thief has never won a race. She almost placed . . . once, but that's only because the horse in front of her stumbled."

Squatting down beside the horse, Eli ran his hand down the animal's leg, speaking softly in Pennsylvania Dutch as he did.

"Eli has taken good care of Car"—Esther stopped, swallowed, and tried again—"*Carrot Thief's* leg. She is almost better."

"I used ice and changed her bandages each day, but it is my wife who made your horse well." Eli guided their attention back to the horse and the young woman she was now nuzzling. "Carly loves Esther. It is as if she knows Esther is with child."

Sure enough, the horse lowered her head from its resting spot alongside Esther's and gently nuzzled it against the growing mound beneath Esther's lavender-colored dress.

"My sister is the one thing Carly loves more than my root beer candies," Hannah said between sniffles.

Slowly, step by step, Valerie returned to the stall, her full attention trained on her beloved Carrot Thief and a tear-ridden Esther. "Carrot Thief may not be a good racer, but she has always been an excellent judge of character. At one race, in New Jersey, she rebuffed the attempted pet of another horse's trainer. And by rebuffed, I mean *rebuffed*—as in nearly bit this man's hand off. I was positively mortified. I'd never seen Carrot Thief conduct herself like that."

Esther whispered something in Carly's ear and then turned to look at the horse's rightful owner. "That does not sound like Carly."

"I agree." Valerie stopped next to Esther and lifted a gentle, reassuring hand to Carrot Thief. "Two days later, a local paper revealed that this particular man had been brought up on animal cruelty charges."

Esther drew back. "I do not understand."

"This man was mean to the horses in his care."

"That is not right!"

Valerie looked from Esther to Carrot Thief and back again. "It was as if Carrot Thief sensed evil." The woman grew silent as she returned to petting her horse. After several long minutes, Valerie dropped her hand to the top of the half wall and readdressed Esther. "Likewise, Carrot Thief senses true goodness. It is why she loves you whether you are holding her favorite candy or not."

Esther's throat moved with a swallow, but she said nothing.

"That is why," Valerie continued, "I am certain this is where she must spend her retirement years."

Claire sucked in her breath so quickly, so loudly, that Carrot Thief's head shot up. "I . . . I'm sorry," she stammered. "Please. Keep going."

"Carrot Thief isn't a racer. Not a good one, anyway." Valerie smiled up at her horse. "Oh, don't get me wrong, she tried. Gave it her all each and every time. But she's really just a great big teddy bear—far more interested in people than in flowers and a fancy sash she can't read anyway."

Eli and Esther traded confused glances, prompting Jakob to step forward, his arm around Claire's shoulders. "What are you saying, Ms. Palermo?"

"I'm saying I want Carrot Thief to live here, with Esther and Eli. I want her to have a chance to get to know their child and the many children that will surely follow."

Esther brought her hands to her face, her gaze on no one but Valerie. "Y-you want us to keep your horse?"

"I want you to keep *your* horse, Esther."

"M-my horse?" Esther repeated as Carly, again, nuzzled her stomach. "I cannot accept such a gift!"

"My business is racehorses, Esther. Carrot Thief—I mean, Carly—is not a racehorse."

"But—"

"Will you and Eli take good care of her?" Valerie asked.

Eli rose to his feet and came to stand as close to Esther as the half wall between them would allow. "Yah."

Wiping the back of her hand across her tear-soaked face, Esther echoed her husband's words with a simple, yet no less meaningful nod.

"Then this is where I want *Carly* to remain . . ."

"I'm sorry, could you, um, read that one more time, please?"
Winnie Johnson rested her elbows on the edge of Charles
Woodward's desk and willed herself to concentrate. "I've
been a little scattered these last few weeks and I think my
mind is playing tricks on me."

For a moment she wasn't sure he'd heard, but, eventually, he nodded, cleared his throat, and began rereading
from the semi-tattered paper in his hands.

"I, Gertrude Redenbacher, being of sound mind and body,
do bequest my precious angel Lovey to my sweet neighbor
Winnie Johnson. I'm sure, given time, Lovey will come to
adore Winnie just as much as I have these last two years."
Charles glanced up, his tired eyes pinning hers. "Are you
still with me, Miss Johnson?"

All she could do was nod, his focus shifting back down
to the paper as she did. "Additionally, having never been

blessed with any children of our own, I also must bequest to Winnie, my late husband's beloved vintage ambulance. He may not have finished restoring it to its true original grandeur, but it runs and it will keep Winnie from having to walk to the bakery in the rain."

Nope. Her mind wasn't scattered. She'd heard every last word exactly the same way the first go-round. Only this time, when the attorney's monotone delivery came to an end, it touched off an almost maniacal laugh track in her head.

"Miss Johnson? Are you alright?"

She glanced around the room, her gaze falling on a miniature bonsai tree on the corner of the man's desk. "Oh, I know what's going on here . . ." Without waiting for a reply, she reached over, parted each branch, and then moved on to a complete and thorough inspection of the soil in which the tree was planted.

No camera . . .

"Miss Johnson, I notarized Gertrude's wishes myself not more than six months ago." Charles pulled the pot closer to his chair and brushed the disturbed soil back into place. "Her body was failing her, but her mind was sharp as a tack as you well know. This is what she wanted."

"Wait." She fell back against her chair, a new and different laugh making its way past her lips. "Mr. Nelson put you up to this, didn't he?"

"Mr. Nelson?" Charles parroted.

"Yes. Parker Nelson. My downstairs neighbor." Suddenly, it all added up. Mr. Nelson was always playing tricks on her—whoopee cushions on her porch furniture, toy mice on her steps, even hiding her newspaper in a different place each day . . . She felt the smile spreading across her face and didn't bother to hide it. "Okay, how'd he get you to do it?"

"Excuse me?"

"Mr. Nelson. How'd he get you to read that one instead of the real one?"

Charles let her finger guide his attention back to the paper on his desk before he pushed his chair back and stood. Then, leaning across the polished mahogany surface, he pressed the intercom button on the side of his phone. "Susan? Could you please bring in Miss Johnson's items?"

"I'll be right in, Mr. Woodward."

Releasing the button, he spun the paper around and scooted it across the desk to Winnie. "I'll need to keep the original, of course, but I'll see that Susan makes a copy for you before you leave. That way you don't have to worry about taxes on the vehicle in the event the government should ever question—"

A door opened behind her and she turned to see the same kind yet efficient woman who'd whisked Winnie into the attorney's inner sanctum within moments of her arrival. This time, though, instead of Gertrude's file and a mug of steaming black coffee, the secretary handed her boss a pair of keys and a brown and white tabby cat who promptly turned and hissed at Winnie.